"Why don't you just go home and leave me alone?"

She spun away from him. "You're not my keeper. Go back and save someone else's life."

Gently but firmly, he grasped her by the upper arm, stopping her in her tracks. "The way you've been pushing yourself you need a keeper." His voice had a ragged edge. Turning to face her, he clasped her other arm. "It might as well be me."

"I don't think so," Becca retorted, a shiver rippling through her when he raised his hand to cradle her face. "You're the last person…"

"Be quiet for once." With that he very effectively shut her up himself, by covering her mouth with his.

The MD's Mistress
by Joan Hohl

The Money Man's Seduction
by Leslie LaFoy

"My sources say you paid cash for this building. Where did you get that kind of money, Miss Raines?"

Sources? She considered him again. Finely chiselled nose and brow, a perfectly square, utterly masculine jaw. Dark eyes with lush lashes. And his mouth… His lips might be full and soft in the rare moments he wasn't scowling. But none of that really mattered now. No, what mattered was drawing a line of acceptable behaviour and then holding it.

"Mr Preston, my personal finances are none of your business."

"I can find out," he countered.

"Well, you just put your pet ferret right on that," she challenged. "Do let me know what he turns up. I'm sure it'll be fascinating stuff."

He gave her a long, hard look. "I'm absolutely certain of it."

THE MD'S MISTRESS

BY
JOAN HOHL

THE MONEY MAN'S SEDUCTION

BY
LESLIE LaFOY

⊚™MILLS & BOON®

First published in Great Britain 2009
Harlequin Mills & Boon Limited,
Eton House, 18-24 Paradise Road, Richmond, Surrey TW9 1SR

The publisher acknowledges the copyright holders of the
individual works as follows:

The MD's Mistress © Joan Hohl 2008
The Money Man's Seduction © Leslie LaFoy 2008

ISBN: 978 0 263 87107 4

51-0809

Harlequin Mills & Boon policy is to use papers that are natural, renewable and recyclable products and made from wood grown in sustainable forests. The logging and manufacturing processes conform to the legal environmental regulations of the country of origin.

Printed and bound in Spain
by Litografia Rosés S.A., Barcelona

THE MD'S MISTRESS

BY
JOAN HOHL

Joan Hohl is a *New York Times* bestselling author. She has received numerous awards for her work, including a Romance Writers of America Golden Medallion Award. Joan lives in eastern Pennsylvania with her husband and family.

Dear Reader,

Hello, dear friend, I hope this finds you well and happy.

The MD's Mistress is the first in the four-book series, GIFTS FROM A BILLIONAIRE. All four stories centre around a mysterious billionaire who gives four unsuspecting heroines a monetary gift destined to change their lives…and bring them unexpected love.

I hope you will enjoy all of the stories, written by myself and three of my very good friends and fellow authors: Leslie LaFoy, a terrific writer of historical and contemporary stories; Mary McBride, another writer with a large following; and Kasey Michaels, a writer known for her contemporary, historical and mystery stories. This talented lady happens to be one of my very best friends…in addition to being very funny.

So, there you have it, gentle reader. I sincerely hope you enjoy all four books…starting with the one you are now holding in your hands.

My best always,

Joan Hohl

To the gang: Kathie, Marcie, Leslie and Mary.

Thank you all for being my friends. Life would be
duller without the four of you wacky ladies!
Love you all.

Prologue

And to wrap up our first column of the New Year, darlings, that delicious rumor has bubbled to the surface yet again. Remember the one about the reclusive billionaire who anonymously surprises the worthy with tax-free million-dollar checks each Christmas season? Well, boys and girls, it would seem that last year was no exception.

Or so we hear.

This time, however, our rumor's got a new twist.

Supposedly, our RB—that's Reclusive Billionaire, darlings—actually starts small, sending anonymous gifts throughout the year to each of those who have impressed him in some way, then sits back to watch what happens next.

Continue to make Santa happy, and maybe there's a cool million in your Christmas stocking. Do those who don't continue to live up to RB's unknown standards get a sack of coal? Or perhaps just a note saying, "Sorry, maybe next time you'll be nice, not naughty." Details! We need details!

Who knows exactly how this generous Santa operates? After all, this is only the latest whisper on the same rumor that's been tickling our fancy for years. Your favorite columnist, who would be *moi,* is still on the story but, so far, all of Santa's helpers have been mum.

In the meantime, you read it here first. It could be fiscally sound to be nice this year, darlings!

The clipping was muttered over, then dropped to the already crowded desktop.

"Yes, I saw that one, too, Uncle Ned," said the man sitting at ease on the other side of his wide teak desk. "We see a handful of stories in one form or another after every holiday season. Are you worried? Do you want to discontinue the program?"

One

It was raining. Again. It wasn't a downpour, but a gentle rain, wet just the same, and chilly.

Becca, shoulders hunched with exhaustion, trudged back to her lodging, such as it was in the tiny African village that everyone, including God, seemed to have forgotten.

After over eighteen months in the village, Becca was beyond weary. There were times when she wasn't sure she could keep going, but the people needed her as much as the small hospital, which had been built by the generosity of American philanthropists. And she had come to love the people, es-

His answer was a frown that would have other men ducking for cover under the closest c

This man merely smiled, and shook his head. " I didn't think so. You're such an old softie, *Santa* pecially the children, with their sweet faces and innocent dark eyes.

Rebecca Jameson had been an O.R. nurse at the University of Pennsylvania Hospital for several years before volunteering to go serve in this small hospital in Africa. Working ten, twelve and sometimes as many as fourteen hours a day, every day, was beginning to wear on her.

Becca knew she should heed the advice of just about everyone urging her to accept a replacement and go back to the States for a long rest. But since Dr. Seth Andrews, the very talented but equally arrogant surgeon, had all but demanded she go, she stubbornly refused to leave.

Grateful for about the hundredth time for being advised to bring boots with her, Becca slogged along the squishy ground, her mind replaying the long shift she had moments ago completed. She sighed. For some reason Dr. I'm-The-Boss-And-You're-Not Andrews had been exceptionally cranky throughout the entire day.

Head lowered, concentrating on putting one foot in front of the other, Becca frowned as her sight became gray, darker than the overcast sky. What—

It was her last thought as darkness closed in, enveloping her. The next moment, she toppled over onto her face, out cold....

Becca surfaced slowly from unconsciousness.

Her head ached. Her entire body hurt. Her mind felt fuzzy, as if it were stuffed with cotton.

Her first thought wasn't, *where am I?* It was, *pain, so much pain.* She made a soft moan of protest.

"Oh, finally awake are you? I told you that you were exhausted."

Even with her mind cloudy, Becca recognized the barely civil voice of Dr. Andrews. "I guess so," she replied, her voice an unfamiliar croak. "So, I suppose I'll live to irritate you another day." She decided her brain must have been rattled, or she'd have never had the nerve to speak to the Great One that way.

"No, you won't, smart mouth." His tone was menacing.

"I'm going to die?"

"No, Rebecca, you're not going to die." Now his tone carried a note of amusement. "You're going home."

Home? *No!* The word rang loud and clear inside her muddled head. Despite his obvious dislike of her, and his equally obvious desire to get rid of her, Becca didn't want to leave. She just couldn't leave the children. And, secretly, she didn't want to leave him, and not see him again, either.

Besides, as grumpy as he was, Seth Andrews was the very best physician and surgeon she had ever worked with, in and out of the O.R.

"I…don't…want…" she began, her throat tight with anxiety.

"I don't care what you want," he said, his voice flat and adamant. "You are worn-out. The next time you'd go down…" He paused, drew a sharp breath. "Well, there's not going to be a next time. I've called for transport. You're going stateside, like it or not."

"But…" she tried to protest.

"No *buts,* Rebecca. You're going home. Period. Now, shut up while I examine you."

Becca closed her eyes to hold back the tears welling behind them. Damn him. She flinched slightly at the cold feel of the stethoscope on her bare flesh.

Her bare flesh.

A sudden, unwanted tingle slid the length of her body at the realization of her breasts being bared to him. He's a physician, for pity's sake, she reminded herself, gritting her teeth to contain the sensation. She sighed with a mixture of relief and disappointment when she felt her gown once again covering her.

"You're a little congested." He frowned. "Still, you're good to go."

Her eyes popped open. "Can I get up?" She stared at him. He appeared exhausted, strained. Lines of weariness scored his thin, chiseled face. If anything, he looked worse than he had the last time she had seen him. When was that, she wondered… yesterday, maybe?

"No." He shook his head, setting his too long thatch of dark hair in motion.

Becca had always thought he had beautiful, shiny hair. But now, he badly needed a decent haircut. She wasn't about to tell him that. She wasn't up to his scalding rebuke.

She closed her eyes again.

"That's right. Sleep, you need it."

As if he didn't. Becca kept the thought to herself. His lack of rest was his problem.

She was out again in moments. This time she fell into a deep, normal sleep.

When Becca woke the second time, the headache was gone, or mostly gone, very likely from whatever medication he'd ordered running through her IV. Her body still hurt all over, but not as much as before.

"Feeling any better?"

Not his voice. With a sigh of relief, Becca opened her eyes, smiling at the pretty, coffee-colored face of the young nurse standing by her bed. "Yes," she answered, her voice still a dry croak. "I'm thirsty."

The nurse, Shakana, smiled back. "I'm not surprised. You've been asleep a long time." Her English was flawless, not only because she had attended an American university, but also because she had diligently practiced it…with Becca's help ever since she had come to Shakana's village.

Watching as the young woman filled a cup with water for her, Becca asked, "How long have I been here…I mean since I keeled over in the road?"

"You went down the day, or evening, before yesterday."

"Two days." Becca croaked, gratefully excepting a few sips of the cool water from the straw Shakana offered her. "I'm concussed?" It was obvious, of course she was concussed. She had done a header, hadn't she?

"Yes, a mild concussion." Shakana smiled. "How's the headache?"

"Better." She managed a faint smile. "But the memory lingers on."

"You were exhausted, Becca, or you wouldn't have collapsed. You simply couldn't go anymore."

Becca sighed, and blinked at the tears misting her eyes. "And now he's sending me home," she said, her voice still faint, but hard-edged with bitterness.

Grabbing a tissue from a box next to the bed, Shakana wiped away the tears running down Becca's face. "Don't cry," she said. "It's for the best."

"Best for who?" Becca cried in a croak. "For me or him?"

"Whom." Shakana smiled.

"Who, whom, what the hell difference does it make?" She was crying harder. "I don't want to go, and he knows it. I want to stay here, work with you…" She was now sobbing. "He doesn't like me, so he's using my fall as an excuse to get rid of me."

"Oh, Becca, no," Shakana said, still mopping away the tears. "You didn't fall, you collapsed. Dr. Andrews doesn't dislike you…" She hesitated, bit her lip. "I think. He is a physician, and he is right about your condition. You're worn-out."

"But I could rest here," Becca protested. "A couple days of rest and I could—"

"No, Becca, you couldn't," Shakana interrupted. "It won't be enough. Have you looked at yourself in a mirror lately?"

"Well, of course I have, every morn—"

Shakana again cut her off. "No, I don't mean a quick glance while brushing your teeth, or your hair. I mean really looked, stark naked."

Becca shook her head, wincing at the stab of pain. "No, why in the world would I do that?" she asked with sharp impatience.

"Why indeed?" the nurse drawled. "Gee, you don't know you're practically down to nothing but skin and bones, do you?"

"Oh, come on, Shak," Becca protested, using the nickname she had given her friend. "I know I've lost a little weight, but…" In truth, she was well aware she had lost a lot of weight, but still she felt compelled to deny it.

"A little weight?" Shakana repeated in astonishment. "Becca, you are skinny, hardly any flesh on your bones at all. Your clothes hang on you." She gave Becca a shrewd look. "Oh, I know you've been wearing smaller tops, but your scrub pants literally hang on your hips, and despite the elastic waistband, I think the only thing holding them up is your protruding hip bones."

Becca bit her lips, admitting, "I was going to get a smaller pair of pants, when I got around to it."

Crossing her arms over her ample breasts, Shakana gave her an arch look, murmuring, "Uh-huh."

Becca couldn't help a weak smile. "Well, I thought about getting a smaller pair."

Shakana shook her head, her dark eyes sad. "Oh, Becca, I'm going to miss you so much. But it's time for you to go home, rest, put on some weight. Dear friend, it hurts me to see you like this."

Tears welled in Becca's eyes. "Come with me, Shak, please."

Those sad dark eyes grew misty. "I can't, Becca. You know that. This is my home."

"I know." Becca heaved a deep sigh, coughing with what she thought was the emotional tightness in her chest. "I know," she repeated, accepting another tissue from her best friend.

Crying softly after Shakana had left to check on her many other patients, Becca fell into a deep dreamless sleep once more.

At the jostling of her body, Becca was startled awake. What…? she thought, her eyes opening wide as she realized she was being moved onto a litter.

Shakana was there, and Dr. Andrews, directing the procedure, of course.

"Shakana?" she croaked from her dry-as-dust throat. "Why am I being moved?"

"The plane is here for you," Dr. Andrews said, his voice devoid of inflection.

"But, my stuff…" she began.

Shakana squeezed her hand. "I packed your things for you, Becca."

"But…" Heaving a long sigh, Becca gave up, knowing protest was pointless. She glanced around at the men handling the litter. From their uniforms and insignia, she could tell they were an American rescue team.

"I'm so thirsty, can I have some water, please?" She looked to Shakana, but it was Dr. Andrews who moved, holding up his hand to halt the crew. Taking the cup Shakana handed him, he put the straw to Becca's lips. His fingers lightly brushed her chin. The light touch rippled through Becca like a minor earthquake.

Shaken by the odd sensation, she quickly gulped the cool water and moved her face away from his hand, settling her head on the pillow. "Thank you," she murmured, not daring to look at him.

"You're welcome." His voice was harsh with an angry tinge.

Confused by his tone, and the possible reason for it, Becca stole a glance at him. He had turned away, again motioning the men to go.

Before they started to roll the litter away, another man walked into her line of vision. Becca frowned in confusion, because the man was wearing scrubs and a white coat. Stopping beside her, he took her wrist into his hand to take her pulse.

Becca frowned.

He smiled. "I'm Dr. Devos. And your pulse is a little rapid."

"She's a little anxious and upset, Doctor," Shakana said. "She doesn't want to leave."

"It's best, Ms. Jameson." He smiled again. "If you'll excuse the expression, you look like hell."

Somewhere around forty, he looked so kind, his smile was so gentle, she had no choice but to smile back. "I'll excuse you...this time."

"I told you she was exhausted, Jim."

Becca shifted her gaze to Dr. Andrews. In her opinion, he looked worse than she felt. Apparently Dr. Devos agreed with her assessment.

"So are you, Seth. That's why I'm here to replace you."

"What?"

Becca was shifting her glance from one to the

other, her mind echoing Dr. Andrews's angry and sharply voiced question.

"You've been ordered home. You can take all the time you need to gather your things." He paused, grinned and added, "So long as you do it within the hour."

"Jim, this is ridiculous."

"Sorry, Seth, it's out of my hands." He turned to smile at Becca. "You may spend some time with your friend here—" he indicated Shakana with a nod of his head "—until Dr. Andrews is ready."

"Thank you, Doctor." Her voice was thick with gratitude. She was ill and had just met him, yet Becca already knew she liked this soft-voiced man. Besides, he had thrown Dr. Andrews a curveball! She smiled.

"You're welcome." Smiling back, he turned to the rescue squad. "Take the litter to one of the empty examining rooms, so the nurses can get this bed ready for another patient." From the men, he looked at Shakana. "You have permission to stay with your patient until Dr. Andrews is ready." With a smile to both women, he strode away.

Holding Becca's hand, Shakana walked beside the litter to the empty examining room. Tears welled in Becca's eyes as the rescue team closed the door behind them. Shakana was ready with a tissue to mop up the flow.

"Where did that nice Dr. Devos and the crew come from? The States?" She sniffed. "And how did they know Dr. Andrews needed a replacement, too?"

"The doctor and the crew came by military jet from the States, and the helicopter came from Israel." A self-satisfied smile shadowed her lips. "Dr. Andrews asked me to make the arrangements. I'm the one who told them he needed a break as badly as you."

Becca wanted to laugh. Instead she started crying all over again, which brought on a fit of coughing. "I'm sorry." She sniffed, accepting another tissue to blow her nose. "But…I feel so, so…"

"I know," Shakana said, her smile now soft, gentle. "I want to cry with you."

"You'd better not," Becca cautioned, trying to sniff and smile at the same time. "What would those guys on the team think, finding two blubbering women when they come for me?" She felt the tears well again, and impatiently swiped her hand over her cheeks. "I'm over it," she said, drawing a breath and sighing. "Resigned to going."

"It really is best for you, Becca. I can't tell you how very concerned I, as well as all the people in the village, have been about you."

"They've all noticed me slowing down, I suppose."

"No, you haven't slowed down, that's your problem," her friend answered. "We've all noticed you dwindling down, week after week."

Becca coughed again, on the tears clogging her throat, she figured. "I love them, Shak."

The other woman's smile was warm with affection. "I know. We all love you back."

Fortunately for Becca, she was saved from completely breaking down by the rescue team returning to collect her. She squeezed Shakana's hand, hard, as if afraid of letting go.

Shakana squeezed back. "I can't walk with you to the plane. I must get back to work." She hesitated, tears beginning to seep down her face. "Get well soon, Becca. I'll miss you."

"I'll miss you, too." Becca was crying again. "I'll be in touch online," she promised, reluctantly releasing her hand.

"You'd better." Shakana was openly crying now. "Goodbye, Becca." She stepped back to let the men move into place at the litter.

Miserable, hating Seth Andrews, she waved goodbye to the people crowded outside the hospital and along the road to the small airfield where a large rescue helicopter sat waiting. She never noticed the two photographers in the midst of the people, snapping away as she passed by.

Dr. Andrews was already in the chopper, looking angry and disgusted. Becca hoped he hadn't found out Shakana had been the one to turn him in...so to speak.

Within minutes, the experienced crew had settled her comfortably inside the craft. Not wanting to look at Seth's grim expression, she closed her eyes and turned her head away.

They made two stops en route, one in Israel where she was given a light meal of broth and coffee. From Israel, they were flown by jet to a military base in Germany. While there, Becca learned there had been a discussion on whether or not to fly her and the doctor straight home to the U.S. or hospitalize them there overnight.

At the time, tired, not caring about anything, Becca had no idea who made the decision to fly directly back to the States. Without argument, she ate the light meal she was offered and drank the vitamin-enriched drink handed to her. When finished she settled back and closed her eyes. All she wanted to do was sleep.

And sleep she did, deeply. She roused as the large plane began its descent at another military base near Philadelphia.

Having turned in her sleep, the first thing Becca saw when she opened her eyes was Seth Andrews. He was sound asleep, and asleep he looked like an altogether different man. Though still haggard, in repose the sharp features of his face appeared softer and younger. His enviably long dark lashes blended in with the darkness underlying his eyes.

He looked approachable.

Uh, yeah, Becca chided her fanciful thoughts. She knew better than most how very *unapproachable* Seth Andrews really was. The term *sleeping tiger* sprang to her mind, causing a frown to crease her brow.

The plane's wheels touched down. His eyes sprang open, and he appeared ready to spring to his feet.

"We're landing," she said, her voice rough from her dry throat.

"So I see." He stared at her, hard. "How are you feeling, Rebecca?"

"About as good as anyone after making such a long flight," she answered. "What about you, Doctor? Oh, and everyone calls me Becca," she added, as if he hadn't known that since the first day they had met.

"Matter of fact, Becca, I feel lousy," he admitted, to her surprise. "And, my name, as you well know, is Seth." This statement surprised her even more. "And whether or not you knew it, you were coughing in your sleep."

"I didn't know it." Not about to call him by name, she eyed him warily. The plane was taxiing, somewhere. "Where do we go from here, do you know?"

He nodded wearily. "Yeah. We'll be ambulanced to the U. of P. hospital."

"But…" she protested. "I want to go home. I don't want to go to another hospital."

"Too bad, because you're going." His voice was adamant.

"But…" she began again.

The door of the plane was opened. Hot air rushed into the interior, reminding Becca it was nearing the end of summer in the northeast.

"Save your objections, Becca." He grimaced. "I don't want to go, either. But we're under orders."

"Orders—whose orders?"

The latest crew was coming for them to deplane.

"The head honcho of the hospital," he answered, as she was lifted onto an ambulance gurney. "He wants a complete workup on both of us."

Becca caught the last of his words as she was lowered from the plane.

Damn, she thought, she wanted to go home.

Seth was in a foul mood, not at all happy with the situation. Dammit! He'd screwed up everything. All he had wanted was to get Rebecca out of Africa for her own good.

She coughed as they were sliding the gurney into the ambulance. He frowned. He didn't at all like the sound of that cough. He should have requested rescue for her sooner, even if he had known the administrator of the University of Pennsylvania Hospital would conclude if Rebecca needed to be sent home, in all probability Seth needed a break as well.

Seth had been on staff at the U. of P. for a couple of years before Rebecca had come to work at the hospital. She was one of the best nurses with whom he had ever worked.

She was one of the most lovely and appealing, too. He had felt an attraction to her almost at once— an attraction both physical and emotional that Seth told himself he neither needed nor wanted.

That being the case, he deliberately constructed an invisible shield around himself, a facade of cool detachment and disinterest. Yet, no matter how hard he fought it, the attraction grew stronger. He even tried blaming her, but that wouldn't wash, even to himself, because in all truth, Rebecca had always been efficient, withdrawn and every bit as cool, if not more so.

He hadn't gone to Africa because of her. He was in line to take over for the doctor there within the year she had started at the hospital. But he was relieved when the notice came for him to clear his schedule in preparation for going.

But putting distance between himself and Rebecca hadn't changed his feelings for her in the least. They had grown stronger; he missed her next to him in the O.R., cool detachment or not.

And then, a month after he had arrived in Africa, Becca had shown up to work with him.

He wanted…*wanted*… Well, he sighed, it didn't matter what he wanted.

Rebecca obviously didn't want anything, especially from him.

So, here he was, back in the States, with her and still so far away.

Life sucked.

Two

Two days later, Becca was still in the hospital, in bed, with pneumonia. Her cough had subsided, and yet she still felt weak. As much as she hated to admit it, if only to herself, Dr. Andrews was right in having her shipped home. And she had no intention of admitting it aloud, especially to him.

Seth.

His name swirled inside her mind, along with an image of him as he had looked the last time she had seen him, right before the attendants had slid her gurney into the ambulance.

He hadn't looked good. Becca couldn't help but wonder if he also had pneumonia, or was simply exhausted. Either case was worrisome. It didn't fit with the image she carried in that secret place in her heart.

To Becca, Seth Andrews was the most attractive and sexy man she had ever met. Over six feet tall, lean and rangy, although not as lean as he had grown lately, he exuded a calm self-confidence and a raw sensuality. Becca couldn't have missed the hungry glances he'd received from the other nurses, as well as female doctors, merely by walking along a hospital corridor or stopping by a nurses' station.

And he was the only man she had ever seen with dark-amber eyes. Too bad those eyes never glanced at her with anything other than irritation or impatience.

Becca sighed, thinking it was also too bad she had felt, if not actual love, then a deep infatuation.

She sighed again, afraid the emotion was the former and not the more personally acceptable latter. One hopefully recovered more quickly from infatuation.

Into her disquieting thoughts, Becca was unaware of someone entering the room, until a familiar voice jarred her alert.

"Are you awake?"

Trying to contain the shiver dancing down her spine, Becca reluctantly opened her eyes.

"Yes, I'm awake." She was rather proud of the calm tone she had managed, considering he looked better if not completely well. He had had his hair trimmed, and the wavy mass gleamed in the sunlight that poured into the room.

"How are you feeling?" Coming to a stop beside the bed, he lifted her wrist to take her pulse.

"Rested, a bit stronger," she said, thinking she felt strong enough to gobble him up with a spoon. Shocked by the thought, she quickly asked, "How are you feeling?"

Seth was staring at her blood pressure and heart rate monitor. "A lot better," he said, frowning as he slid his glance from the screen to her face. "Your pulse and heart rate are a little rapid."

Damn. Becca blurted out the first thought to zip through her mind. "I was dozing. You startled me." She held her breath, wondering, hoping he bought her excuse.

"That explains it then." He shot another look at the screen. "Heart rate's leveling." With a flourish, he waved a newspaper in his left hand that she had failed to notice because of her focus on him. "You've made the headlines."

Becca blinked. The headlines? What...? She frowned "I don't understand."

"You're a celebrity," he said, holding the paper up so she could see the article. "At least, you're one below the fold." He handed the folded paper to her, the bottom half displayed.

There it was, under the heading of the article,

her name and a picture of her being carried to the helicopter on the litter.

Pennsylvania Nurse a Heroine in Africa

Becca quickly scanned the article, then went back to reread it more carefully. The contents described in detail her experience, both in nursing before volunteering to go to that small village in Africa, and her service there until she was airlifted home, exhausted and ill. When she had finished reading it the second time, she looked up at Seth Andrews in bewilderment.

"Where?" Shaking her head, she frowned. "How? Why? Who?" Becca's voice shook with emotion. She didn't consider herself any kind of heroine.

"I don't know who gave out the story," he said, anger edging his voice. "I had asked Shakana to request the transport." A small, cynical smile touched his tight lips. "I now realize she ratted me out, but I find it hard to believe she would have alerted the media, as they say, about you and your condition."

"No, she wouldn't have," Becca said with absolute conviction. "Shakana and I are friends."

"I am and was always well aware of that," he said in a soothing tone, because it had to be obvious she was very upset. "No, it was either leaked here or at the jumping-off site in Israel."

"But the picture was obviously taken in Africa, as I was being lifted onto the helicopter." Becca frowned. "Where did the photographers come from?"

Seth shrugged. "Who knows? It seems these days they are everywhere."

Her frown deepening, Becca looked at the paper again. "I don't like this. I'm not brave. I'm not a heroine." Her voice rose as she slipped into a full rant. "They had no right…now I know how celebrities feel. It's an invasion of privacy, my privacy—"

"Becca…" His voice was low, soothing. It didn't stop her flow of angry words.

"I feel foolish. I'm a nurse, dammit! Nurses are supposed to care for people. If I'm a heroine, then every nurse in the world doing their job is a heroine. I…"

"Becca," he repeated, his voice stronger, almost commanding. She appeared not to hear him.

"I want a retraction," she railed on. "Or at the least, recognition of the good work being done by nurses everywhere." She finally paused to draw breath. Seth struck before she could say another word.

He shut her up very effectively by bending over the bed and covering her mouth with his own.

Becca went stiff at the gentle touch of his lips on hers. Giving a half sigh, half groan, he deepened the kiss as his lips went firm, draining the stiffness from her body and infusing softening warmth.

Becca's body melted against his chest.

Seth slid his arms beneath her to lift her, holding her closer to his hard body.

Her head spinning with sensations, Becca raised her trembling hands to grasp his shoulders, clinging to him, lost in the wonder of the shiver-inducing heat of his mouth, the flicking touch of the tip of tongue. His mouth was demanding, his tongue tormenting.

Within an instant she was hot, burning for him with all the secret passion locked inside her. Tightening her grasp on his arms, she arched in need of getting closer, closer to the heat radiating from him.

A soft cry escaped her when he released her mouth and drew back.

"I'm sorry," Seth said, his voice harsh, his expression stern. Shaking his head, he stepped away from the bed. "That won't happen again." A wry smile eased his tight expression. "It was the only way I could think of to shut you up."

He had kissed her to shut her up? Appalled by his reasoning, Becca could do no more than stare at him.

"You were getting too worked up over the newspaper article. It wasn't good for you in your condition."

And being kissed like there was no tomorrow was good for her? Becca wondered. Blinking in confusion, she refused to recognize or let the tears stinging her eyes fall.

"I'm tired." It was all she could think of to say to him. "I'd like to rest now." There was no way she would admit to him her utter devastation.

For an instant, he looked as if he wanted to say something, then he shrugged and turned away. When he reached the doorway, he glanced back at her. "I'll be back to check on you tomorrow morning."

Becca wanted to protest, call out to him not to stop by, but it was too late. He was gone. She could picture him, striding down the corridor, utterly unaware of the tentative smiles and longing glances sent his way.

Calmer now that Seth was out of the room, Becca replayed in her mind those few magical moments he had held her in his arms, and taken command of her mouth.

She sighed with the same kind of longing so many other women felt for him. And she had thought to call him back, tell him not to stop by the next morning? Ha! She couldn't wait to see him again…fool that she was!

The next moment, Becca frowned. She couldn't believe he had actually explained away his kissing her as the only way he could think of to shut her up. That had to be the most overused, clichéd line in romance fiction. Either the man secretly read too many romance novels, which she seriously doubted, or he had never read any, which she felt certain was the case.

Poor Seth. He didn't even realize he was clichéd and outdated with his approach with women.

Becca couldn't control a small smile at the thought. The sizzling way he kissed, Seth didn't have to worry about his statements being outdated. Hell, he really didn't need to speak at all.

Drowsily, Becca savored the lingering taste of Seth on her lips. His tongue had done a thorough job of teasing the inside of her mouth. The memory triggered a shivery sensation on every nerve ending in her overheated body.

What would making love with him be like?

She quivered at the very idea, before pulling herself together. Get a grip on your imagination, Rebecca, she chided herself in frustration.

Seth Andrews is not interested in you in any personal way. She grimaced. *Matter of fact, he very likely did kiss you to shut you up!*

Damn you. Standing in the corridor not far from Rebecca's room, Seth berated himself for the third, or maybe the fourth time since walking out moments ago. He stared at her chart, as if studying her stats.

What in the world had he been thinking, kissing her the way he had? Admitting to himself he had kissed her because he had wanted to for so long, Seth refused to excuse himself for acting so precipitously. He had had no right to simply grab her and kiss her.

Oh, but she had tasted so good, even with the hint of coffee on her tongue. He had wanted to taste her ever since she had become a member of his surgical team.

And now he had…and almost wished he hadn't. Becca had tasted like heaven, and Seth wanted another taste. No, he wanted to own her mouth, have it for himself alone, have *her* for himself, all to himself.

The mere thought of having Becca, making love to her, shot tongues of fire through Seth's body, directly to the most vulnerable part of his being.

A shudder of hungry desire brought Seth to his senses, to what he was and where he was.

He was a doctor, a surgeon, standing in the hospital corridor fiercely aching for a woman…no, not just any woman, a certain woman.

Rebecca.

Merely thinking her name moved him. He made a half turn to go back into her room, when he caught himself short. What the hell was he doing?

Seth was tempted to laugh. He was driving himself crazy over one kiss, that's what he was doing.

Not too smart, Andrews, he chided himself, as he strode down the corridor, immune to the speculative sidelong glances following his every step.

True to his word, as he always appeared to be, Seth entered her room as Becca was finishing her breakfast. Without asking, he examined the contents of the tray, taking note of what she had eaten.

"You didn't drink your juice."

"I don't like grape juice," she muttered in annoyance. Who did he think he was anyway?

Seth raised his eyebrows and observed wryly, "I see you drank all your coffee."

"I do like coffee." She gave him her sweetest smile. "Matter of fact, I've asked for a second cup."

His gaze lingered on her lips for an extra moment. Becca was hard put not to shiver in response to the heated look she thought she saw in his eyes.

Ridiculous. She rejected the very idea. Seth Andrews giving her a heated look? Yeah, right.

"You have company."

His remark scattered her thoughts, silly as they were. "I have company? Who?" She couldn't imagine. Her parents had retired to a lovely retirement complex in the region around Williamsburg, Virginia. Her sister, Rachael, lived and worked in Atlanta. How would they have known she was back in the States from Africa…?

That damn newspaper article.

"Do you want to see them?"

His voice, now edged with impatience, once again broke into her thoughts.

"Yes, of course I want to see them," she said, every bit as impatiently. "When did they arrive?"

"Yesterday."

Yesterday? Becca frowned. "But, why didn't I see them then?"

"You weren't allowed company yesterday."

"You—"

"No," he said, cutting her off. "Not me. Pulmonary. Dr. Inge decided you needed more time."

Becca sighed. "The head honcho of Pulmonary."

"I see you recall the staff here." He smiled. As slight as it was, his smile went straight to her heart and lungs. She started coughing.

In the next instant, he was pressing the cold stethoscope against her chest. Without speaking, or asking, he lifted her up once again, this time to press the cold instrument to her back.

"Deep breaths."

"I only swallowed the wrong way," she lied, grabbing at the first excuse to enter her empty head.

"Uh-huh, don't talk, deep breaths."

Becca didn't need to be told again; she knew he wouldn't give up until she followed his order.

"Well?" she asked, when he lowered her back onto the bed. "It's clear, isn't it?"

"Yes, fortunately."

She eyed him suspiciously. "Why…fortunately?"

"Because, if there had been the lightest hint of a rustling sound," he answered in a stern tone, "I'd have sent your company packing until tomorrow…maybe."

She heaved a dramatic-sounding, long-suffering sigh. "Since there wasn't, may I see my family now? Please," she muttered through clenched teeth.

"Sure." With that too breezy reply, he sauntered from the room.

If Becca had had something heavy at hand, she'd have hurled it at his head.

Moments later, Seth ushered Becca's parents and sister, Rachael, into the room. "Keep an eye on the time," he said, before walking away.

Becca might have frowned, maybe called out a question to him, but she was caught up in being hugged by her parents and sister, hugging back while tears filled her eyes and overflowed onto her cheeks. As her mother and sister clung to her, her father stood by, holding her hand, as if to say, *I'm here.*

Crying, laughing, everyone spoke at once.

"How did you know…?" Becca began.

"Dr. Andrews called minutes before we saw the article in the paper," her mother answered.

"I learned about it on the TV news, and then Mom called me," Rachael said.

Becca was appalled. "It was on the TV news?"

"Yes." Rachael nodded, grinning. "Prime time, both network and cable." Her grin grew into a quick laugh. "You're a genuine heroine."

"But I'm not," Becca protested. "I'm no more a

heroine than any other nurse." Her voice rose in agitation. "If I'm a heroine, then so are they!"

"Calm down, honey," her father murmured soothingly, squeezing her hand. "Do you want us to get thrown out of here?"

Shocked by his question, Becca glanced up at him as her mother and sister released their hold and stepped back. "Thrown out?" she yelped. "What do you mean? Why would you be thrown out?"

"The good doctor warned us not to upset you," her father said, annoyed. "As if we would deliberately do or say anything to upset you." He stared at her, visibly concerned. "How are you feeling, honey?"

"I'm okay, really," she quickly declared when he appeared skeptical. "I'm still a little tired, but my lungs are clear and I feel okay."

"You look more than a little tired, Rebecca," her mother said, frowning at her.

Becca sighed, but she had to agree. "Yeah, I know. I saw myself in a mirror for the first time this morning. I know I look like death warmed over." And at the time, she had wondered what had prompted Seth to kiss her. She looked a mess. Oh, that's right, she recalled. How could she forget? He kissed her to shut her up.

"Don't even say such a thing," he mother said, bringing Becca's flashing thoughts to a sudden stop.

"What?" She blinked, catching up to what she had said. "Well, it's true, I do look a sorry sight," she defended herself, fighting a grin. She lowered her voice ominously, and said, "Like the face of death."

"Rebecca, that is not funny."

"No?" She gave her mother a wide-eyed, innocent look. "Then why is Dad chuckling, Rachael nearly choking on suppressed laughter, and your lips twitching?"

Her mother tried to look stern, and failed. "You always were a handful," she said, shaking her head as in despair of her youngest.

Her father's chuckle deepened and Rachael lost it, laughing out loud.

"And you weren't much better," her mother said, switching her mock stern look to Rachael.

Rachael laughed harder. Her laughter was contagious and soon her father and Becca joined in. Finally, her mother gave up trying to appear stern and laughed along with the rest of her family.

It was like old times, the four of them laughing together. They had always been a close-knit unit, and it was obvious they loved her as much as Becca loved them.

"We've missed you all these months, Becca," her mother said, her eyes growing misty.

"I missed you, too," Becca replied, feeling the sting in her own eyes.

"Are you going back?" her father asked, always the practical one.

"I'd like to." Becca sighed. "But I really don't believe I'll be allowed to go."

Rachael took her remark personally. "But…why?" she demanded. "Not that we wouldn't miss you just as much as we did before, but I could tell from your letters and e-mails that you loved working there. Why shouldn't you be able to go back when you're fully recovered?"

"I'll tell you why." The low voice came from the doorway.

Becca didn't need to look to see who it was. Only the sound of that one low voice could send chills skating up and down her spine.

"Why then?" Her mother and Rachael turned in unison to confront Seth Andrews, challenge in both their voices. Apparently, her father was prudently going to wait for an answer before he challenged anyone. Becca smiled as he gave her hand another light squeeze.

"Because," Seth calmly answered, "Rebecca is too dedicated or too bullheaded to take care of herself. That's why she was sent home."

"You sent me home," Becca corrected challengingly, swallowing when he slid a look at her.

"You're damn right I did."

Three

The next day, while absently sipping her lunchtime coffee Becca mulled over the events of the day before, most particularly her family's reaction to Seth Andrews's comment about Becca being bullheaded.

Were there angry outcries against his assessment of her? Oh, no, she mused, scowling into her now empty cup. Laughter, each and every one of them. Mother, father and sister agreed with him.

Traitors. The thought wiped the scowl from her lips, replacing it with a smile. It was rather funny, Becca had to agree, at least to herself. Hadn't the three of them been saying the exact same thing, telling her she was bullheaded, since she was in middle school? Truth be told, they had been saying that before she was out of diapers!

Still…they hadn't had to agree with the man, wiseass that he was!

Said wiseass picked that moment to stroll into her room, looking far too attractive for her own good.

"Mail call," he said, holding a cream-colored envelope out to her as he came to stop beside the bed. "And hand delivered, at that."

"Hand delivered?" She was beginning to frown when the light went on in her brain. "Oh, you mean by you."

Shaking his head, as if in despair of her, Seth answered, "No, by a delivery man. You know, the kind of person hired to deliver something."

Condescending jerk, Becca inwardly raged, feeling a need to smack the superior look from his face. But since she was in bed and couldn't reach it, she plucked the envelope from his hand instead.

The very first thing that struck her was the weight and texture of the paper. Expensive stuff, she mused, sliding a fingernail under the flap. Removing the note from the envelope, she quickly scanned it, softly gasped and slowly reread the contents. It began…

Ms. Jameson,
It's my pleasure to inform you that due to

your sacrifice and dedication in giving of your service to the people of Africa, you have been chosen to be awarded by the person to be known as an admirer.

Your award will consist of the use of a fully equipped cabin in the Appalachian Mountains until you are fully recovered or for as long as you wish to stay. Although directions are included, you will be transported to and from your destination. The cabin will be fully supplied, along with a housekeeper/part-time nurse for your care.

We sincerely hope you are well and hearty again soon. Meanwhile, a telephone number is also listed, in case you need anything at all. Please, do not hesitate to call if you do.

That was it, other than a second sheet with the directions.

"Well, damn," Becca muttered, once again reading the missive.

"There's a problem?"

Becca was just getting an inkling that Seth was possibly behind this invitation, but his expression, his tone of voice, doused the idea.

"This is incredible," she answered, frowning down at the sheets of paper in her hand. "I don't know whether to take it seriously or laugh and tear it up."

"May I?" He held his hand out for the letter.

She shrugged. "Sure, why not."

Taking the papers from her, he carefully scanned both sheets before looking at her. "Take it seriously."

"Why should I?"

"I take it you've never heard of the anonymous billionaire?"

"Obviously not," she said, a tad sharply. "But, also obviously, you have. And what does an anonymous billionaire have do to with this letter?" She arched her brows.

He smiled. Well, almost.

"Yes, I have heard of him, but I'm sure whoever it is, he is your benefactor. No one knows who he is, except of course, those who work for him. The person is considered an eccentric, reclusive, generous older man who, in his later years, is sharing the wealth, so to speak."

"Well, naturally, I can't accept this offer."

"Why not?" It was his turn to frown.

"Why not?" she repeated in surprise. "Because it would be like being rewarded for doing my job."

"And…?" Again he pulled that aggravating look of superiority.

"And why should I be?"

Seth leveled an impatient look at her. "Rebecca, you have gone above and beyond the duty of other nurses."

"But…"

He silenced her by simply raising one hand. "I was there, remember? I witnessed your devotion to caring for those people, your genuine affection for them. In the process, you wore yourself out…completely. This generous person is offering you a retreat, a quiet place to rest and rebuild your strength."

Becca was on the verge of protesting once more, but reality intruded. He was right, of course. She was tired, even after several days in bed. The nurse inside her knew she needed more than a week or so to get back to normal.

Besides, she knew Seth, along with her family, would nag her until she agreed.

She let out a soft sigh of defeat. "Okay, I'll go to the mountains," she said, quickly adding, "but only until I feel up to par again."

"Good girl." Seth actually smiled. Amazing. "And you missed a third sheet." He held the paper aloft before handing it to her.

"I did?" Becca frowned, taking the sheet from him. She read the page, then sharply glanced up at him. "This is ridiculous."

"Why?" He arched one eyebrow at her.

She rattled the paper impatiently. "It says a limo will be waiting for me here at the hospital the day I'm released."

"Yes, I read it…so?"

Becca let out a loud sigh. "So…so? So, I have to go home, to my apartment."

"Why?" He raised an eyebrow.

"Why?" she repeated, waving a hand in agitation. "Because I have to pack my things…hell, I need to wash the clothes I brought home with me."

He smiled.

She stifled an impulse to jump from the bed and slug him a good one. "What's so amusing?"

"You are." His smile matured into a grin. "You are very easy to rile. Rebecca, your mother and Rachael can take care of everything."

"Oh." It was stupid—no, it was downright asinine—but damned if she didn't bristle at hearing him say her sister's name. Stupid maybe but… could he possibly feel an attraction to Rachael? Becca smothered an urge to sigh, or cry. She closed her eyes.

It was blatantly obvious Seth Andrews did not feel any kind of an attraction to her, Becca thought, despite that kiss…to shut her up. Why wouldn't he feel an attraction to another woman? Being the eldest, Rachael was beautiful, bright, single and closer to his age. Becca suspected Seth was at least ten years her senior. And, while the difference didn't bother her, it might bother him.

"Hello?" His voice was soft, curious. "Have you fallen asleep on me?"

I wish. Becca shook her head.

His smile vanished, replaced by a look of concern. "Are you feeling all right?"

"I'm a little tired," she said, determined not to admit exactly how tired she felt.

Suddenly he was at the side of her bed, his fingers on the pulse in her wrist, his glance directed to the blood pressure and heart rate monitor to one side.

"I'm okay," she insisted, wanting nothing more than for him to stop touching her. No, what she really wanted was to be swept into his arms for another scorching kiss.

Ain't gonna happen, Becca told herself, except in her dreams.

"Well, your vitals are normal," Seth admitted, gazing down at her in concern. "Do you see now why I insisted you accept that billionaire's offer?" Before she could respond, he added, "The mountains are ideal for resting and recovering. No distractions, fresh air and a housekeeper to take care of you."

"I suppose," Becca said, blinking against the tears misting her eyes. While she knew he was concerned for her as a doctor, she couldn't help feeling he would be happy to see her go.

Her eyelids were losing the blinking battle, so she closed them to staunch the flow. "I think I'd like to take a nap now."

"I think you should."

He didn't move for long seconds. Becca felt sure the gathering tears were about to escape and embarrass her. Finally, she heard the soft swish as he turned and headed to the doorway. "I'll be in later to check on you."

"Umm," she murmured, as if she were half-asleep.

Three days later, Becca was showered, dressed and in a wheelchair, waiting for a nurse to wheel her to the exit where the limo would be waiting for her.

She was tired, from the shower and dressing, she told herself. And though she felt a bit depressed, she told herself it had nothing to do with not having seen Seth in three days.

Becca firmed her lips into a flat, determined line. She would not allow herself to go into a blue funk over an arrogant, overbearing…absolutely wonderful man. Uhh, scratch the last adjective.

As if summoned by her thoughts, the man haunting her dreams strolled into her room.

"Ready to go, I see," Seth said, coming to a halt mere inches from her chair.

"Waiting for someone to wheel me down," Becca said, somehow managing to sound cheery…when all she really wanted to do was weep, and tell him she didn't want to go.

"It may be a few minutes. I understand the staff is very busy." He simply stood there, looking at her, so close, yet so far away.

For a minute.

Becca stopped thinking, breathing, when he leaned forward over her. He placed his hands on the armrests of the wheelchair, to lean closer.

"Wha...wha..." she muttered, unable to force the full word from her suddenly parched throat.

"You will let the housekeeper take care of you," he said, so close now his breath whispered over her lips, causing havoc in every cell she possessed.

Beyond speech, Becca nodded.

"Good." He smiled; she smelled mint on his breath, and yearned to taste it. "I'll miss you in the O.R."

Becca deflated like a pierced balloon. Of course, hadn't he at one time admitted she was the best O.R. nurse he had ever worked with?

She shut her eyes in private misery, and wasn't aware of him closing the inches between them. The touch of his lips on hers startled her and set her pulse pounding.

Seth's kiss was soft, gentle, undemanding and heart-wrenchingly sweet. Within a moment, before she could even think to respond, he moved away.

Becca lowered her head and her lashes.

With the tip of his finger, he tilted her face up to

meet his steady gaze. His amber eyes had darkened to a shade of brown she had not seen before.

"Get well," he said. "Take care of yourself, little girl."

Girl? Little girl!

A wave of anger crashed over Becca, washing away her misery along with her caution and good sense.

"Little girl," she protested, her voice elevated. "I'm not a little girl, Doctor. I'm a woman."

"Tell me about it."

As he finished speaking, a nurse breezed into the room, distracting Becca from wondering about the odd note in his quiet voice, the flash of emotion in his now dark eyes.

"Hi, I'm Jen, sorry to keep you waiting," the young woman said, bending to flip the locks from the chair's wheels. "It's been a busy day." Smiling, she moved to the back of the chair. "Ready to go? Your chariot awaits outside."

Seth stepped back as Jen rolled the chair to the doorway. "Doctor," she said politely, smiling as she moved past him and started down the corridor.

"Come back healthy, Rebecca. I need you…in the O.R."

Seth's quiet voice floated down the corridor after her.

Clutching the chair arms, she fought against the

sting in her eyes. She had known all along he wasn't interested in her in any personal way. She was a good O.R. nurse.

No! she thought, lifting her head and angling her jaw. She was a terrific O.R. nurse. And when she was completely back up to speed, she silently vowed, she would not torture herself by returning to work for him.

Maybe.

When Jen rolled the chair outside the electric doors, Becca couldn't get out of the chair and into the impressive black stretch limo fast enough. She did not look back.

Seth stood rigid behind the large, heavy plate-glass door. A strange sensation invaded his stomach—emptiness? He shrugged the thought aside.

He didn't have time to worry about a stubborn woman. He didn't really need her in the O.R.; there were plenty of good—no, excellent—nurses waiting, hoping to take her place.

Yet he didn't move away from the door. He stood there, watching until after she had disappeared inside the limo. Hell, he was missing her already and the car hadn't yet pulled away from the building.

Becca. A pang in his chest startled him.

Dammit, she never so much as glanced back.

* * *

In a word, the limousine was plush. There was a small cooler holding snacks, and a bar with an ice-filled bucket chilling a bottle of champagne.

Curious, and hungry, as the lunch carts had just started to be pushed along the hospital corridor as she was being wheeled out, Becca investigated the bounty. Caviar, she marveled, the outrageously expensive stuff.

Expensive but gross, she thought, making a face. Thankfully there were several different kinds of cheeses and crackers and a bunch of plump black grapes. Yum, that was more like it.

Popping the cork on the bottle, she poured the golden, bubbly liquid into a real crystal flute and made a meal of the cheese, crackers, fruit and champagne…three glasses of champagne.

After sealing what was left of the champagne with the foil cap and packing away the remains of the food, Becca made herself comfortable by curling up on the butter-soft seat and promptly fell asleep.

Becca didn't know where she was; the setting was lush but unfamiliar. She was in a freshwater pool, serenely floating naked in the cool water.

It was a peaceful, quiet place, a secret bower with heavy foliage and masses of bright-hued flowers on the banks surrounding the pool. And there was a waterfall, a gentle flow cascading into the sparkling water.

Lovely. She was alone but unafraid, somehow knowing this was where she belonged.

There came a splash, not loud, but as if a fish had leapt with joy in the pool. Small ripples blurred the water, drawing closer to her.

The next instant he was there, his lean bare body gliding along hers.

"Seth." Her eyes closing, she breathed his name, as if she had known he would be there.

"Yes." His lips were close to her ear. "Have you been waiting long?"

"Forever," she murmured against his jaw.

"I'm here now...for you." A slight turn of his head and his mouth took hers. A gentle, tender kiss, for a moment.

Becca curled her wet arms around his neck, and arched her body into his, murmuring low in her throat when he deepened the kiss, taking complete command of her mouth with his lips and tongue.

Without thought, she lifted her legs and coiled them around his hips, feeling the strength of his need, and loving the feel of it.

"You want me," he whispered against her lips.

"Yes..." she sighed, arching higher into him. "Yes, please."

"Then I'm yours." He moved into position between her legs. She felt him there, and…

"Ms. Jameson."

The soft, unfamiliar voice broke the spell. Becca opened her eyes, and nearly cried out in protest.

She was lying on the seat of the unmoving limo. She raised her eyes to see the driver, his expression both concerned and compassionate.

"We're here, at the cabin." He smiled. "Sorry to have to wake you. You were sleeping pretty soundly."

"Yes," she said, blinking herself fully awake and aware.

"I—" she began, only to have him interrupt.

"You obviously needed the rest," he said, getting out of the car to open the door for her.

She needed something, Becca thought wryly, and right that minute rest didn't come close.

"Well, there you are," a voice called out, startling Becca. "And just in time for supper, too."

Becca looked up at the woman standing on the wide porch running along the entire front of the…cabin? Ha! This place was the last thing Becca would call a cabin. The word *resort* jumped into her mind.

"Come on in, honey, and get acquainted. I'm Sue Ann, but folks just call me Sue."

"Hi, Sue," Becca said, stepping out of the car and mounting the four steps to the porch. She held out her hand. "I'm Rebecca." She smiled. "But folks just call me Becca."

Sue returned the smile, and turned to the driver, who stood patiently waiting at the base of the steps, his hands full of Becca's luggage.

"I'm Dan," he offered. "Sorry I can't shake your hand, ma'am."

"My name's Sue," she said, laughing. "And you two come right on inside."

Becca liked the woman at once. In her mid-fifties, Becca judged, nice, down-to-earth, the solid type.

"I'll show you to the room I've prepared for you," she said, striding to a hallway and motioning Becca and Dan to follow. "'Course, if it don't suit, you have your choice of any of the four others."

"Only five bedrooms?" Becca said, laughing. "What kind of cheap dump have I been subjected to?"

Dan chuckled.

Sue laughed along with Becca. "Yeah, shame, ain't it?" She swung open a door. "You'll just have to rough it for a while, I suppose."

Becca caught her breath as she stepped into the room. It was simply gorgeous, luxurious, down-right, flat-out decadent. A room fit for royalty.

"Sheesh," Becca whispered in awe.

"Think you might be able to make do?" Sue asked, in mock concern.

Becca nodded. "Yeah, for a while, at least."

Laughing, Sue headed from the room. "Just drop the bags, Dan. I'll take care of them later." She glanced at Becca. "Why don't you freshen up, then come out to the kitchen, before supper dries up. You, too, Dan."

Dan thanked her, but demurred. "I'd better to be on my way, ma'am."

"You not going to drive all the way back tonight, are you?" Becca said.

He shook his head. "No, just an hour or two. All the arrangements have been made for me. Matter of fact, I think I'll be going, while it's still light."

Impulsively, Becca hugged him as she thanked him. Within minutes the limo was smoothly moving away from the house.

"Well, then," Sue said. "Let's you and I get to know each other over supper."

Four

The first week at the so-called cabin went well for Becca. Sue appeared determined to spoil her rotten. Surprisingly, independent as she always had been, Becca reveled in the pampering. Sue insisted she rest, so Becca rested. Sue insisted she eat, so Becca ate…and very well, too.

On her first full day there, Becca unpacked, delighted to see Rachael had stowed her laptop and several novels in her cases, along with plenty of clothing. After putting everything neatly away, she had lunch and then a nap. Later, she explored the house, and was not surprised to find that every room was as beautifully decorated as her bedroom, if not as luxuriously. Obviously, she figured her room was the master suite.

Two days later, she felt quite at home, and was already fond of Sue. But then, she thought, who wouldn't be? Sue zipped about like a teenager. And she was one terrific companion, not to mention a great cook. Becca was certain she would be a lot heavier when she left the cabin than when she arrived.

Once she'd gotten comfortable at the cabin, she began exploring the outdoors, starting with the long porch. From the position of the house halfway up a foothill, Becca could see a town nestled in a narrow valley below. Curious, she brought up the subject of the town over supper.

Sue was happy to give Becca a short history of the town, named Forest Hills, for obvious reasons. There were a lot of forested hills, not to mention mountains completely surrounding it.

"That town dates back to the eighteen eighties," Sue began. "It started up when veins of coal were discovered."

Sue paused, and Becca inserted, "I didn't see anything while on the porch that looked like a mine."

"That's 'cause you can't see it from here," she said. "It's located in a fold of the mountains nine or so miles from here." She smiled, sipped her tea and said, "I was born in this town. My ancestors settled here before it was a town. They were farmers, heading west, this little valley looked good to them. So they stayed, settled. We've been here ever since."

Becca took the opportunity to ask another question when Sue took another sip of tea.

"You've lived here all your life?"

"Lord, no," she replied with a quick head shake. "I shook the dust of this place off my shoes right after I graduated high school. I went to the city to college to become a nurse."

"Really?" Becca smiled. "That had to take courage. I mean, growing up in a small town, then going off alone to a big city." She hesitated, but asked outright, "Did you make it—the nursing, I mean?"

Sue gave a proud smile. "Sure I made it, even got my bachelor's degree in science."

"Good for you. That's wonderful." Becca returned a small shy smile. "I did, too."

"Oh, honey, I know," Sue said, giving her a thumbs-up. "I know all about your work in Africa, too. I hear you almost worked yourself right into the ground."

Sighing, Becca shook her head. "No such thing."

Sue pulled a skeptical expression. "That isn't the way I heard it."

"Overplayed by the media." Becca shrugged.

So it was all well and good—for the first week. There was one little problem with Becca: she continued to dream about Seth every night, erotic fantasies that made her blush come morning. Night after night, in each dream, she was alone and naked, always in a beautiful but different setting than the first. In every dream, he was suddenly there.

They would not talk. His naked, slim, muscular body was impressive in full arousal. Becca would open her arms to him at once, and he would lie next to her, holding her, his hands caressing her, his mouth tormenting her. In desperation, she would tug at his hair, his shoulders, urging him closer, closer. He'd murmur without speaking, and move sensuously between her thighs. His tongue would thrust deep into her mouth, drawing a moan of need from her throat into his. His mouth and tongue owning hers, he'd move and…

Becca would awaken, her breathing ragged, her body moist all over, longing, longing. Frustration became her constant companion.

She wanted…she wanted…Seth—all of him.

Toward the middle of the second week she confided to Sue some of her restlessness. She wasn't about to describe her dreams. She was embarrassed even thinking about them. Not that she wanted them to end. Oh, no. Since she knew the dreams were all she would probably ever have of him, she cherished each and every one…but her frustration grew. It had been a long time—back to her college days, in fact—since she had been intimate with a man. The experience had not been earth-shattering.

"I'm getting antsy sitting around here," she said, between bites of a delicious stew. She was almost amused by the understatement.

"No kidding," Sue said, rolling her eyes. "I'd have never known, if not for seeing you prowling back and forth like a caged animal." She grinned.

Becca grinned back. "Can I help with your work, if only a little?"

"Absolutely not," Sue said resolutely. "I'm getting paid for taking care of this place and you, and paid very nicely, thank you."

Becca's shoulders drooped. "Oh, well, I might as well pack up and leave. I'll go flaky with nothing to do. I'm getting cabin fever already."

"Weeelll," Sue began, pausing as she got up to pour coffee for both of them. "Maybe I can help you find something light to do."

"The dusting?" Becca asked eagerly, accepting the steaming cup.

Sue shook her head. "No, I told you, this place is my job for now. But…"

"But?" Becca prompted.

"I have another job, part-time, and I was thinking you might be able to help there."

"Where?" Becca asked, and immediately added, "Doing what and with whom?"

"Nursing." Sue paused for a reaction. She got it as the word left her lips.

"Nursing, where?"

"At the small clinic in town."

"I didn't know there was a clinic in town." Becca was anxious to hear more. "Tell me about it."

"First let me give you a thumbnail background." She slid her soup plate aside and cradled her coffee cup in her palms. "The clinic is run by Dr. John Carter. He was raised here—I've know him most of my life. John was ahead of me in school. Like me, he left after graduating high school to attend college, followed by med school."

She took a tentative sip of her drink before going on. "Unlike me, he came back here to set up a practice. He's been serving the community ever since."

"And you work for him?"

Sue nodded. "On a part-time basis."

Becca frowned. "But you said something about a clinic. Where does that come in?"

Sue laughed at her eager tone. "There were times, accidents and such, when John's small office was overcrowded with hurt or sick people. There were a few times with mine accidents when it was chaos. You see, the nearest hospital is over a half an hour away."

"But that means…" Becca began, appalled.

"Yes," Sue nodded. "Some men died in transit." She drew a breath and took a swallow of coffee. "So, ten or so years ago, the mine owner paid to have an addition attached to John's building, which he owns and lives in, in the apartment above. I must admit, the owner, Carl Dengler, didn't skimp. The clinic is well-equipped, not state-of-the-art, but good. John does X-rays and blood work. Everything except surgery. It has saved more than a few lives."

"Oh, my gosh!" Becca said. "That's right up my alley."

Sue smiled. "That's what I thought."

"When can I go to meet Dr. Carter?"

"How 'bout tomorrow morning?"

"Yes!" Becca punched the air. "Please."

Two days later, Becca was back to doing the work she loved. No, it wasn't the precision work of being next to Seth in the O.R., but it was satisfying nonetheless. Best of all, it kept her mind engaged and busy, as well as her hands. The edge was taken off her frustration.

Becca liked Dr. Carter at once. Nearing sixty, he was still in excellent physical shape, and still handsome. She could just imagine how attractive he must have been to the female population when he was young.

He appeared to live alone, as Becca heard no mention of a wife, nor was introduced to anyone.

Curious, she asked Sue about his possible marital status.

She was happy to clarify. "John married his college sweetheart right after graduation. He brought her home with him. Apparently, she had other dreams of life being married to a doctor. She lasted not quite two years, then she packed up and left." She grimaced. "So far as anyone knows, except to sign the divorce papers her lawyer mailed him, John hasn't heard a word from her since."

"And no local lady friend?"

"Oh," Sue said. "John has lots of female and male friends, but no lady friend in the way you mean."

"Skittish, huh?"

"Yeah, and it's a shame. He's a great guy." Sue sighed and walked away, ending the discussion.

Becca watched her, curious. Her sigh had not only a note of compassion, but a touch of longing as well. Hmm, she thought, interesting.

As Sue had explained Becca's situation to John, he agreed to her working three half days a week to begin. She was tempted to argue for more time, but gave in gracefully, as she somehow knew she wouldn't win, anyway.

By Saturday, working her third half day of the week, Becca had settled in as if she had worked in the small clinic for years. She was back in form and loving it.

* * *

It was hot and humid in Philadelphia. Summer was hanging on to the east coast like a leech to a blood vessel. There were frequent storms; with each one, the air seemed to get hotter and more humid.

Seth was tired. He was tired of the heat. He was tired of the humidity. He was damn sick of feeling tired. He knew most of his problem was mental, not physical.

Physically, Seth was feeling pretty good. He wasn't back to performing surgery yet, but he had been helping his practice partner, Colin Neil, by doing hospital rounds checking on the progress of Colin's pre- and post-surgical patients.

No, the problem wasn't physical…except in one particular and vulnerable part of his body. But, sexual frustration aside, his health was much better than when he had left Africa weeks ago.

Truth to tell, Seth felt fine as long as he was inside the hospital. Talking to patients, checking charts, reading test results along with discussing individual patients with Colin kept him too busy to think or brood about other, personal matters.

Actually, there was only one matter, and that matter's name was Becca. The moment he stepped through the hospital doors at the end of the day, her name filled his mind and senses.

Thinking about her, wondering about her—how

she was feeling, what she was doing, who she might be meeting—was driving him nuts. And underneath the relentless, nagging thoughts was an emotion he refused to recognize.

Seth had tried evasive action. He did something he had never done before. He had dated another doctor. Her name was Kristi and she was doing her internship. He had agreed to let her trail behind him, observe as he did his daily rounds.

That had been a few days after Becca had left. Seth had hoped having an intern with him, answering her questions, explaining his and Colin's procedure, might keep his mind centered.

And it had worked, so well that he figured if it worked during the day, maybe...

Anyway, Seth had asked Kristi out to dinner. She didn't so much as hesitate—she said yes immediately.

All well and good, Seth figured. They could share a nice dinner and possibly, very probably, some professional conversation. He fully expected her to pick his brain, and why not? He didn't mind.

Kristi was a very attractive woman. Any man would be proud to be seen with her. She was pretty, slender and petite, very feminine.

She was also very bright, which was what appealed to Seth even more than her looks. In his opinion, she would make an excellent physician. In addition, she had a good sense of humor. All and all, Seth found her a wonderful dinner and conversational companion.

On seeing her home, Seth had even kissed her, not a friendly peck but a real kiss.

He felt nothing.

Oh, it wasn't horrible or even unpleasant. But it was bland, ho-hum, not at all the shockingly erotic physical and emotional impact he had experienced when he had kissed Becca.

Dammit.

It wasn't her fault. Kristi simply wasn't Becca. The most ridiculous part was he had actually felt as if he had cheated on Becca.

Talk about being tired.

He missed Becca and Seth was, in a word, miserable. Still, he soldiered on, making rounds, checking charts, answering Kristi's questions.

Seth lasted until near the end of the third week after Becca left. Then he caved to the urge gnawing inside him. He had to see her, be convinced she was taking care of herself, resting, eating, getting well.

On Friday of that week, he told Colin he would be leaving town for an end-of-summer vacation, and that hopefully he would be ready to go back into active practice when he returned. His partner agreed it was an excellent idea, and that he'd hold down the fort…so to speak.

Packing enough clothes to last about a week, Seth set out for West Virginia near dawn on Saturday morning.

The trip was long and tedious, with a short break for breakfast. Finally, around lunchtime, he brought his car to a stop at the cabin. Some cabin, Seth thought, shaking his head in near disbelief at the beautiful structure. But then, it belonged to a billionaire, he should have suspected more than a mere cabin in the woods.

Leaving the car, he mounted the steps to the wide porch and knocked at the solid oak door. The door opened to reveal a sober-faced, middle-aged woman.

"Yes?" Her eyebrows rose.

Seth smiled. "Hi, I'm Seth Andrews. I'm looking for Rebecca Jameson," he said. "Is she here?"

"You're Dr. Andrews," she said, smiling back. "Becca didn't say she was expecting you."

A funny sensation trickled through him. "Has she mentioned me?"

"Oh, yes." She nodded. "Said you worked together in Africa."

"That's right…and before Africa." He frowned. "Isn't she here?"

"Oh…my goodness, where are my manners," she said, sounding flustered. "My name is Sue, I'm the housekeeper. Come in, Doctor, come in." She stepped back, swinging the door wide.

Once inside the lovely room, Seth tried again. "Is Becca here?"

"No, she isn't," Sue answered. "She's working."

For an instant, everything stopped cold inside Seth. He arched his brows. "Working?" He had to work to keep his voice calm. "Where is she working?"

"She's helping out part-time with our doctor at the clinic in town." She glanced at her watch. "Matter of fact, I was about ready to go pick her up."

"I'll go," Seth quickly offered. "If you can point me in the right direction?"

"Oh, it's easy to find," Sue said, grinning. "Fact is, it's hard to miss. You follow the road at the other side of the house down the hill to town, it's called Forest Hills, the clinic is right along West Street, the main drag."

"Thank you, Sue." He turned to leave. She brought him to a stop at the door.

"Dr. Andrews, have you come to take Becca home?" Sue's voice had a note of disappointment.

He looked back to offer her a wry smile. "Only if she is ready to go, Sue. It's up to her." Without waiting for a possible response, he opened the door and walked out.

Working. *Working*. Seth fumed and sped down the winding road as if there were no tomorrow.

Dammit, had the woman completely lost her mind? He barely felt ready to go back to work, and she had been in a lot worse shape than him.

Seth found the clinic easily, just as Sue said he would. He found a parking space along the curb, then walked to the nondescript building and stepped inside. The first thing he saw was the back of Becca.

She was slightly bent over a woman who appeared to be weeping. He hesitated, waiting until she turned to walk to a door set in the far wall next to a reception desk, unattended at the moment.

When she opened the door and stepped through, he followed her, sparing a concerned frown for the softly crying woman.

Following Becca through the door, he saw her, shoulders slightly drooping, about to enter another door farther along a hallway. Even in profile, he could see the tension on her face, the tired, anxious look.

Exasperation immediately turned to impatience. Searing anger spiraled through Seth's entire being. Without thinking, he snapped at her.

"What the hell are you doing?"

Five

For an instant, Becca froze in surprise and shock at the sharp sound of Seth's voice. The sensation swiftly changed into a quick burst of joy inside at the reality of him being there. Then the present reality intruded.

As mere moments passed, she kept her hand curled around the doorknob and turned to scowl at him.

"I don't have time for this, Doctor," she said, anger rising to replace all other feelings. "There's a young boy choking in here."

Turning the knob, she entered the room, fully aware Seth was right behind her. Dr. Carter stood next to the examining table, on which a boy lay unconscious and gasping for every breath. The doctor was very carefully working a breathing tube down the boy's nasal passage.

"Foreign object?" Seth quietly asked from where he had come to a stop right beside her.

"No." Becca shook her head. "Allergic reaction to a bee sting."

"Have you administered epinephrine?"

"No," she repeated. "The doctor's receptionist is looking for—"

"Becca, who is this man, and what's he doing in here?" Dr. Carter interrupted. He didn't look up from the boy, but his tone gave clear indication of his impatience.

"The name's Seth Andrews, I'm also a physician. I worked with Rebecca in Africa."

Dr. Carter gave Seth a quick glance.

"Have you called for an ambulance?" Seth asked, keeping his gaze on the boy. "He's still struggling to breathe. He should be in a hospital."

"I agree." John sighed. "Problem is the closest hospital is over a half hour away. He wouldn't have made it there."

"Not without the epinephrine," Seth responded caustically. "Why is there none available?"

"Becca told you my receptionist is looking for one." His tone was sharp. "And I'm beginning to panic here, as I can't get this tube any deeper."

This entire exchange lasted no more than a few

seconds, during which Becca had moved to stand beside the doctor in case he needed her. Both she and John looked up when Seth spoke again.

"He's not getting enough air," he said urgently. "He needs a tracheotomy…now, or there could be brain damage."

John's eyes widened and his face drained of color. "I never…I'm not a surgeon…" He glanced at the boy, swallowed, straightened his shoulders and said, "But I'll do my best."

"I am a surgeon, and while I've never performed this procedure, I know how it's done," Seth said. "Would you prefer I do it?"

"Please."

"Is he sedated or did he pass out?"

"Passed out," John answered. "He was terrified."

Seth nodded. "Where can I scrub?"

"There's a sink behind you." John inclined his head.

Seth turned, saying, "Becca."

That's all he had to say. Becca got busy. By the time Seth turned from the sink, with his hands up, she was masked. She held a lab coat out and he straightened his arms for her to slide it on backwards. Moving behind him, she closed two buttons to hold the makeshift scrub top in place. The next second she was shoving plastic gloves onto his hands, and tying a mask on his face.

"Anesthetic?"

"I've administered a low dose," John said. "We don't need another reaction."

Seth nodded, and without saying another word, or asking any more questions, he moved to the side of the examining table, as if he knew without doubt Becca would have everything he needed prepared for him to begin.

And, of course, she did. Still not speaking or looking at her, he held out his right hand. Becca slapped a scalpel into his palm.

Concentrating on the job at hand, Becca was still vaguely aware of a light tap on the door, the quiet voice of Mary, the receptionist, saying, "I found it, Doctor," and John's equally soft voice thanking her. He then told her to call at once for an ambulance, and also said to tell the boy's mother he would be all right.

In short order, working with his accustomed precision, Seth set aside the instrument and inserted the breathing tube Becca handed to him into the child's trachea. The boy's breathing eased noticeably at once and slowly returned to a normal pattern. John handed the syringe to her and she plunged the needle into the boy.

As Seth stepped back, away from the table, another tap sounded on the door, and a voice said, "Ambulance crew."

Glancing at John, Seth said, "He's about ready to go."

With her usual calm efficiency, Becca dressed the wound around the tube. Just then, the boy's eyelids fluttered and opened. She smiled into his startling and blessedly clear green eyes.

"Mommy," the child cried in a rough whisper.

"I'm here." Tears streaming down her face, the woman from the waiting room shouldered her way by the ambulance crew. "I'm here, baby, Mommy's here."

While the crew gently slid the child from the table to their litter, the woman grabbed John's hands. "Thank you, Doctor, thank you so very…"

"I did very little, it's Dr. Andrews you should thank." He turned her to face Seth.

She repeated her gratitude to Seth, and impulsively grabbed and hugged him.

Not unused to being hugged by grateful patients and family members, Seth patted the woman's back gently. "You're welcome, now go with your boy."

With tears still trickling down her face, she gave him a brilliant smile and rushed after the ambulance crew.

Becca felt misty-eyed but exhilarated…for all of three or four minutes. Then she crashed. Exhaustion, part physical but mostly emotional, struck like a blow. With a last surge of energy, she pulled off the lab coat and the mask from her face. Heaving a heavy sigh, she dropped like a stone onto the chair at the doctor's small desk.

Seth heard her sigh and he turned to give her a probing look, in exactly the same piercing way he would gaze at one of his still shaky patients.

"You look beat." His tone was not kind, more accusing. "You shouldn't be working yet. It's obvious you aren't strong enough."

"I'm okay," she insisted, abruptly standing to prove her point. For a second the room spun around her and her stomach lurched, proving only that she was completely played out.

"Right." Seth shook his head, showing his impatience with her. "Let's go."

"I can't go now," she protested, feeling the need to sit down again. "I have to clean up in—"

"Seth is right, Becca, you've done more than enough for one day," John interrupted. "You look about ready to collapse. Mary and I will do the cleaning up."

"But—" Becca began once again, and again she was interrupted, this time by Seth.

"Don't argue," he said, moving to her to gently but firmly take hold of her arm. "And be still," he went on as she tried to shake his arm off.

In truth, Becca was too tired to argue. She allowed Seth to lead her from the clinic to his car.

It was a nice one, too, and expensive. But she was even too tired to comment on the vehicle.

Becca nearly fell asleep on the drive back to the cabin. Fortunately, she thought, as she roused with a start when the car came to a halt at the house, she hadn't drifted deep enough for her to dream.

The very idea of Seth witnessing her in the throes of one of her erotic dreams was embarrassing. Whatever would he think? She didn't want to find out.

Seth was out of the car and at her door before Becca finished undoing her seat belt. Pulling the door open, he again took her arm, guiding her from the car and up the porch steps.

The door swept open, revealing a concerned-looking Sue. "What happened, Becca? You look awful." She leveled a narrow-eyed look at Seth. "What have you done to her? You, of all people…" That's as far as Seth let her get.

"She's all right," he said, brushing past her to lead Becca inside to a chair. "There was an emergency at the clinic. A child stung by a bee had an allergic reaction. He was asphyxiating when I got there."

Sue's eyes widened and her one hand flew to her chest. "Oh, my lord," she exclaimed. "Is he…" She paused, as if afraid to voice her fear.

"No." Seth shook his head to reassure the woman, but kept his intent gaze on Becca, who had her eyes closed and was resting her head against the back of the deeply padded chair. "He'll be fine. He's being ambulanced to the hospital."

"Thank goodness," Sue murmured, her anxious gaze also fixed on Becca. "She overdid it, didn't she?"

"What else?" Seth's tone was wry. "I believe she thinks she's indestructible...but..." He hesitated before adding, "She was magnificent."

Becca blinked her eyes open. "I was no such thing," she protested, scowling at him. "I didn't perform the surgery."

"Surgery?" Sue jumped on the word. "John performed surgery on the boy?"

Becca shook her head. "No, no, Sue. Seth did it, although John was prepared to do it."

"But John's not a surgeon!" Sue said.

"That's why I did it," Seth inserted. "I am a surgeon. But John would have tried."

"Of course he would," Sue agreed. "John is a devoted, caring..." The ringing of the phone stopped her cold. "I'll get it," she said, turning away.

"Is there any coffee, Sue?" Becca called after her. "I think I need a shot of caffeine."

"Yes," Sue called back. "I made a pot for lunch, but I'll make a fresh pot as soon—"

"No, I'll get it," Becca said, interrupting.

"No, I'll get it," Seth interrupted Becca. "You stay here and rest. Where's the kitchen?"

"Follow me," Sue said from the dining room. "That's where I'm going."

"But…" Becca started to rise.

"Sit down and behave yourself," Seth ordered, in his most I'm-the-boss tone, as he strode after the housekeeper.

Watching the back of his retreating form, Becca began to simmer. That…that…*man,* she thought. Who the hell did he think he was? Well, she continued in her mental rant, she wasn't about to let him order her around. She no longer worked for him. He was not her boss.

Carefully rising, Becca stood still a moment. When her head didn't whirl, or her stomach rebel, she smiled. Moving slowly, she took one step, then another. Ha! She could walk just fine. *Take that, Mister-Big-Deal-I'm-The-Man-Surgeon.*

Feeling proud of herself, which she admitted to herself was pretty childish, Becca sauntered through the dining room to the kitchen. Seth was standing at the countertop, pouring coffee into two mugs.

"You take orders much better in the O.R.," he grumbled, turning to carry the mugs to the table.

"But we're not in the O.R.," Becca said, calmly, seating herself, "are we?"

He raised his incredible amber eyes.

She met his steady stare head-on.

Standoff?

"Doesn't matter," he said, after a long moment. Turning, he went to the fridge to get milk. "Considering your condition, I'm still in command." Giving her a wry smile, he set the carton of milk on the table. "Do you use sugar?" As if he didn't know.

"No, and what do you mean by my condition?" Becca asked, stunned by his blatant assumption. "What condition?" she stormed, in attack mode. "I'm a little tired. I'll be fine. In fact, I'm feeling better already." She pulled a cheery smile, but felt it didn't quite come off. "That's all there is to it. End of story."

During their strained exchange, Becca could hear Sue talking on the phone, even though she couldn't make out her words. Then she heard Sue cradle the instrument.

"Becca…I have sandwiches and a salad prepared and in the fridge for lunch," Sue said in a rush as she approached the table. "And a chicken vegetable pie ready to go into the oven for supper." She hesitated, smiled and rushed on. "Dr. Carter wants to see me…would it be all right with you if I went out for the night?"

Becca was already nodding her head, a smile shadowing her lips, certain Sue's sudden attack of nerves could be attributed to John's invitation…for the night, perhaps? The shadow materialized into a real smile at the thought. She had guessed Sue and

John were interested in each other, and both were tiptoeing around making a bold move.

"Of course, I don't mind. I'm tired, Sue, not half-dead. I'll be fine."

"Oh, thanks, sweetie." Sue actually beamed. "I'll just get my purse and—"

"Sue, wait a moment, please," Seth said, interrupting her. "Before you leave, can you direct me to the closest motel or rooming house?"

"Rooming house!" Sue exclaimed. "Motel? I'll do no such thing." She swept the area with one arm. "Here's this big house, and you're thinking rooming house? Becca has the master suite down here, but there are four empty bedrooms upstairs." She paused to breathe.

Becca jumped in. "Uh, Sue, I don't think—"

"Now don't tell me the owner will mind, honey," Sue interrupted. "What that rich man doesn't know won't be hurting anyone."

She glanced at Seth, who, to Becca's way of thinking, appeared much too innocent-looking. "Now, before I leave, you go right out and get your gear from the car, then I'll show you the place and you can take your pick of the rooms…all with their own bathroom, I might add."

"Well…if you insist."

Becca gritted her teeth at the humble note in his voice.

"I do." Sue gave a definite nod of her head. "No, *we* do. Don't we, Becca?"

No! Becca kept her lips tightly closed to contain the word of denial from bursting out of her mouth. "Yes," she agreed, not too graciously. "We do."

Seth smiled.

Had Becca been closer to him she might have smacked that victorious smile from his face. Wanting only to put some distance between them before she did something rash like face-smacking, she said, "Why don't you get your bags so Sue can be on her way?"

He nodded, smile still in place. "Right." Moving smartly, he headed for the door.

Becca heaved a soft sigh of relief. Still, Sue heard it. "You're still tired. Why don't you lie down for a bit? The sandwiches and salad will keep."

"I'm fine, honestly." This time Becca's smile was genuine. "I promise if I start to feel any worse, I'll rest."

Sue smiled back. "Okay, and it might help if you'd eat a little something."

"That sounds good to me," Seth chimed in, strolling into the kitchen, suitcase in hand. "I haven't eaten since early this morning."

Hanging on to her fraying composure, Becca rose from the table, carrying the still full coffee cup. "Okay, you get settled in and I'll serve lunch."

"Good," Sue said, heading for the archway into the dining room. "Follow me, Seth. I'm sure Mr. Moneybags won't mind how long you stay."

Oh, hell...hell...hell! Becca railed to herself. *Just stay as long as you like, Seth. Have yourself a great time driving Becca to distraction.*

Fuming, she dumped the now cold, bitter coffee into the sink and fixed a fresh pot. While the coffee brewed, she set about slapping place mats and napkins on the table, followed by plates for the sandwiches and small wooden bowls for the salads. She was setting the large bowl of mixed vegetable salad onto the table when Sue hurried back into the room.

"Seth will be down in a minute," she said, grabbing her purse and heading for the door. "I'll be leaving now...okay?"

"Yes, of course—go, Sue." Becca made a shooing motion with her hand, managing a smile for her. "I'll be fine. Dr. Carter is waiting."

"Right." Excitement glimmered in Sue's eyes. "Uh...I don't know when I'll be..."

"Don't worry about it," Seth drawled, sauntering into the room. "I assure you, I'll take good care of her."

Sue grinned, and rushed out of the house.

Becca was simmering. Who in the world assigned Seth Andrews, boy-wonder surgeon, to take care of her? She was fully capable of taking care of herself, thank you.

Carefully setting the sandwiches on the plates, she tried to calm her rising ire, afraid if she didn't she might explode all over the place, or him.

"Do you want a glass of water?" Becca avoided looking at him by turning to go to the cabinet where the glasses were kept.

"Yes, please." There was a trace of hidden laughter in his tone.

"Why are you here anyway?"

"Why else—to check on you."

The simmer was quickly turning into flaring temper. "Have a seat," she said with false calm. Back in Philadelphia, she thought, rather nastily.

Lunch was hardly a pleasant chatty occasion. In fact it was eaten in absolute silence.

Out of pure contrariness, not thirst, Becca drank two cups of the fresh coffee, while simply nibbling at both her salad and sandwich.

Naturally, Seth serenely ignored her while eating every bit of his lunch…not to mention the half of sandwich she left on her plate.

To Becca's further annoyance, he monitored every swallow of coffee she took.

"You know," he said, too casually, "instead of gulping caffeine, you should be resting."

Skirting the edge of serious anger, Becca glanced at him balefully. "Is that a professional or merely personal opinion, Dr. Andrews?"

He appeared unfazed by both her expression and sour tone of voice. "Both."

"Well, you can take both opinions and jam—"

"Careful now, Rebecca," he cautioned. "Let's not get down and dirty here."

Throwing her hands into the air, rather than her fist at his head, Becca shoved back her chair, stood and began clearing the table. "I don't want to listen to you issuing orders or suggestions." Carrying the dishes, she stopped halfway between the table and the sink to turn and face him. "You are not my boss here."

"I am not trying to boss you around." Seth shoved his chair back and circled the table to stand over her. Anger was beginning to color his voice. "Can't you see I'm trying to help you?"

"No." She gave a sharp shake of her head. "All I see is a man trying to tell me what to do and when to do it. Well, I'm tired of it." Becca drew a quick breath, and ranted on, "I have been telling you I am fine. Why can't you let it go at that?"

"Because you obviously aren't *fine,*" he snapped back at her. "If you were *fine* you wouldn't have damn near collapsed in John's office."

Although Becca was well aware that everything he was saying was true, she couldn't admit it.

"Why don't you just go get your bag and go back to Philadelphia, and leave me alone?" She spun to go to the sink and deposit the dishes. "You're not my keeper, you're a surgeon. Go back and save someone's life, for heaven's sake!" She turned again, away from him. Gently but firmly grasping her by the upper arm, he stopped her in her tracks.

"The way you've been pushing yourself, you need a keeper." His voice had a ragged edge. Turning to face her, he clasped her other arm. "It might as well be me."

"I don't think so," Becca retorted, a shiver rippling through her when he raised his hand to cradle her face. "You're the last person…"

"Oh, Becca, shut up." With that, he very effectively shut her up himself, by covering her mouth with his.

Six

At first his kiss was really not a kiss at all, simply his cool lips on hers. Becca went stiff, ice invading her spine, freezing her to the spot with outrage.

Damned if he wasn't doing it to her again, kissing her to keep her quiet. *Oh, Becca, shut up.* Only this time he didn't press his mouth to hers almost as if he wanted to devour her.

And then, all hell broke loose inside her mind, her emotions, her entire body.

Seth's lips grew warm, his mouth taking command of hers as though it was his right, as though she belonged to him, was his to do with as he pleased.

She wanted to shove him away, but at that moment he slipped his hands from her face to wrap his arms around her, drawing her hard against him.

She lifted her hands to scratch at his face, tangled her fingers in his hair to tear at it, pull it from his scalp.

Her rioting emotions, frustration, need, emptiness and a sudden flare of physical response stilled her hands, turning her fury into passion.

She did slide her fingers into his hair, but to tug his head closer. His tongue swept inside her mouth, teased her tongue, sending electrical shock waves throughout her body. The tips of her breasts tightened and tingled all the way down to her feminine core. Without thought or direction, Becca arched into him.

He made a low, almost growling sound in his throat, thrust his tongue deep inside. Tightening his arms around her, he trailed one hand to the base of her spine, crushing her to the hard readiness of his body.

She felt him…all the way from the top of her head to the tip of her now tingling toes. Somewhere, in the very back of what was left of her mind, Becca thought she should stop him.

No, no, she banished the dimming thought. She didn't want to stop him, she wanted… Releasing her fingers from his silky hair, she curled her arms around his neck and hung on, hungrily returning the kiss as if her life depended on it.

With an urgent need to breathe, Seth again lifted

his head. Becca wanted to protest, but she couldn't speak. He didn't loosen his hold on her and she continued to cling to him. Resting her forehead against his heaving chest, she shivered to the excited arousal racing along her nervous system, tangoing up her spine.

"Ahhh, Becca." Raising her chin with his other hand, he again lowered his head to command her mouth with his.

This time his kiss was gentle, teasing, his tongue playing hide-and-seek with hers. Kissed senseless, beyond coherent thought, she simply melted into him, returning the kiss, joining with his playful tongue.

She was only vaguely aware of being lifted into his arms. His increasingly hungry mouth setting her on fire, she clung to him as he strode into her bedroom, kicking the door shut behind them.

"Seth…" she began, only to have him silence her with one finger over her lips.

"Now is not the time for talk, Becca," he murmured, gliding his finger over her bottom lip. "Now is the time for indulgence, of our senses, in each other."

A tremor of longing rippled through her at the images his words evoked. Images right out of her dreams about him, them, together. Without a murmur of protest, Becca raised her mouth to his.

Within minutes, without breaking the kiss, they

slipped out of their clothing. Then finally, skin to skin, they fell onto the bed together.

Seth's body was hot and smooth and hard. She shivered in the heat of him. She trembled as his hands began to move, caressing her body.

A soft protest sprang to her throat when his mouth left hers. Her protest swiftly changed to a moan as his lips tracked the path of his hands.

Following his lead, Becca skimmed her hands over every inch of his body she could reach. She loved the feel of his hot skin beneath her palms. His back was broad, muscles taut with expectation. She traced the length of his spine. Emboldened by the quiver of his body, she smoothed her hands over his tight, narrow buttocks then stretched to slide her palms down his muscled bunched thighs. He made a guttural sound deep in his throat as she skimmed her fingers up the insides of his thighs.

Her own muffled groan echoed his as his one hand cupped one of her bottom cheeks and the other hand cupped her mound.

Without conscious thought, her thighs parted. She gasped with surprised pleasure when his fingers found and teased the most sensitive spot on her body.

"Seth…" That was all she could manage to say between short harsh breaths.

"You like that?" His voice was low, pure temptation. His mouth sought and found her breast, lips closing around the tip.

This time she couldn't manage even one word. But her gasp, the tremor that cascaded down her body, told him all he needed to know. "You like that, too?" His warm breath bathed her wet nipple, causing her to shiver.

Becca was long past denial. "Yes, yes, yes," she said, raking her nails down his back.

"Umm…" he murmured, shivering in response. "And I like that." Sliding up over her, he took her mouth in a soul-stirring, mind-destroying kiss. "And I like that." He deepened the kiss. "And that," he whispered against her lips before drawing a shudder from her by gliding his tongue along the inside of her lower lip. "But I like what's next even more." Kneeing her thighs wider, he settled between them.

She half expected to suddenly wake up, as she always did in her dreams when he slid between her thighs.

But Becca knew she wasn't dreaming when with one thrust he was inside her, filling the aching emptiness.

This was Seth inside her, pleasuring her, driving her higher and higher. It was wonderful. Aroused beyond anything she would ever have imagined herself to be capable of, Becca went wild in response.

Her breathing harsh, her body growing moist with perspiration, she arched up, into his every thrust, wanting more and more of him.

Leaning down over her, his hands covered her breasts as his lips covered her mouth, his tongue thrusting in rhythm with his body.

Becca was certain she was dying, or would if the tension, the friction of their joining, went on much longer. "I...I..." She gulped a breath. "Seth, please, I can't...I can't take any more."

"Do you want me to stop?" His voice was a purr that stroked her senses, incited her hunger.

"No!"

"Then, what do you want?" He had slowed his rhythm. "Tell me, Becca."

"You know." She grasped him by the hips, urging him deeper, deeper. "You know what I want."

"Yes," he whispered, plunging hard and fast. "I know, because I want it, too."

Becca went frantic as the tension built higher... higher...and then it snapped, flinging her wildly into a place she had never been. She cried out with the joy of it.

The very next instant, as if from a far distance, she heard Seth grunt before crying out his own release from the shatteringly wonderful tension.

Collapsing on top of her, Seth buried her face in the curve of her neck. Bearing his weight, Becca cradled him in an embrace of her arms and legs as their labored breathing slowly returned to normal.

Satiated, completely fulfilled and wonderfully drained, Becca closed her eyes, beginning to drift in the area between wakefulness and sleep.

She felt Seth move, shift his body from hers to lie next to her on the bed. She shivered and Seth drew her to him, while pulling the comforter over both of them.

Sighing with the double sensations of warmth and safety, Becca surrendered to slumber.

It was dark when Becca stirred to the delightful sensations created by Seth's hands stroking her now sensitized skin. Barely awake, her body responded to the arousing glide of his hand as it skimmed from her hip to her breasts, caressing one and then the other.

She sighed as his mouth moved over her face, leaving tiny kisses in its wake. She moaned with need when his lips took hers and his free hand delved into the apex of her legs, testing her readiness. Clasping him to her, she returned his kiss, her mouth and body demanding more, more of the ecstasy he had already given her.

With a soft chuckle, Seth obeyed, sliding his body between her parted thighs.

This time there was no teasing play. There was just a mutual urgency driving them. Seth was demanding, and so was Becca. She wanted to wring every drop of passion from him.

Seth didn't disappoint her. His thrusting body drove her quickly to the edge and over it. Becca's near scream of exquisite satisfaction and delicious pleasure was silenced inside his mouth.

She felt as if she had died, and didn't care. Close to unconsciousness, she was barely aware of Seth's tortured breath as he muttered close to her ear.

"That was fantastic."

They were the last words she heard before falling into a deep sleep.

Becca woke alone in the bed. Before opening her eyes, she floated in her dreams. They were like all the others, except this time she hadn't awakened at the most crucial moment. A soft smile on her lips, she opened her eyes, blinking at the bright sunlight streaming through the two bedroom windows.

What time was it? she wondered, yawning and glancing at the beside clock. *After ten? When had she gone to bed?* Her mind still a little hazy, she tossed back the comforter. The ache in her inner thighs, the tenderness in the apex of her legs, brought consciousness and memory flooding her mind.

Seth.

Turning her head, Becca looked at the empty space next to her. She sniffed, then drew a deep breath. She could smell him, the combined odors of sex and sweat and Seth's own masculine scent.

Memories continued to play inside her mind. His kisses, his caresses, his…*twice!* It was all there, in full color. Becca grew warm with a flush spreading from her cheeks to the rest of her body. She felt hot again and needy and…something niggled at the fringes of her mind, something important that she couldn't grasp.

She needed a shower. Not a cold one like men needed to ward off building passion, but a hot one that always left her feeling limp and drowsy.

Moving slowly, grimacing at the pull in her legs, Becca sat up onto the edge of the bed, tentatively getting to her feet. Okay, so far. Standing, she slowly walked into the bathroom. After standing under the hot spray from the shower for several minutes, she emerged, the flush of desire gone, along with much of the stiffness in her legs, the tenderness between them.

Becca stood in the steamy bathroom, blow-drying her hair, when the niggling sensation in her mind burst forth with its revelation. The echo of Seth's murmured words as she had drifted off to sleep came through loud and clear.

That was fantastic.

Meaning fantastic sex. That's all he'd thought it was. Just sex. A chill washed over her, chasing the warmth from the shower, leaving her body shivering. Biting her lip to hold back threatening tears, Becca turned off the dryer and rushed into the bedroom to dress.

Damn him, she raged in furious silence. He had done it again. Only this time, instead of being satisfied with merely shutting her up with a kiss, he had taken it to the limit, using her to satisfy himself with her body. And she, blind fool that she was, had surrendered herself to him.

How could she ever face him again? What must he be thinking of her? She had been eager, wanton, a willing partner in his self-indulgence.

That Seth had given her unimaginable pleasure in return didn't matter. Becca now knew she was not just infatuated with him. She was in love with him, while he…he…

Sniffing, she finished fastening her bra, swiped a hand over her moist eyes and pulled a hot pink T-shirt over her head. Telling herself she absolutely refused to cry over any man, she sniffed again while stepping into jeans, noting that although they were still loose on her, they weren't as loose as they had been two weeks ago.

Slipping into ballerina flats, Becca glanced into the mirror, grimacing at the wild tangled mess of her dark, straight hair. As she tamed her hair with a brush, she caught the aroma of brewing coffee and frying bacon. Sue must be back and cooking breakfast…and it smelled wonderful.

Her stomach rumbled. The eyes reflected back at her from the mirror widened. How could she be hungry at a time like this? Becca frowned at her reflection. Maybe because she hadn't eaten since she had picked at her lunch yesterday. Not to mention the "exercise" in the afternoon and during the night.

But Becca didn't want to think about that. Satisfied with just smoothing moisturizer on her face, she skipped makeup and left the room.

Maybe, just maybe, if she were lucky, Becca thought as she made her way to the kitchen, after what happened between them, Seth had left the house earlier and was on his way back to Philadelphia.

She should live so long.

Becca took one step inside the kitchen and stopped dead in her tracks. Sue was not in the room. Instead, Seth stood at the stove, pouring beaten eggs from a bowl into a sizzling frying pan. He glanced over his shoulder at her, saw her cool expression and raised his brows.

"Good morning." He didn't smile.

"Morning." She didn't smile, either.

He did frown. "Have a seat, breakfast will be ready in a few minutes." He turned away to stir the eggs and flip over the bacon.

Ignoring his invitation, Becca walked to the cof-

feepot and filled one of the mugs set on the countertop. Then she returned to sit down at the table.
Carefully sipping the hot brew, she watched him lay
pieces of bacon onto a towel to drain, then separate
the eggs onto two plates. He was doing the same
with the bacon when she spoke.

"I'm not very hungry." Her stomach clutched at
the bald-faced lie.

Now, Seth ignored her. He brought the two
plates to the table and set one in front of her. "You
must be," he said mildly. "You haven't eaten
anything but those couple of bites of your sandwich
yesterday."

"But—" she began, only to have him cut in.

"Eat, Becca," he ordered. "Or do you want to
make yourself ill all over again?"

"Of course not," she protested, her mouth
watering from the scent of the eggs and bacon
wafting to her. "I'm just—"

"You're just what?" Sharp impatience rode his
tone. "Waiting for the toast? It's on a plate right
there in the middle of the table."

"But…" she tried again, to no avail.

Seth scowled at her, and said coldly, "Becca,
shut up and eat."

Shut up…again? She glared at him.

He glared right back at her. Then he shrugged.
"Have it your own way. I'm hungry and the food's

getting cold." Looking away from her, he calmly began to eat.

For a moment, her mind and her stomach battled. When he reached for a piece of toast and slathered strawberry jam on it, her stomach won. With a soft sigh of defeat, Becca dug in to her breakfast.

They ate in tense, uneasy silence. Even so, Becca finished every morsel on her plate and two pieces of toast. She moved to get up to refill her mug. Seth was faster. Rising, he walked to the countertop and brought the pot back to the table with him. After filling both mugs, he set the pot down and turned to look at her.

"Okay, what's your problem?" he said, continuing before she could think of a response. "Regret? Remorse? Shame? Guilt?"

She held his steady gaze while corralling her thoughts into a cohesive reply.

"All of the above?" he asked.

"No. Yes." Becca shook her head at the demanding note in his voice. "I don't know."

Seth gave a deep sigh. "Becca, I don't understand. This morning you give me the cold shoulder. After last night I thought—"

"Yes, I know what you thought," she snapped back at him. "You thought it was great sex."

"No," he denied. "I thought it was fantastic sex. So, what's wrong with that?"

What was wrong with that? Becca asked herself, raking her mind for an answer. Well, in all honesty, nothing was wrong with fantastic sex. In fact, fantastic sex was…well, fantastic…between two committed people. But they—she and Seth—weren't committed. She now realized she was in love with him, crazy in love with him. So then, wasn't she committed?

Maybe she ought to be committed, into a room with padded walls, she chided herself.

"So?" Seth prompted her after her lengthy silence. "I asked what's wrong with that?"

"I…" She shook her head, shrugged, desperate for a coherent response. "I don't…" She was interrupted by the kitchen door swinging open, Sue practically dancing into the room.

"Good morning," she said, her voice light with a happy note.

Becca's immediate thought was that it would appear Sue had enjoyed some pretty good sex, as well. "Good morning, Sue." She and Seth spoke in unison. Relieved at being saved from answering him, she asked, "Have you had breakfast?"

"Yes." Pink tinged her cheeks. "John and I had the breakfast buffet at the Coffee Shop."

"This Coffee Shop does breakfast buffet?" Seth arched his brows. "Every morning?"

Sue shook her head. "No, only on the weekend.

They lay it on, too. The place gets packed." The color deepened in her cheeks. "John made reservations last night to make sure we could get in."

"Hmm, I'll keep that in mind." He shifted a glance at Becca. "Where is this place located?"

"Halfway down the street from John's office." Sue flushed again, obviously with the mere mention of John's name. "Is there any coffee?" she asked, neatly changing the conversation.

"It's gone cold." Becca slid her chair back. "I'll make a fresh pot."

Seth's chair scraped back at the same time. "No, I'll make it."

Becca stood and favored him with a patently fake smile. "You can clear the table. I'll get the coffee." She turned her attention to Sue before he could utter a protest. "So, how was your dinner?"

"It was wonderful, John cooked it." The flush was back. "How was the chicken veggie pie?"

Pie? Becca stopped cold, her mind a momentary blank. Memory returned, and her cheeks flushed. Oh, heavens, the supper Sue had prepared for them. They had completely forgotten, with good reason. She flashed a quick look at Seth. A tiny smile played at the corners of his lips, and arching a brow, he blandly returned her look.

No help from that quarter. Facing Sue, she plastered a smile on her lips. "I'm afraid I never got to it. I made do with lunch, then went right to my room." She shot Seth a smug look and an innocent tone. "What about you, Seth. Did you have the pie for dinner?"

"No, I didn't want to bake it just for myself," he returned, his voice smooth, unruffled. "I didn't have much of an appetite anyway." He gave Sue a charming, disarming smile. "The three of us can have it for dinner tonight, if you're planning on being here."

"Oh, I am, but—" Sue hesitated, before looking at Becca and rushing on "—I hope you don't mind, Becca, I've invited John to dinner. I'm sure there'll be enough pie for the four of us."

"Of course, I don't mind," Becca said, silently sighing with relief. Hopefully, the tension between her and Seth would dry up with Sue and John there. "As for being enough, we can always add to the salad Seth and I didn't finish yesterday."

"Oh, thank you." Sue sighed aloud. "I know I should have asked you first but…"

"Don't be silly," Becca said, bringing the coffee-pot and a clean mug to the table. "Coffee's ready. Do you want a refill, Seth?"

"Yes, thank you," he eyed her warily, as if not sure from her pleasant tone what her mood was.

"Well, I've had enough coffee this morning. I think I'll collect my laundry and wash it." Despite

Sue's arguments, Becca had insisted from the day after she arrived at the house that she would do her own wash. She was walking through the archway into the dining room when she leveled a zinger at Seth over her shoulder. "I think I'll launder the sheets, as well."

"But I thought you just changed sheets three days ago," Sue called after her.

Becca halted, a wicked smile feathering her lips. "I did, but I had a couple of nightmares last night, and I was perspiring all over the sheets. They now have a bad smell."

Seven

"Sweaty and smelly from nightmares, are they?"

Becca froze at the sound of Seth's low-pitched voice. Her fingers curled into the bottom sheet she had been tugging from the mattress.

"Strange…they didn't seem like nightmares to me. They were a lot more pleasurable than nightmares."

Oh, why had she left her bedroom door open? she wondered, afraid Sue might be able to hear him. Bracing herself, she turned to face him. He was standing at the doorway. He hadn't taken one step inside.

"May I come in?" Seth's smile was wry. "Even though it's mighty tempting with those sheets all rumpled and smelling of sex, I promise I won't pick you up and toss you onto the bed."

Damn right you won't, Becca thought. "I didn't suspect you would," she said.

His brows went up. "Then…?"

"Why, what do you want?"

Now the smile that crept over his alluring mouth, the sudden darkening of his amber eyes, said volumes without him uttering a sound. "I think we need to talk."

"All right, come in." She sighed. "But…" There was a warning note in her voice.

"You have my word," he murmured, stepping inside and quietly closing the door behind him.

"Okay, talk away," Becca said, turning back to continue stripping the bed.

Unfazed, he circled the bed to the padded boudoir chair set next to the window. "May I?" He indicated the small chair.

Becca didn't look away from what she was doing, only yanked harder on the sheets. "If you must," she said, sighing loudly.

He chuckled softly, seating himself.

His laughter tickled down the length of her spine and back up to the nape of her neck. Why did the man have such a melting effect on her? He always had, and Becca had worked hard all the years she'd assisted him not to betray her feelings.

Watching him with quick sidelong glances as she worked, she saw him stretch his long legs out and cross his ankles. While she mused that by rights he should look uncomfortable in the small chair, he managed to appear completely relaxed.

How did he do that? Puzzled by his apparent comfort in the lady's chair, Becca slid another long glance at him and immediately wished she hadn't, for he was watching her.

"You said you wanted to talk." Irritation, more at herself than him, shaded her tones. "About what?"

"First, I'd like to know why you had to mention anything to Sue about having to change the sheets? I was thinking we had a great time making those sheets sweaty and smelly. But then, I had believed you were thinking the same."

Her mind a sudden blank, Becca stood there by the bed staring at him, the soiled linens bundled in her arms.

Of course, she knew the answer. She'd said it because she felt hurt, used and longing for something more than sex. She loved him. She wanted nothing more than to repeat their night together every night for the rest of her life.

But Seth didn't love her. It didn't take a genius to figure that one out. Oh, she supposed he liked her okay, in his own gruff way, and certainly he respected her ability as his assistant in the operating room. But he had never once indicated any personal interest in her before. So why now, and here?

Suddenly she realized she had been quiet too long, simply staring into his now closed expression. What had he said? Oh, yeah, something about him believing she'd enjoyed their lovemaking as much as he had.

"I admit I did enjoy our night together," she finally replied. "It had...uh, been a while for me," she blurted out, at once regretting the admission.

His expression went from closed to hard and cold. "I see...I was a handy convenience." His voice was every bit as hard and cold as his expression.

Becca felt almost as though he had slapped her. Without a thought, she retaliated. "It appears we were handy conveniences for each other."

"Umm." That was the only sound he made. Slowly, his gaze still locked onto hers, his expression softened, his eyes warmed with sensuality. "In that case, while I'm here, why not continue the arrangement?" A half smile formed on his lips. "Sex is a healthy outlet for tension and stress, and we've both endured plenty of that for some time."

Stunned speechless, Becca simply stared at him, unable to believe he had actually said that to her. But then, he was a man and she'd read somewhere that men thought about sex every few minutes. Seth had very likely been celibate for a long time. At least she felt sure he hadn't been with a woman during the time he had been in Africa. As small as the village was, the grapevine was always up and running and she'd have heard about it if he had been seeing a woman.

Of course, Seth had been back in Philadelphia for a month now. He could have… Becca didn't want to think about what he could have been doing.

"I hate to intrude on your introspection, but is your silence a way of saying no to my proposal?" Now his voice was bone-dry, and a little gravelly.

Becca felt stuck between a rock of pride and a hard place of desire. Which did she need more, her pride or…? Pride lost the battle hands down.

"How long are you planning on being here?" she asked, avoiding giving him a definite answer.

"I told Colin I'd be gone a week." He shrugged. "Colin has held it together long enough. It's time I got back to work."

"I like Colin," Becca said, fully aware she was biding for extra time.

"So do I or I wouldn't be in practice with him," he said, giving a brief shake of his head. "But that has nothing to do with the subject at hand. All I want, Becca, is a yes or a no."

She drew a breath, a deep one, once again avoiding an answer by saying, "I'll think about it and let you know." What a coward you are, Becca derided herself. Too gutless to grab what you want.

"Your call," Seth said, rising to nonchalantly stroll to the door, where he paused to glance back at her. "While you're thinking, keep in mind that we're both adults," he said. "At least, I am." He walked out, closing the door quietly behind him.

"Damn," Becca muttered, flinging the bundle of sheets to the floor. She stood still for a moment, breathing hard. He was right. He was an adult. She was the one acting like a child...a bad-tempered one at that.

She opened a dresser drawer to take out a set of clean sheets and proceeded to remake the bed.

As she hadn't eaten breakfast until late morning, Becca skipped lunch and spent the rest of the afternoon in her room, relaxing and reading, but in plain truth, she was hiding from Seth.

In an attempt to keep her thoughts at bay, she took a long, hot bath, scrubbing every inch of her body with a single-mindedness that left her skin tingling.

By the time Becca had done her hair and was dressed in wide-legged flowing pants and a loose pullover top, she had made up her mind as to exactly what her answer to Seth was going to be.

Finally leaving her bedroom, Becca's steps were light as she walked into the kitchen. Sue was bent over, her head stuck in the fridge.

"Are you caught in there, Sue?" she said, laughing as she crossed to the older woman. "Can I help?"

Laughing along with her, Sue backed out of the fridge, the chicken vegetable pie in her hands. "Yes, you can get the salad and cut up more ingredients to toss into it to stretch it to make enough for four." She raised her eyebrows. "You did remember that John is coming for dinner?"

"Yes, I remembered." Becca took Sue's place in the fridge, gathering veggies from the bottom drawer. "What time do you expect him?" she asked, straightening and shutting the door with a swing of her hips.

Sue was sliding the pie into the oven. "I told him six," she said, closing the oven door. "Did you have a nice nap?"

"Not really." Becca grinned. "I guess I wasn't as tired as I thought." She glanced around and into the dining room and the living room beyond. "Where is Seth?"

"John invited him into town for the grand tour, which shouldn't take very long." Sue smiled. "I suppose they're in the clinic and he and Seth are having a gabfest." She glanced at the clock. "It's five now." Her smile turned into a laugh. "I suspect they'll be here in time for dinner."

"They'd better be," Becca said, holding a strainer under running water, rinsing the grape tomatoes inside the bowl. "This is going to be one hummer of a salad."

* * *

It was a fine September Sunday afternoon, the perfect weather for a stroll around the town of Forest Hills. After making the circuit, John invited Seth back to the clinic for a cup of coffee and some conversation.

Seth sat in the chair beside John's desk. They were sipping John's strong coffee, getting to know one· another, biding time until they were due to return to the house for dinner.

"You know, I've heard of your father," John said out of the blue. "It's said he's one of the best heart surgeons in the world."

"You heard correctly." Seth smiled. "In the operating room, my father's a power to be reckoned with. He beats the odds more often than he loses."

"I heard about you, too." John smiled at him. "You started up the hospital in Africa your father and a few other doctors built."

"Correct again." Seth laughed. "I presume you heard of me because of all the attention Becca received when I sent her back to the States."

John shook his head. "Oh, yes, I couldn't have missed that as it was all over the news. But I had heard of you before, in connection to the hospital, as well as the reputation you've built in your own field of expertise."

Seth shrugged off the praise, addressing only his

work in Africa. "I didn't do anything spectacular. A doctor was needed in that village and I offered to go. No big deal."

"You did nothing spectacular except bring much-needed hope and medical care to those people in that town," John said.

"Yeah, but my dad and his friends made it all possible by financing the hospital," Seth said. "Becca's the heroine of that story."

John nodded in agreement. "From what I read, she gave her all to those people and her profession."

For a moment, Seth felt a twinge of the familiar fear. "She damn near killed herself." His quavering voice betrayed his feelings. He cleared his throat and said, "And even so, she argued about leaving."

"You like her, don't you?" John said, obviously noting the concern hiding behind his rough tone.

"Yes, of course," Seth answered, thinking, no, *like* didn't even come close to the depth of what he felt for Becca. It was a feeling he wasn't about to confess to John, or anyone except Becca—maybe.

"She has been a great help to me here since she arrived," John said. "After she leaves, I'll be back on my own...unless I can talk Sue into taking Becca's place. Sue is a nurse, you know."

Seth shook his head, frowning. "I don't...wait a minute. The letter Becca received did mention that Sue was a nurse. I suppose I thought she had retired from nursing, and was supplementing her income by being the housekeeper for the person who owns that lodge they dare call a cabin."

John laughed. "Yeah, some cabin, huh?" Still chuckling, he clarified, "Sue had retired from nursing to come home here to take care of her mother after her father passed away." He sighed. "She had been helping me out in the clinic now and then before she was offered the job of housekeeping the cabin, keeping it neat part-time between visitors and full-time while someone was there and…at a salary you wouldn't believe."

Seth grinned. "Yeah, I would. Whoever this person is who owns the place has to be a multi-millionaire or even a billionaire. That dump is something." He chose not to mention that his own father had a place that put the so-called cabin to shame.

John grinned back at him, and said in a soft, conspiratorial voice, "I have spent a few nights there with Sue when nobody was in residence."

Seth laughed, both at John's naughty-boy tone, and in a bid to conceal the shudder rippling through him at the vivid image of he and Becca sharing that big bed in the master bedroom.

Seth felt the stirring in his lower body. If he got hard now, John would think he was as horny as a teenager. Instead, John saved Seth's pride by glancing at his watch.

"We'd better be going," he said, standing. "Sue said six and it's ten of now. She won't like having to hold dinner. Besides, I'm hungry." Striding to the door, he opened it for Seth.

Seth was thinking he was hungry, too, but for Becca. His body calming down somewhat, he strolled from the room and the clinic to his car, which was parked right behind John's ten-year-old vehicle.

Food first, Seth thought, then…Becca's answer. He could only hope it would be the one he wanted to hear.

Sliding the tray of dinner rolls into the oven, Sue set the timer then glanced at the clock. "They had better get here soon," she muttered.

Becca glanced up to smile at the frowning woman. "There's time, it's only ten minutes till six," she said, glancing back at the table to make sure she hadn't missed anything.

As Sue had decided to eat dinner in the kitchen instead of at the much larger and formal dining room, Becca had set the table with the everyday dishes, the ones she and Sue had used ever since Becca had arrived.

Everything was ready. The white wine was chilling. Becca had uncorked the red to allow it to breathe. The large salad bowl was set to one side, four smaller matching bowls next to it. A selection of dressings sat behind the grouping of salt-and-pepper shakers and a crystal butter dish.

Satisfied, Becca went to the counter to shake out and place a napkin inside a basket for the rolls. She looked up, her heart beginning to race as the doors of two separate cars were slammed shut. Moments later came the sound of footsteps up and onto the porch.

She turned as the kitchen door was opened, repressing a shiver as the men entered the room. The shiver grew, chilling her spine as Seth's eyes immediately sought her out with a heated amber stare.

"We're back," John announced, voicing the obvious. "And with a few minutes to spare till six."

"You two can go wash up," Sue said, a warm smile on her lips for John. "Dinner is ready."

"Yes, ma'am," John said, his smile as warm as hers had been. "Let's go, Seth."

"Yes, sir," Seth replied, shooting a grin at Becca. "I'm right behind you."

His grin, both amused and intimate, played tricks with Becca's senses. Heat flared in the deepest part of her body. She was at once uncertain of the decision she had made about the answer she planned to give him. When a mere grin was all a man had to do to turn her on…well… The men's return to the kitchen scattered her already tumbling thoughts.

"Ahhh," John murmured, inhaling deeply. "That smells wonderful, Sue."

The Sue that Becca had come to know had seemed unflappable, but one minor compliment from the good doctor did the trick. Flushing, Sue set the large pie on the table and with a breathy "thanks" quickly turned to the stove to slide the tray of rolls from the oven.

Smiling in sympathy for the older woman, as Becca was still feeling a bit breathless herself, she retrieved the salad from the fridge. While Sue took a carafe of water from the fridge, Becca got the wine bottles and set them on the table.

To her surprise, the men waited to seat them before seating themselves. Becca assumed Seth had followed John's lead, as he had never held a chair for her in all the years she had worked for him, and they had taken lunch and dinner together many times before.

The meal was wonderful, the conversational topics all over the place. Sometimes serious, more often amusing, they lingered over their coffee and the apple pie Sue warmed in the oven before plopping big slabs of vanilla ice cream on top of each large slice.

By the time they made a move, seemingly as of one mind to leave the table, it was . early seven forty-five. Becca felt about to burst, but she also felt mellow from the delicious food, the wine and the sense of camaraderie and contentment.

Both men began to collect the dishes. Sue put an end to their efforts to help.

"Becca and I'll do the clearing away," she said, making a shooing motion with her hands. "You two go watch the news or a football game or something."

"But you and Becca had the work of prepar—" That's as far as she allowed John to go.

"And Becca and I will clear it away. Now go," she ordered. "The sooner we get started, the sooner we'll get finished."

Neither Becca nor Seth said a word. They just stood by, smiling and watching. Well, Becca was smiling and watching Sue and John, but the sensation of the raised hairs on her arms, the tingle at the back of her neck, made her feel certain Seth was watching her. But while she felt as though she could feel his intent gaze on her, there was no way she could discern if he were smiling or frowning at her.

It was not a comfortable sensation. While doing her best to appear unaware of his stare, Becca lost track of the tug-of-war between Sue and John. She caught up with it just as John threw in the towel.

"Okay, okay, we'll go into the living room." John raised his hands in defeat. "Come on, Seth, let's get out of here before this comes to blows."

"As if," Sue retorted, laughing.

John and Seth sauntered from the room. Becca exhaled in relief, glad to be out from under the microscope of Seth's speculative gaze.

Starting to clear the table, she gave Sue a curious look. "Why were you so insistent on the men not pitching in to help out in here?"

"Because I wanted a minute to talk to you in private," Sue answered, her cheeks growing pink again. She carried a load of dishes to the dishwasher.

"Okay," Becca said, following her with the knives, forks and spoons. "About what?"

Sue straightened up from the dishwasher. "Becca, you're a nurse and a mature woman, and I hope you'll understand…" She trailed off, then burst out, "Oh, hell, Becca, I've asked John to stay over at my house tonight." She grabbed a breath. "Will you be all right alone here again tonight?"

Now Becca did laugh, gently. "Of course I'll be all right. And I won't be alone, you know, Seth will be here with me."

Hearing her own words squelched her laughter. She quivered inside, remembering how they had spent the night, and his proposal.

"Whew," Sue said, beaming at Becca. "You'd figured out where I had spent last night, hadn't you?"

Becca lips quirked in a half smile. "Well, I had my suspicions."

"Oh, Becca, I have been in love with John for as long as I can remember." Noting Becca's quick frown, she hurried on. "Oh, don't misunderstand, I loved my husband dearly, but a tiny piece of my heart always belonged to John. And now…" Tears misted her eyes.

"Now he has discovered you?"

"Yes." Sue sniffed, followed by an uncertain smile. "We're both in our fifties and we don't want to waste any more time. Does that make sense to you?"

"That makes perfect sense, Sue." Becca smiled. "How did that old line go…something about only going around once?"

"Yes." Sue laughed. "You're right, so let's get done so John and I can get out of here."

It required less than twenty minutes to put the kitchen back in order. Appearing casual, Becca and Sue joined the men in the living room. They were watching a football game on TV.

Seth glanced up at Becca, a wry smile on his lips. "The Eagles are playing the Giants."

"Oh, that's nice." She didn't give a rip about football, and Seth knew it. "I think I'll get a book to read." She started for her room, but turned back to give Sue a pointed look. "Did you say something about you and John going out for a while, Sue?"

"Yes, I did." Sue returned the smile. "Are you about ready to go, John?"

"Whenever you are," he said, pushing out of the chair's deep cushions. "I'm a baseball fan myself."

Seth moved to rise.

"You don't need to get up, Seth," John said, offering him a man-to-man grin. "We know our way out."

"Well, 'bye now," Sue called, leading John by the arm to the door.

Seth stared at the doorway with a "what did I miss?" expression. Stifling a laugh, Becca turned again to go for a book. But she couldn't resist a mild teasing jab.

"You're missing the game." Before he could turn to her, she took off down the hallway to her room.

Seth was right behind her.

Although she didn't hear him, she knew he was there. The tingle up her spine gave warning. Arching her eyebrows in question, she turned to look at him.

Once again he stood at the doorway, not entering without her permission, still wearing the slightly baffled look on his face.

"What was that all about in there?"

Not wanting him to see the smile flitting across her mouth, Becca turned away again, simply asking, "What was what all about?"

"That exchange there in the living room just now," he said, impatience riding his voice. "That byplay between Sue and John...and you, too?"

The smile escaping, she slanted a sidelong glance at him. Umm, he looked sooo good, she thought.

"They were being coy, Seth. Sue and John are going to spend the night together." She chuckled. "I suspect they did last night as well."

"Sounds good to me," he said, his voice low and much too seductive.

"I feel sure it would sound good to most men," she murmured, expecting an argument as she turned fully to face him once more. He didn't give her one.

"Have you reached a decision?" His voice was softer, his eyes wary.

Becca drew a deep breath. "Yes, I'll spend the rest of the week with you."

"Good," his voice held a soft sigh of relief. Stepping inside, he crossed to her, halting abruptly when she held one hand up, palm out.

"But not tonight."

His eyes narrowed and one brow lifted in skepticism. "You have a headache?"

Eight

Becca gave him a wry look. "No, I don't have a headache, Seth."

"Then—" he began.

"But I ache everywhere else in my body."

"Oh…" He frowned.

Becca could tell by the sudden chagrined look on his face that he understood she was sore from their sexual exercise through most of the night.

"Yes," she said, allowing him a small smile. "So tonight I just want to read my book a while then get a good night's sleep."

"Of course." Seth nodded, smiling sympathetically. "Will you bring your book into the living room, sit with me while I watch the game?"

"If you'll recall," she pointed out to him, "I said that's what I was going to do."

"Good." Turning, he walked away.

Shaking her head in bemusement, Becca picked up the historical romance paperback from the bedside stand and followed him into the living room.

Earlier, Seth had been sitting in the butter-soft leather lounge chair. Now, he was on the sofa. He patted the cushion next to him when she entered the room.

"Come, sit beside me," he invited, soft and low.

Becca arched her brows.

"I'll behave," he said, grinning, and again patting the cushion. "I promise."

"Weelll…" she said, dragging the word out. "If you promise to keep your promise." Becca grinned back at him, as she settled on the couch beside him.

"Hmm," he murmured, appearing sad. "Does behaving include no kisses or hugs?"

His teasing and downcast look were so far out of character, it was simply too much. Becca burst out laughing.

"Is that a yes or a no?" His attempt to look and sound stern was pathetic.

She laughed harder. "I never knew you could be fun to be with," she admitted.

Seth jerked back, one hand flying to his chest, as if he had been shot. "You wound me, woman. Are you insinuating last night with me wasn't fun?"

Still laughing at his antics, Becca covered her mouth with one hand and shook her head in the negative.

This time he managed a killer, sensual smile. "You are so sexy when you laugh, did you know that?"

"Sexy! Me? I am?" Becca was stunned. "I'm not at all sexy," she declared, so thrilled by the compliment, the words seemed to tumble out of her mouth. "At least, no one has ever given me the slightest hint they thought I was sexy."

"You're not serious…are you?" One dark eyebrow arched in disbelief.

"You think I'd kid around about something like that?" she said, a tinge of annoyance in her voice, a cover-up for her sense of inadequacy. She made a move to get up, put some distance between them.

"Whoa, you stay right where you are," Seth ordered, curving his arm around her waist. "Better yet, come here, closer to me." He drew her stiffened body against him, raising a hand to turn her face to his.

Becca tried to move her head. He held her still, staring deeply into her eyes.

"To me, Becca, you are the sexiest woman I've ever set eyes on." He moved closer, brushing his lips over her mouth.

Becca shivered in response and inched closer to him for more of the same. "Really?" she whispered, returning the favor by brushing her mouth over his lips.

"Hmm," he murmured. "I've been wanting to get you into my bed, be inside you, ever since you became a member of my surgical team."

Becca inwardly cringed against a pang in her chest. He wanted her, physically, nothing more. She closed her eyes against a rush of hot tears as Seth took possession of her mouth, and thrust his tongue between her teeth.

For a moment she went still in his arms, his kiss was physically thrilling and emotionally devastating. She wanted to push him away, but clutched him to her instead. He hadn't lied to her, but had honestly admitted he wanted an affair, a week together of sexual fun and games.

While she, like a romantic fool, loved him with everything inside her being.

Desperately needing to release the tears gathering in her eyes in a long self-pity party of weeping, Becca pushed gently against his chest.

Seth was frowning when he lifted his head to gaze at her in confusion. "What's wrong?"

"I did tell you not tonight, Seth," she said, wincing at the painful tug of her lower back and inner thigh muscles as she rose from the sofa. "Now things are getting too intense. Not only do I still ache all over, now my head is beginning to pound."

"Let me get you some Tylenol or something stronger," he said, rising to stand next to her, and sliding his arm around her waist. "You are a little pale."

"Tylenol will be fine, thank you." Unable to resist, she rested her now throbbing head on his shoulder. "I don't like to take stronger pain medication. I'm just tired. I'll be okay after a good night's sleep."

"I'm not so sure about that," he muttered. It was only then she felt his finger on her wrist. "Your pulse rate is rapid. Looks like you've managed to overdo it once again."

"No, the rapid pulse is your fault," she admitted, managing a tiny smile. "That's the effect your kisses have on me."

He smiled. "That's a good thing." He immediately grew sober again. "I'm going to get my stethoscope." He started to turn away.

"No," she said, catching him by the arm. "It's not necessary." She frowned. "You brought your stethoscope with you on vacation?"

"Habit." He grinned.

"Uh-huh." Becca sighed, knowing full well he had come for the express reason to check on her. That also would have been a good thing, if he hadn't bluntly told her he wanted her to get well because he needed her in the operating room.

She sighed again. While the tears in her eyes were now gone, she still felt the urge to cry. "I think I'll forget reading tonight and go on to bed."

"Maybe that's best," he agreed, peering at her in his patient probing way. "You go ahead, I'll get the Tylenol and a glass of water."

Seth sat sprawled on the sofa, staring blindly at the TV screen. He didn't see the game in play, or hear the noise of the crowd of football fans or the chatter of the commentators.

The fire in his body had finally calmed down. The concern for Becca remained, worrying him. He didn't understand. She had seemed fine last night in bed, so sweetly responsive, ready...no, eager to share her body with him. Shivering, he grew warm remembering the honey of her mouth, the tight peaks of her breasts, the satin softness of her skin, her smooth thighs curled tightly around his waist.

Seth heaved a long sigh. He wanted to be lying next to her right now, not for the sex, although that would be wonderful, too. Most of all, he wanted to hold her close to him, make her completely well, keep her warm and safe, protect her for the rest of his life.

But Becca had made it obvious, many times, if not by words but attitude, that she was impervious to him and, apparently, any man. She was and had always been cool, calm and remote.

Except last night.

Last night. Closing his eyes, Seth rested his head on the back of the sofa, reliving every minute of the night before, every kiss, every touch, every cry of release and heady satisfaction.

He had never experienced anything even close to the euphoria he had shared with Becca.

She had given him this week. One week of being together day and night. On the spot, Seth vowed to make it the best week of his, and hopefully Becca's, life.

Her head throbbing, Becca lay across the bed fully dressed, but did not immediately fall asleep, as she had hoped she would. Slowly, the Tylenol eased the pain in her head, but it didn't induce sleepiness. Her mind was restless, spinning from one thought to the next, always coming back to the most important of all her jumbled mental meanderings.

She wanted Seth so very badly…body, heart and soul. Having been with him, in the most physical, intimate ways a woman can be with a man, she felt bereft without him next to her, holding her, loving her.

Loving her.

A sob rose in Becca's throat. She swallowed hard, attempting to force it back. Instead, it broke from her lips. She buried her face in her pillow to muffle the painful sound.

Until recently, Becca rarely allowed herself the indulgence of tears. In her teens, she had concluded giving way to tears only ever got two results—puffy eyes and a pale, blotchy face. Who needed that?

She had cried with Shakana before leaving Africa, but that was because she was ill and weak. Now, Becca was no longer ill or weak, at least physically. Emotionally, she was a basket case.

And so she cried, sobbing into the pillow until there were no more tears left inside her. She felt empty and she found peace in the haven of deep sleep.

Hours later, Becca woke, feeling washed out and used up and cold. Her eyelids felt heavy and odd. She hadn't closed the drapes and the light from a nearly full moon filled the room. She could see clearly. What she saw confused her for a moment.

She was fully dressed lying on top of the covers. Becca frowned. What was she doing in bed in her clothes? She moved her head on the pillow, grimacing at the wet touching her cheek. Why was the pillow... Oh. Dawn broke, not beyond the window but inside her now fully awake mind.

She had soaked the pillow with her useless tears.

She no longer wondered why her eyes felt funny. Sighing, she dragged her body from the bed, made her way to the bathroom and flipped on the light.

The image that stared back at her from the mirror was not encouraging. Her eyes were red-rimmed, the lids swollen. Her complexion looked like it had developed a bad rash while she slept.

"This is what you get for allowing yourself to become involved with a man who wants nothing from you but casual sex, even if he is the most skilled and exciting lover and otherwise wonderful man you have ever met."

Somehow, berating herself aloud had little effect on the ravaged image before her. Shaking her head in despair of the pitiful-looking creature in the mirror, Becca turned the faucet on until the water running from it felt almost icy.

Soaking a washcloth, she held it against her face, applying pressure to her eyes. She repeated the process several times, until her face felt numb with cold. After patting her face dry, she glanced into the mirror once more. She was red as a beet, but the swelling in her eyelids was down.

Knowing the cold-induced color would fade, Becca returned to the bedroom and switched on the bedside lamp. The digital number on the clock read 4:11 a.m.

Becca was wide-awake, shivering with the cold,

and suddenly hungry. First things first, she thought. Pulling off her clothes, goose bumps rising on her skin from the chill air, she slipped on an equally chilled silky nightgown. Grateful to Rachael for packing her ankle-length velour robe, she shrugged into its warmth and tied the belt snugly around her waist.

Now...food, she thought, sliding her cold feet into fuzzy, flat mule slippers. Before leaving the room, Becca went to the window to place her hand against the pane. Uh, yep, the night had turned very cold. Why she was surprised, she didn't know. It was September, and hard as it was to believe, two months had passed since she had returned to the States from Africa.

Time flies when you're having fun, she mused, grimacing as she left the room. And even if you weren't having fun.

Becca stopped in her tracks as she entered the living room. Seth was lying half on and half off the sofa, as if he had fallen asleep sitting up and slid down flat with his legs hanging over the edge. He appeared sound asleep. Becca could see he was now wearing pajama pants and a well-worn University of Pennsylvania sweatshirt. His feet were bare.

Realizing he was probably cold, Becca quietly walked to the sofa and carefully lifted his long legs onto the sofa. Taking the faux fur throw from the back of the sofa, she covered him, tucking the throw around his cold feet. Seth didn't wake up. He grunted and snuggled into the throw. Smiling, she backed away, turned and walked to the kitchen.

Becca was sitting at the kitchen table, chewing on a piece of toast and cradling a hot cup of tea in her hands, when Seth strolled into the room, the throw draped over his shoulders like a cape.

She raised her eyebrows. "Did I wake you when I covered you?"

He shook his head and smiled. "No, the smell of the bread toasting woke me. Smells good."

"Help yourself," she invited. "The bread's on the countertop, and bring a cup if you want some tea. I made a full pot." A flick of her hand indicated the fat china pot set close to her on the table.

"Thanks, I think I will."

Becca continued to eat her toast as she watched him make his own. She was finishing the last bite when he seated himself opposite her, pulling the throw around him like a robe.

"Turned cold during the night," he said, biting into a piece of toast.

"Yes," she agreed. "I guess Indian summer is over. I'll have to turn on the heat tomorrow…later today," she said, correcting herself.

"Hmm." Seth nodded, eyeing the teapot. "That tea smells good, too."

Unwilling to play either employee or hostess,

she refilled her cup, then slid the pot to him so he could pour his own tea.

"Thanks," he drawled, taking another big bite of the bread. "Couldn't you sleep?"

"I did sleep," she said, raising the cup to sip the hot brew. "I fell asleep on top of the covers. The chilly air, along with a pang of hunger, woke me."

"Oh." Seth continued to eat.

Becca concentrated on her tea, unable to think of another thing to add to such scintillating conversation.

Finishing off the last of his toast, Seth concentrated on his own tea…for a few moments. "You look tired, Becca," he said, sounding more the lover than the doctor.

A tingle attacking her spine, Becca lowered her eyes, murmuring simply, "I am tired."

"Come to bed with me, Becca." His voice was low, seductive, so very tempting.

The tingle in her spine flared into a full-fledged sizzle. She raised her eyes to stare into the depths of molten amber. "I…" She hesitated.

"Please." An imploring note added inducement to his passion-roughened voice.

"Seth, I—"

"I promise I'll be gentle, careful of your sore, aching muscles."

She paused, sighed and gave in to the hunger clawing at her body. "Yes."

Seth stood, pushing the chair back, and started toward her, his arms reaching for her.

"Seth, wait." Becca help up a hand. "I've got to clear away our dishes."

He rolled his eyes, sighed in exasperation. "Becca, the dishes can wait," he said, plucking her plate from her hands before taking her in his arms. "I'm not so certain I can."

Becca didn't struggle.

He swept her up into his arms, and started for her bedroom. The throw fluttered to the floor unnoticed.

Curling her arms around his neck, Becca rested her head against his shoulder, inhaling the spicy scent of his cologne and the even spicier natural scent of Seth beneath.

Nine

Seth carried Becca into her bedroom. A light nudge of his hip shut the door after them.

Setting her on her feet, he opened the belt on her robe. It slid silently down to the floor. Stepping back, he ran a head-to-toe look over her. A smile touched his lips. "Cute slippers."

Becca smiled back. "They're warm and comfortable." Her smile grew. "And, yes, cute."

Seth ran another glace the length of her. "The slippers are cute," he repeated, his eyes heating as his smile faded. "The nightgown is lovely...but I prefer you in your glorious natural state."

"Seth..." His name was all Becca could get past

her suddenly dry-as-dust throat. Her pulse jumped when he grasped the edges of his sweatshirt and pulled it up and over his head. He stood there, naked except for the cotton pajama pants riding low on his slim hips.

Lifting her eyes to his, Becca held his gaze as she drew the nightgown straps over her shoulders, allowing the gown to slide down her body to pool around her feet.

Once more Seth ran a slow look over her body.

Becca stepped out of the slippers and into his arms. A tremor skipped through her at the feel of his hands outlining her form.

"You're still too thin," he murmured close to her ear. "I can feel your hip bones jutting out."

Becca sent her own hands exploring. "You're still thin yourself, Doctor," she whispered. "Your hip bones jut out as far as mine."

She could feel his smile as he glided his lips from her ear to the corner of her mouth. "Your skin is silky again," he said, laughter in his tone. He brushed his mouth over hers. "Your lips are sweet."

Becca speared her fingers through the thick strands of his hair. "It's the jam I had on my toast."

He laughed aloud. "Ah, Becca, never without a comeback." He taste-tested her lips again. "Nope, it's not the jam. It's the essence of you."

She gave a light tug on his hair. "Are you going

to kiss me for real, or are you planning to put me back to sleep?"

"You talked me into it." Lifting his hands, he captured her face and took command of her lips. His tongue claimed the inside of her mouth.

Heat seared Becca, leaving her weak, needy. She clung to Seth, arching into him, thrilling to the hard pressure of his erection against her belly.

"Oh, I need you." Grabbing a corner of the rumpled covers, he tossed them all the way down to the bottom of the bed. Then, he swept her down to lie gently on the mattress. "I need you now."

"Yes…please."

Standing by the bed in a pool of moonlight, Seth pulled the string of his pajama bottoms. They slid over his hips and down his long muscular legs. The sight of him, in full arousal, stole her breath. Stepping out of the pants, he slid onto the bed and between the thighs she parted in anticipation for him.

He lay there, staring into her face, allowing her to see the passionate need eating at him. His erection just touching the apex of her thighs, he braced his forearms on the mattress on either side of her head and crushed her mouth with his own.

Becca kissed him back with everything in her— her love, her need, everything. She dueled with his tongue, scraping her nails over his shoulders and down his back, thrilling to his grunt of pleasure.

Raising his body up onto his hands, Seth lowered his head to her breasts, laving the tips with his tongue before suckling first one then the other, driving her to the very edge of completion. She cried aloud in protest when he lifted his head to smile at her.

"Seth…" There was a note of pleading in her passion-roughened voice.

"Just one more kiss," he murmured, lowering his mouth to hers.

Becca parted her lips for his kiss and gasped with pleasure as he thrust his body into hers as he thrust his tongue into her mouth.

Curling her legs around his waist, Becca hung on to him, arching into the rhythm he set. Her breathing grew steadily harsher as tension spiraled tighter and tighter inside her.

When Becca was sure she couldn't take any more, the tension snapped, flinging her over the edge of reason. She cried out with the intensity of pleasure. A moment later, Seth's cry echoed her own.

When he rolled to the mattress beside her, she curled close to him, snuggling into his warmth. The air in the room was even chillier than before. She shivered.

Still, she protested when he disentangled himself from her, saying, "I'm cold."

"I know." Laughter tinged his voice. "I'm about

to take care of that." Sitting up, he pulled the covers up and over them, not neatly but effectively.

Becca murmured her appreciation in a near purr as he drew her to him, tucking the covers around them both. She was sound asleep within minutes.

Seth lay holding Becca in his arms, satiated—for the moment. A smile played across his lips. He had thought he was past the age to get hard again so soon after experiencing such a mind-bending orgasm.

Apparently not. His smile vanished and a very vulnerable part of his body jerked as Becca—still sleeping—slid one leg over his, her thigh resting against his hardening erection.

Damn, he thought. While it felt good, it was also a form of delicious torture. What to do. Without conscious direction, he moved his hand to stroke her thigh. He was further torturing himself with the feel of her soft skin against the hardest part of him.

Seth froze when Becca murmured and snuggled closer, when he didn't think it was possible for her to get any closer. Now her breast was pressing against his chest. He felt the sensation throughout his entire body. Oh, hell. He didn't want to wake her, while at the same time, he feared he'd burst if he didn't wake her.

What to do?

"Seth?"

Her soft voice was like balm to his body and soul. "I'm awake." In every particle of his body, he thought, suppressing a tremor.

"I…uh…" She hesitated and shifted around, damn near drawing a groan from him.

"What is it?" he asked, managing to sound reasonably calm, when he was anything but. "Bathroom?" he added when she shifted again. He silently sighed.

"No."

He could feel her shake her head. He swallowed, feeling her slide her leg back and forth against that most tender of spots. "More?" He hoped.

"Yesss," she said drawing the word out in tones of satisfaction for his understanding.

Seth began to caress her, make love to her. To his vast relief, Becca would have none of it. Grasping his hips, she pulled him over her, right between her legs.

"I don't want to wait, Seth," she said, kissing the corner of his mouth. "Next time…maybe."

That was encouraging, he thought. He was happy to oblige her every whim. Still, he took time to thoroughly kiss her senseless.

Unbelievably, it was even better than the first time. Seth fell asleep a very contented man.

It was barely light when Becca woke the second time. This time she did need the bathroom. Next to her, one arm circling her waist, Seth was softly snoring. Smiling, she carefully moved his arm and slid away and over the side of the bed.

Shivering in the chill air, she answered nature's call, made fast work of a washup, and quickly brushed her teeth. Practically running, she made a beeline back to the bed, slipping beneath the covers to snuggle close to Seth again.

To her disappointment, he slid out of the bed on the other side. "My turn," he said, flashing a grin at her before striding into the bathroom. Five minutes later, he got back into the bed and snuggled up next to her.

"Damn cold out there," he muttered, drawing her tightly against him.

"I know," Becca agreed, catching the smell of her soap on his skin and the minty scent of her toothpaste on his breath. "Warm in here though."

"Yeah." He smoothed a hand down the side of her body. "Were you thinking of going back to sleep?"

"Eventually," she said, gliding her palm down his chest, smiling when he sucked in a breath. "Did you have something else in mind?"

"Well—" he began.

"Would you like to discuss the world situation?" she interrupted to ask, managing a straight face and somber tone. "The economy?"

Thrilling her with his bark of laughter, Seth rolled on top of her. "Oh, I think we can come up

with something much more interesting than that."
His smile was blatantly sexy. "And I do mean
come up with."

Feeling wonderfully wanton, Becca slid her hand
farther down his torso to curl around the hard length
of him. "I see…er, feel what you mean."

Seth was laughing when he kissed her; his
laughter quickly ceased, his kiss becoming gentle,
coaxing, luring her into participation…as if she
needed any coaxing or luring.

This time, he made slow, exquisite love to her,
arousing not only her body but her emotions as well.

Murmuring his appreciation of her complete acceptance of him, Seth turned her on her side, away
from him, and curled up behind her, spoon fashion.
Becca sighed as he stroked her body, and drifted
into a deep sleep.

It was near noon when Becca woke once more.
Bright autumn sunlight streamed through the bedroom windows. Next to her, Seth yawned and
stretched.

"Time to get up already?" he asked, running his
fingers through his hair.

"Already?" Becca said, laughing. "It's nearly
lunchtime."

"Humph," he mumbled, "that must be why I'm
feeling half-starved."

Shaking her head, Becca tossed back the covers. She shivered and Seth yelped at the touch of chilly air against his bare skin. He reached for the comforter. Taking it with her, she jumped from the bed.

"I'm going to shower." She laughed again at his pained expression. "I suggest you do the same."

"What if I want to go back to sleep?" he called after her as she stepped into the bathroom.

"Do it in your own bed upstairs," she called back. "I'm going to pull the sheets again after I shower and dress."

"You changed the sheets just yesterday," he shouted as she shut the door.

"And I'm changing them today," she shouted back. "So take a hike upstairs." Grinning, she turned the water on for the shower full-force. She started as the door was suddenly pushed open and Seth stuck his head inside.

"Why can't I shower with you?" He gave her a dangerously sexy smile.

Becca didn't bother to answer, simply because she felt he wouldn't take a refusal anyway. "Seth, get out of my bathroom," she ordered. "I'm freezing and I want a hot shower. Get your own shower. Oh, and on your way upstairs, turn the thermostat up on the heater."

Heaving a heavy sigh, he pulled his head back and shut the door. But even over the sound of the shower spray she heard him call, "You don't know what you're missing, Becca."

"You mean it gets better?" she yelled to be heard, nearly choking on a burst of laughter.

"Oh, do I have 'better' waiting for you," he yelled back, laughter in his voice. The door shut with a telling bang.

Becca was still smiling when she stepped from the shower. Her smile fled as the still cold air brushed her naked body and dripping wet hair. Wrapping one towel around her head, she grabbed another to dry her shivering body. Dry, she tossed the damp towel in the hamper and hurried into the bedroom to dress and blow-dry her hair.

By the time she had stripped the sheets from the bed and remade it, Becca could feel warm air wafting from the vents in the floor.

Dressed in jeans, a cotton knit pullover sweater and her fuzzy slippers, Becca left the bedroom, tugging the rolling hamper behind her. She went directly to the laundry room to dump the sheets into the washer before heading to the kitchen.

"What kept you?" Seth said as she entered the room. "I was about to eat without you."

Becca raised her eyebrows at the sight of him. She wasn't surprised to see he had fixed the coffee, as she had smelled it the moment she'd left her room. But she was surprised to see he had also fixed breakfast. Without a word, she observed his handi-work. Seth simply stood there, looking casual yet terrific in snug-fitting jeans and a dark-brown sweatshirt, a smile on his face as he watched her.

Ignoring the little flutter inside at the mere look of him, she shifted her gaze to his domestic handiwork.

There were strips of fried bacon draining on a paper-towel-covered plate. She caught the scent of cinnamon coming from the four slices of French toast cooking in a large frying pan.

The table was set for two, large glasses of water and small glasses of orange juice set at each place. She watched, bemused, as he turned to neatly flip the bread over in the pan.

"Do you cook often?" she asked, dryly. "Or is French toast and bacon your limit?"

"I've been a bachelor for a long time," he said, just as dryly. "It was either learn to cook for myself, eat frozen dinners, or in restaurants every day. I decided to learn to cook." He lifted a piece of the toast with a spatula. "Perfect, I'll dish up. You can pour the coffee."

Hungry, and tingling from his attention, Becca was happy to comply.

"Hmm, delicious," she murmured with her first bite of toast. "Did your mother teach you to cook?" It seemed a natural assumption, as Becca's mother had taught her at an early age.

"Good grief, no." Seth laughed. "My mother is a lousy cook. Fortunately, my father can afford to pay for an excellent cook. I learned, trial and error, from a number of cookbooks."

Becca laughed with him, then grew quiet as she devoured every morsel he had served her. After lingering over second cups of coffee, they made short shrift of cleaning up the kitchen.

"Is there someplace I can get a newspaper around here?" Seth asked as Becca started for the laundry room to switch loads.

"Yes." She flashed a grin at him. "At the end of the driveway there's a mailbox. The paper will be in it." She stopped him as he headed for the door. "If you want to wait till I put on shoes, I'll walk along with you and get some fresh air."

"I was gonna take the car." A smile teased his lips and his eyes.

Becca merely gave him a look. His smiled graduated into a laugh.

"Okay, we'll walk."

"Damn straight," she muttered, chuckling as she bypassed the laundry room to walk to the bedroom. Along with her shoes, Becca took a lightweight jacket from the closet, just in case.

It was a cool but beautiful late September day, sunlight sparkling off myriad colors of the changing leaves of the deciduous trees on the mountains.

At the mailbox, Seth collected the paper and arched a brow at her. "How about a walk before we go back inside?"

"Okay," Becca agreed, slipping the jacket over her shoulders. "Which direction?"

"Let's just follow one of those side paths we passed on our way down," he suggested. "See where they lead, if anywhere."

"Fine." She turned, heading back up the drive, and started as, falling into step beside her, Seth curled his long-fingered hand around hers.

Controlling her breathing pattern with effort, she strolled along, as if walking hand in hand with him was an everyday occurrence. Her pulse leapt when he laced his fingers through hers.

They talked as they strolled, following where the path led them. They discussed the nice weather, the beautiful mountains, the town below, but not at any time did the conversation flow into their personal lives. Not one word was mentioned about their work, or the agreement they had struck to spend the next five days of his vacation together both in and out of bed.

They laughed at the realization that the path had meandered around in a wide circle, ending at the house, near where it had begun.

Becca, aching inside, smiling outside, loved the

sound of Seth's laughter, loved laughing with him…loved him more than she cared to acknowledge.

But, there it was, glowing like a light inside her. She loved him unconditionally, with every cell and atom in her mind and body.

And yet, as much as she was enjoying every minute of being with him, Becca had come to a hard-made decision. When Seth left at the end of that week, it would be the last she would see him.

The very idea of never seeing him again hurt badly, but loving him as she did, Becca knew she could not keep going in the role of his mistress, nor could she work so closely with him as his assistant under those circumstances. When Seth left on Saturday, he would unknowingly be taking her heart and love with him.

On the other hand, when she left the cabin, and she knew it would be soon, she would not be returning to Philadelphia, possibly not even Pennsylvania.

As they neared the house, Becca vowed to herself to live to the fullest, savor ever minute of these few remaining days with him. She was certain they would have to last her the rest of her life, for she could not foresee any other man ever taking his place in her heart.

"You've grown very quiet," Seth said as they mounted the stairs to the porch. "Something wrong?"

"No." Becca shook her head, and worked up a smile and an excuse for her silence. "I noticed that Sue's car isn't here, so I've been thinking about what to make for dinner later."

He came to an abrupt stop at the door, a frown drawing his dark brows together. "Do you think they might have had an emergency at the clinic?"

"Oh, I never thought of that," she said, rushing into the house and straight to the phone. "I'll call down there and…"

"Wait a minute," Seth said, bringing her up short with her hand on the phone's receiver. "Sue must have been here while we were out." He held up a piece of paper. "There's a note on the table from her."

"Read it, please," she said, walking back to the table as he read aloud.

"'Becca and Seth…although I may be wrong, I doubt it.'" Seth glanced up from the note to grin at her before reading on. "'But I believe you two have a thing going on, the same as John and I have. So, I've decided to give all four of us a break. John and I will be staying at my house until Saturday. Becca, you won't need to come in to the clinic this week, either, as I will be working there with John all week. Have fun, Sue.'"

Seth glanced up at her when he'd finished, his

eyes bright with laughter. "How thoughtful of Sue," he said, laughing aloud.

"Hmm," Becca murmured, nodding in agreement. "But whatever will we do with all that time together?" she mused aloud, her lips quivering with laughter.

"Well, right now, you are going to go toss the sheets into the dryer."

The look Becca gave him clearly indicated she couldn't believe he'd said that. "I see." Of course, she didn't, and said so. "And what will you be doing while I busy myself with the laundry?"

"I'm going to turn down the thermostat," he answered, in apparent seriousness.

She frowned in confusion. "Why?"

"Because I'm going to build a fire." He pulled a broad, laughable leer. "After that, I'm going to spread the furry throw on the floor in front of it."

Warmth and excitement begun to bloom inside Becca. As if puzzled, she fluttered her eyelashes as she repeated in all innocence, "Why?"

He wiggled his eyebrows suggestively. "So we can have an orgy. Or twelve."

Becca, suppressing a shiver of expectation, leered right back at him. "Or even a dozen."

Laughing again, he circled the table to take her in his arms. "You are something else," he said, kissing her soundly. Turning her away, he gave her a light nudge toward the laundry room. He strode into the living room, calling back, "It won't take be long to start a fire, so get it in gear. I'm aiming for a full baker's dozen." He turned to flash a smile at her.

"No kidding," she said, flashing one right back at him. "I can't wait."

Ten

It was late Saturday morning, Becca stood next to Seth beside his car. His bag was in the trunk, the driver's-side door was open. Soon he would slide behind the wheel and drive away, out of her life.

Since Monday, the days had flown by. Becca, determined to stick to her agreement to spend the remainder of the week with him, had put everything from her mind but Seth. They cooked, took walks, talked and laughed, made near desperate love at the merest suggestion…and there were many.

She wanted to cry. She wanted to grab ahold of him and beg him not to go. She did neither of those things. Instead, she schooled her expression into one of calm composure. There would be plenty of time for crying later after he was gone.

After she was alone.

"I wish you'd come home with me, Becca," Seth said, chasing away her troubling thoughts. "Your physical condition is back to normal." A wisp of a smile touched his lips. "That's obvious from the way you kept up…with our long walks, and other exercise."

"I'm not ready to go back yet," she said, thinking she very likely never would be.

"I know you're not ready to go back to work," he said. "I could tell that from the way you reacted after we were finished treating that boy. Emotionally, you appeared ready to pass out."

"I know." She managed a smile.

"I need you beside me…" His voice was rough, a little strained. "I need you beside me in my bed, and in the operating room."

If he had left it at the first part, Becca might have given in, surrendered to her own need to be with him. But she wanted more, she wanted to be with him in every way, not just as his bed partner and operating-room assistant.

"I'm not ready, Seth," she repeated, her throat thickening and her eyes stinging with tears, longing for him to stay, wishing he would go.

"Okay." Stepping to her, Seth drew her into his

arms, crushing her to him, his mouth to hers. He reluctantly released her. "Take as much time as you need, and keep in touch to let me know how you're feeling."

She made do with a nod. "Goodbye, Seth. I'll…miss you. Drive safely."

"I always do." He smiled and slid behind the wheel. "I'll miss you, too." Holding her gaze for long seconds, he started the car, waved and drove away.

Tears rolling down her face, Becca watched his car until it disappeared around the curve at the end of the driveway.

He should have told her he loved her.

The thought tormented Seth all the way back to Philadelphia. *Why hadn't he?* That thought always followed the first one. Of course, he knew the answer. Fear of her rejection kept him silent.

Becca had never given him the slightest hint she felt anything for him but respect for his expertise as a physician and surgeon. His lips twisted in a bitter smile. Oh, she had obviously appreciated his expertise in bed. She had been as eager for his body as he had for hers.

She had admitted she had been a long time without a man, and he was certain she had not been with a man the entire time she had spent in Africa. So her physical response to him was normal and understandable.

Becca had given him no indication whatsoever love had anything to do with their time together.

Seth sighed. Even so, he longed for her to come home.

Should she have confessed, told Seth she loved him—had loved him almost since first joining his surgical team? Becca had lost count of the times she had asked herself that question. The answer that sprang to mind was always the same. Had she told him, even hinted at her feelings for him, in all probability she would have been standing in the driveway, choking on his dust as he drove hell for leather away from her.

Seth was in his thirties; apparently he didn't want to get seriously involved with any woman. Sex, even fantastic sex, was one thing. Obviously love didn't factor into his life, his work.

Becca didn't keep in contact with Seth. He tried to reach her, but she didn't answer either his calls or e-mails. What could she say to him? She knew that soon she'd have to tell him she had no intention of going back to Philadelphia, or possibly even Pennsylvania. But she kept putting it off till later.

By the end of the second week after Seth had left, Becca was certain she was pregnant. All the signs were there. Not only had she missed her period, her breasts were tender and felt a bit larger, and she was tired and sleepy most of the time.

It was time to leave the cabin. Sue, having come back to stay at the house with Becca after Seth departed, fussed over her, but at least she didn't pry into why Becca wouldn't take his calls.

Becca didn't hesitate. She told Sue she was leaving that same evening over dinner. "I've loafed around long enough," she said when Sue protested. "It's time I got back into the swing."

"You're going back to work with Seth?" Sue asked, a hopeful note in her voice.

"First, I'm going to visit my parents in Virginia," she said, avoiding a direct answer. "Afterward, maybe I'll drive to Atlanta to see my sister. I'm going to call the number given to me and thank whoever answers for the use of this lovely house, but I'm going to pass on the limo. Is there anywhere I can rent a car?"

"Yes, in the city," Sue said, smiling. "Where the hospital is located. And you're in luck. I was planning to drive into the mall there later this week." Her smile softened. "John's birthday is next week and I want to get him something special. You can go with me if next week is okay for you."

"That's fine, I'm really not in a hurry," Becca said, thinking a few days wouldn't make any difference.

"After you leave, I'll close the house," Sue went on. "As I'll be working full-time with John, I'm not going to be available to be the standby housekeeper anymore."

Four days later, Becca stood hugging Sue in the parking lot of the car rental firm. Her luggage was already stowed in the trunk of the late-model compact she had rented.

"I'm going to miss you, Becca," Sue said, sniffing as she stepped back. "So is John."

"I'm going to miss you and John, too." Becca swiped a hand over her moist eyes. "You've spoiled me rotten over the past two months."

"It's been fun." Sue's smile was watery. "Hard to believe it's late autumn already." She glanced around her. "The leaves are falling and before you know it, it'll be Christmas." Saying the word seemed to perk her up. "Hey, as long as I'm shopping for a birthday present, I might as well look for a Christmas present for John."

"Then you'd better get at it." Becca laughed. "And I'd better get moving if I hope to arrive at my parents' house before dark." One more hug, and Becca got into the car and drove away.

The test was positive, as Becca was certain it would be. It was only then, in the bathroom of her parents' lovely home, that the full impact of it hit her. She was pregnant. A part of her and Seth was already forming inside her body. Her baby.

Seth's baby.

The thought brought her up short. Seth's baby. He didn't have to know. In all probability, he wouldn't want to know, she rationalized.

Becca had saved her money since her first job at sixteen, when she had worked part-time in one of the shops not far from her home in Philadelphia. She had a very healthy bank balance, more than enough to last her until the baby was born, and for some time after. With her credentials, she could find a job almost anywhere, in any number of hospitals or doctors' offices in Pennsylvania.

The idea wasn't at all scary.

Becca spent a week with her parents. She played a round of golf with her father. She went shopping with her mother. And the three of them enjoyed a lovely day in Colonial Williamsburg, always a thrill for Becca as she was an American history buff.

She had to forego her visit to Rachael. Her parents told Becca that her sister was on a business trip to San Francisco.

When the week was over, Becca started back for Philadelphia, using the long trip to plan for her eventual move from the city. There would be so much to do—look for another location, then a job, after that a place to live, sublet her apartment, pack and arrange for shipping her furniture.

It made her tired simply thinking about it.

The Philadelphia area was enjoying mild late October weather. Lugging her cases from the car to her apartment, Becca felt too warm in the turtleneck sweater she had pulled on that morning.

Inside her apartment, she dumped the bags, leaned back against the door and sighed. It felt good to be home. "We're home, baby," she whispered, splaying her hand protectively over her belly.

Pushing away from the door, she made a quick glance around the place, satisfied with the job done by the lady that cleaned for her once a week. The place was dust-free and smelled fresh.

After the long hours of driving, with stops only to grab a bite to eat, Becca was tired. Picking up the cases once more, she carried them into her bedroom and let them drop again. The next moment she herself dropped, onto the neatly made bed.

Expecting to have a nap, she closed her eyes, but sleep eluded her. Several thoughts she had determinedly ignored for several days finally broke through her mental barrier.

First and foremost was the acknowledgment that she had to tell Seth she was pregnant. As the father of the baby, he had a right to know. Not once did she so much as consider the idea that he might deny responsibility, or at least his part in it.

Secondly, she admitted to herself that she didn't

want to relocate. She wanted to remain in Philadelphia, and she wanted to work at the University of Pennsylvania Hospital, if not with Seth, then as a floor nurse. She didn't want to—*couldn't*—work with another surgeon.

Knowing what she had to do, Becca heaved a sigh of defeat, pushed herself up to sit on the edge of the bed and reached for the phone on the nightstand.

Seth's private secretary, Judy Miller, answered on the second ring. "Hi, Judy, it's Becca Jameson," she said. "Is Dr. Andrews available?"

"Oh, hi, Becca, how are you?"

"I'm fine, good as new," Becca answered, injecting a jaunty note into her voice. "I need to talk to Seth."

"I'm sorry but he's not here. He cleared his calendar for today and Monday. May I leave him a message?"

"Yes, please, Judy. Tell him I'd like to talk to him at his convenience."

Feeling deflated, Becca sat for a long time.

Knowing she'd now not be able to nap, she got up and began unpacking her bags. Later, she would make a run to the supermarket to restock her fridge. After that, she'd do her laundry, then find other things to do, every day until Seth called her.

Her telephone didn't ring the entire weekend or

for most of Monday. But her doorbell rang late Monday afternoon. The ring was immediately followed by a sharp rap on the door.

Knowing who was on the other side of the door, Becca drew a deep breath, wet her suddenly dry lips and went to the door to open it.

"Where in hell have you been?" Seth demanded, storming past her into the room.

"I was visiting my parents," she answered as calmly as she could.

"Yeah, for one week." He looked about to explode. "Dammit, Becca, I know up until you left for Virginia you were at the cabin. Why didn't you answer my calls or e-mails? I was going nuts worrying about you."

Oh, the doctor was back on duty, she thought. "I…er, needed some time to myself. Why were you worried? You knew where I was," she said.

He exhaled, as if to let off steam. "Becca, you didn't answer my phone calls, you didn't respond to my e-mails. I didn't know what to think. Hell, you could have died for all I knew."

"But—"

"I'm not finished," he interrupted, on a roll. "Friday, I drove down there, only to find the cabin dark and deserted. So, I went to the clinic. Sue told me where you'd gone and that you were fine. I got back to my apartment not half an hour ago, to find a message from Judy on my voice mail, telling me you had called me Friday."

"Yes, I did." Becca was having difficulty maintaining her composure. His rant was beginning to unnerve her.

"Why?" he nearly yelled at her.

"Why, what?" She was starting to tremble at the idea of telling him about her condition when he was obviously so very angry.

"First off, why didn't you answer my calls or e-mails?"

"Because I didn't want to talk to you." Now she was getting angry. Who did he think he was, yelling at her? "And before you can ask, I'll tell you why. I didn't want you to know I wasn't planning on staying here, or working here with you anymore."

His eyes narrowed. "Why not? After the week we spent together..." His softened voice was almost scarier than his shouting.

"Because I had no intention of being your assistant in the operating room during the day, and your bedmate at night."

"You certainly made no objections about being my bedmate at the cabin." Seth's voice was harsh. "In fact, you appeared to revel in it."

"That was before I knew the reveling would make me pregnant," she shouted at him.

"I made you pregnant?"

He was clearly astonished, which made her madder. "Yes, you did it! Who else?" she retorted, getting angrier by the second.

"And so you were simply going to take off for parts unknown," he snapped back at her. "Is that it?"

Becca angled her chin defiantly at him. "Yes, I was planning to take off."

In a blink he went absolutely statue-still. His features went rock-hard. His eyes were like amber chips in ice. "You were thinking about an abortion?"

As if he had struck her, Becca recoiled, but recovered quickly. "No! Never! This is my baby. You have nothing to say about it."

Within two long strides he was standing inches in front of her. "I have plenty to say about it, dammit!" His voice was tough, adamant. "If you're pregnant, I'm pregnant, too."

Stunned by his flat authoritative statement, she stared at him, speechless. Seth took advantage of her momentary silence and, fortunately, in a more reasonable tone of voice.

"I'm relieved to hear you weren't considering abortion, Becca. The idea of you wanting to get rid of my baby sickened me."

"I never gave it a thought, Seth." Suddenly, Becca was exhausted, physically and emotionally. "I wasn't going to tell you. I was just thinking of relocating and taking care of the baby myself."

He closed his eyes and an expression of pain flickered across his face. "Oh, Becca…"

"I'm sorry for ever thinking you wouldn't care." Her voice held a soft sadness. "I realized Friday that you had the right to know, and I had to tell you. That's why I called your office."

"You believed I wouldn't want my baby, our baby?" He placed a palm on her still flat belly. "Of course I want it. I love the baby already, almost as much as I want and love you."

"Wh-what?" she could barely whisper.

He cradled her face in his hands. "Becca, I love you, I have been in love with you for what seems like forever."

"But…you never said…" Tears filled her eyes. "You never…I thought…"

"That I just wanted sex, your body?" Seth's smile was heartbreaking.

"Yes." Becca met his gaze steadily, bravely.

"I did." He kissed her. "I do." He kissed her again. "But I want more, I want all of you, you heart, your mind, your soul." His smile now teased. "Your body and the fantastic sex we have together."

"Oh, Seth," she murmured, sighing.

"And if you don't soon tell me you love me, too," he said in warning, "I'm going to ha : a freaking nervous breakdown right here."

"I love you, Dr. Seth Andrews," Becca confessed, nearly choking on rising laughter. "We've been such idiots all this time, we deserve each other."

Although he was laughing with her, both their laughter was silenced when his mouth took hers.

Becca and Seth were married at her parents' home the day after Thanksgiving. Seth stole her breath away, looking so handsome in a dark suit and white silk shirt. He claimed she stole his breath in the plain midcalf-length, high-necked, long-sleeved white velvet wedding dress. They left Virginia the day after the wedding, to honeymoon in a place known only to them.

They arrived at their destination in late afternoon. It was unfamiliar to Becca, though it was very familiar to Seth. It should have been. The honeymoon site was the condo Seth had bought and lived in for years.

Perfect. They didn't leave the apartment or answer the phones, cell or landline. Other than switching the cooking of meals every other day, they rarely left the bed. Perfect indeed.

When Becca and Seth returned to her apartment to begin packing her things to be moved to his place, she found an intriguing-looking envelope among her weeklong pile of mail. It contained an invitation that was both terse and formal. It read:

The honor of your presence is required at an undisclosed location, December twenty-fourth of this year, at eight o'clock in the evening, for a black-tie affair, at which time an explanation concerning your recent anonymous gift will be offered.

Enclosed are the pertinent travel arrangements for both you and one guest of your choosing.

That was it. No signature. The travel arrangements listed a limousine to collect her and guest at her apartment, which meant the location was in or around Philadelphia.

Becca read the invitation aloud to Seth. When she finished, she glanced up at him, frowning. "What do you think?"

"Sounds intriguing, I think we should go," he said, using the excuse of scanning the invitation again to come to stand behind her, coil his arms around her waist, press close to her and read over her shoulder. "What do you think?"

"From the feel of something back there," she drawled, "I think we should go to bed."

He laughed, turned her around, drew her into his arms and soundly kissed her. "I think that's a great idea. But, do you want to go to the gala?"

"Oh, that, yes, let's go. If not fun it should at least prove interesting."

"Okay, but you must wear your wedding dress."

Becca smiled. "Okay, if you insist, but why?"

"Because your tummy is still flat, and you looked so beautiful in it."

Her smile softened. "I knew there was a reason I loved you," she whispered, giving him a quick kiss. "I'll wear the dress on one condition."

"Fine. Name it."

"We go shopping for something to relieve the stark white." Her eyes brightened. "I know, something festive, a pin maybe…no, a sash in silver, red and green."

"Anything you want." Seth swept her up in his arms. "But first we make use of the bed, then we go shopping."

Wrapping her arms around his neck, Becca sighed in delicious contentment.

* * * * *

THE MONEY MAN'S SEDUCTION

BY
LESLIE LaFOY

Leslie LaFoy lives in a small town on the Kansas prairie with her husband, two dogs and four cats. With a bachelor's degree in the administration of justice and a master's in sociology (criminology), Leslie serves as the unofficial poster child of over-education. Having taught social studies for fifteen years, she turned her creative energies to writing historical romances and the rest is, as they say, history.

Between her sixteenth and seventeenth published book, Leslie and her husband bought two commercial buildings on the National Historic Register and committed the rest of their lives and all their fortunes to restoring them to their 1884 glory.

When not up to her chin in sawdust, plaster and paint, Leslie writes books, serves on the City Council and the board of the local Main Street Association, and sends care packages to her son who serves his country in the United States Navy.

You can contact Leslie at her website, www.leslielafoy. com.

Dear Reader,

It has been such a treat to work on the GIFTS FROM A BILLIONAIRE series. An intriguing premise, the chance to collaborate with creative friends, and an editor who trusts our visions and voices...it's the stuff of a writer's dreams.

And the stuff of dreams is precisely what this series is all about. Take one good person trying to make the world a better place, add an unexpected gift from an anonymous donor, and then stir in the sweet tumult of finding the love of their lives along the way... Ah, how wonderful life can truly be.

It's my pleasure to present you with *The Money Man's Seduction*, the second story in this series. I sincerely hope you enjoy the story of Emily Raines, a nationally renowned artist and crusader for elder services, and Cole Preston, a successful venture capitalist who firmly believes that most social angels are really scam artists in disguise. The dreamer and the cynic. The do-gooder and the money man.

They say that opposites attract. Or is it really more a case of two open hearts finding common ground in the pursuit of what really matters in life?

I'll let you read Emily and Cole's story and decide for yourself. Happy reading!

Leslie LaFoy

For Mary, Joan and Kasey,
friends and fellow storysmiths.

And for MJ,
the best and most patient editor in the world.

Prologue

Well, my darling devotees, it's just a few months into the RBGS—that's Reclusive Billionaire Giving Season for those of you who have only recently joined the ranks of Inquiring Minds. Taking most seriously my responsibilities as your trusted purveyor of vital information, I assure you that I have had my ear constantly tuned to hear even the slightest whisper of rumor and speculation about who this year's lucky largesse recipients might be.

And while the tidbits are absolutely stunning, my dear fans, I'm not quite yet prepared to let the names of this crop of golden kitties out of Santa's bag. But for those of you who have been inspired by *moi* to collect tidbits on your own… Well, darling, call me; we'll do lunch and compare our notes. Reporting most definitely has its rewards, you know.

Sam Balfour placed the newspaper clipping on the desktop. "Have you seen this? The last item." He didn't wait for a response. "I warned you this barracuda isn't going to let you alone. She doesn't know anything concrete yet, or at least I hope she doesn't. Otherwise she wouldn't be trolling her readership to get names. Hell, I should call her myself. Then maybe you'll realize that it's time to stop this crazy game."

S. Edward Balfour IV, known to his nephew as Uncle Ned, only smiled as he trumped Sam's newspaper with the dark green manila folder he removed from the top desk drawer. "Deal with this, please, before you rush out to call the woman and set a date for your luncheon rendezvous."

Sam sighed as he looked at the folder. Green, for giving. How many more folders just like it did Uncle Ned have sitting in that drawer? "I talk, but you don't listen. I'm only trying to protect you, you know."

"And I appreciate your love and concern," Ned told him. "That does not, however, mean I'm ready to abandon Maureen's project. Please see that the usual funds are delivered within the week."

Sam only glanced at the Letter to the Editor his uncle had circled before checking the top of the page and the name of the newspaper. "You keep having to cast your net wider and wider to find candidates, don't you? I never heard of this place. Is it even on the map?"

"I could send you instead of Bruce, and then you could find out for yourself."

"And be more involved in your project than I am now? Thanks, but I'd rather have a root canal," Sam said, and gave up the argument. Santa Ned wasn't going to be convinced. At least not yet. He closed the folder and tucked it under his arm. "I'll have Bruce take the company jet."

"Bruce is a good man. Very discreet."

"Three cheers for Bruce." Sam was about to turn and leave his uncle's office, but then hesitated. "You know what, Uncle Ned? I don't know if I should be hoping this Emily Raines is a good pick or a bad one. I don't know which result would be better for you."

"You think too much, Sam. Better you should learn how to feel. True joy is in the giving, not what happens once that gift is given. Anything beyond the giving is out of our hands."

One

There were no half-naked nymphets scattering flower petals and the red Porsche wasn't exactly a classic chariot, but the man getting out of it was a certified Greek god. Emily Raines rested her forearms on the handle of the still-unplugged industrial floor sander and watched the stranger through the front window. Tall, broad shoulders, narrow hips and dark hair just long enough to blow in the light breeze. The easy way he moved as he reached back inside the car for his suit jacket....

Emily smiled appreciatively and wondered if he had his pants tailored so that they pulled extra nicely over his gym-honed muscles when he bent over. Lord Almighty, if he was here in Augsburg, Kansas, taking nymphet applications, she just might be tempted to fill one out.

"Emily!"

Half her brain recognized her friend's arrival from somewhere in the old building. The other half went on with a fantasy of see-through togas, reclining sofas and grapes.

"I'm telling you," Beth declared, "this whole deal is a bona fide case of no good deed going unpunished."

Ah, he was looking up and down the street. Maybe he was lost. "You are such a pessimist. Such a CPA." Maybe she should be a nice person and wander out to see if he needed directions.

"Realist," Beth countered, waving a handful of papers. "Estimates tend to do that for most people. Fifteen thousand or fifteen-five for a new roof. Your choice."

"Which roofer looked more interested in doing it?" she asked as Mr. Adonis's attention came to her building...and stayed. Her heart added a happy little beat in anticipation.

"Quite frankly, they both looked like they'd rather take a beating."

Okay, he was crossing the street. She had just enough time to do a setup. "Speaking of contractor beatings," she said, quickly turning to Beth. "Would you go back and talk to the electrician until I can get there?" She nodded toward the street. "It looks like we're going to have a visitor."

Beth glanced toward the glass front doors, arched an auburn brow, tucked a fiery red curl behind her ear and grinned. "Scream if you need help," she offered, laughing and heading for the door at the back of the office. "Loud if you're serious about it. It's a big building."

Need help? Ha! Emily glanced back toward the front just long enough to gauge her timing, and then began to ever-so-casually unwind the cord of the sander. The bell over the door jangled. Emily put what she hoped looked like a serene-but-pleasantly-semi-surprised smile on her face and looked up.

"Hello," Adonis said.

Oh, be still her heart. A voice that rumbled, deep and slow and low. "Hi," she vaguely heard herself reply as she watched his gaze slide slowly down to openly marvel over the fact that she'd bought her T-shirt in Jackson Hole. It moved lower still to the frayed edges of her cutoff jeans and right on down, smooth as silk, to the tops of her leather work boots. It returned upward—every bit as appreciatively—to finally meet her own.

He smiled, lopsidedly, the light in his eyes a delicious combination of guilt and pleasure.

Emily reined in her own smile and managed to tamp the more obvious notes of hope out of her voice as she asked, "What can I do for you?"

The guilt part evaporated out of his smile and his eyes sparkled with clear understanding. "I'm Cole Preston and I'm wondering if you've seen my grandmother this morning. She said she was coming here. Ida Bentley?"

Well, this was even better. Hardly a stranger at all. Emily grinned. "Ida's an absolute sweetheart. A truly incredible woman."

Sadness replaced the easy pleasure in his smile as he nodded. "She's also got a few screws that aren't quite as tight as they used to be. And I have the checkbook to prove it."

"Well, yes," Emily allowed diplomatically as her stomach fluttered and went a little cold. "I have noticed that Ida's mind tends to drift a bit every now and then."

"More than a bit," he countered. "And every now and then is more like often."

"I think she maintains very well for an eighty-something-year-old woman," Emily offered brightly in her elderly friend's defense. "Ida is always dressed not only impeccably, but also perfectly appropriately for the weather and the occasion. And she's gracious, delightful company. She's been coming in every day since we started working on the building and she has some wonderful ideas for classes once we're up and running."

"That would be the classes on modern interpretive dance." Cool, distant, definitely disapproving.

"Well, of course," Emily answered. "Your grandmother was a professional dancer. Judging by the scrapbooks she's shown us, she was very highly regarded in her time."

"That was then. This is now. Her time is over."

Over? "I beg your pardon?" she asked as in her mind's eye she saw Ida huddled on an iceberg being shoved out to sea.

"People need to stop filling my grandmother's head with the idea that she can still dance."

So much for the hope of Mr. Wonderful wandering in off the street. The man certainly looked like the stuff of feminine dreams, but the nice suit and the well-toned body only disguised the fact that he had all the emotional sensitivity of…of…well, she'd think of something really cold and heartless later.

At the moment, all she could really think about was how pathetically desperate she was. To think she'd been willing to drop her toga and share her grapes with him. Shaking her head and silently mourning the untimely— and not to mention brutally quick—death of the most inspiring fantasy she'd had in years, Emily plugged the cord of the sander into the wall socket.

"We obviously disagree on your grandmother's capabilities," she countered with a shrug. "It's clear, though, that she's a considerably kinder and less judgmental person than her grandson."

He blinked and opened his mouth to speak, but she didn't give him a chance to actually spit any words out. "I haven't seen Ida this morning, Mr. Preston. She could be over at the café or the gift shop. You might check there."

"Well, maybe it's a good thing she isn't here yet," he said, either missing the fact that he'd been dismissed, or choosing to ignore it. Neither possibility counted in his favor. "It'll give me a chance to take care of business."

Business? She wasn't a business. She was a nonprofit community organization for the elderly. The rural elderly. Or would be once she got the place fixed up. Not that she needed to tell him any of that. Holding the handles of the floor sander in the classic I'm-busy-let's-get-this-over-with pose, she met his gaze again. Or tried to, anyway. His gaze was taking another Fantastic Voyage to her boot laces and back. Since his attention was otherwise engaged…

Emily considered the long length of his lean legs, the broad width of his chest, the way the dark hair at his nape brushed against the crisp white of his shirt collar. She arched a brow.

Maybe she'd been too quick to give up the torrid affair thing. It wasn't as though she was looking for Prince Charming and the whole forever-in-a-happy-castle deal. Cole Preston was sculpted, hot, and no doubt about it, interested. It would be a real shame to waste such an incredible opportunity.

And not just a shame, either. It could very well be a crime. Like leaving a perfectly fitting pair of jeans in the store dressing room was a crime against the shopping gods. Wonderful things were put in your path for a reason and you took a big chance if you didn't properly appreciate them. And gosh, she certainly didn't want to risk offending the gods of a breathless good time.

She softly cleared her throat. "What kind of business do you need to conduct, Mr. Preston?"

"Do you know if an Emily Raines person is here?"

An Emily Raines person. Well, as Ida would say, how perfectly ill-mannered. The man just couldn't seem to stop digging a hole for himself.

"I'm Emily Raines," she said crisply.

He not only blinked, but actually rocked back a little on the heels of his finely made Italian leather shoes. Emily didn't give him a chance to regain his balance. "You said that you had something you wanted to talk with me about, Mr. Preston. What is it? I have a electrician waiting out back to tell me how much of the Earth it's going to cost to bring this building into the twentieth century."

"In case you haven't noticed," he replied, offering her a smile that looked decidedly strained, "it's the twenty-first century."

Emily sweetly replied, "Actually, I have noticed that, Mr. Preston. But I can't afford to wire this place for the latest bells and whistles. The tail end of the last century will have to be good enough for now."

He looked up at the rusty spots in the tin ceiling tiles. "And where are you planning to get the money for electricians?"

Her shock lasted only a nanosecond. Anger took over after that. Propping her hip against the built-in antique desk and crossing her arms over her midriff, she coolly replied, "The etiquette lessons are being held over at the high school."

His brows knitted for a moment before he quietly cleared his throat and asked, "Excuse me?"

"I said that the etiquette lessons are being held over at the high school. The class is designed for the teenage girls in town," she went on, embellishing the bold-faced lie. "But I'm sure that given your very obvious need for them, they'll let you participate."

His dark eyes sparked and the muscles in his jaw pulsed.

"The class started just a few minutes ago," she added.

"If you hurry, you won't have missed much. I'm sure there will be a section on how it's considered grossly impolite to ask total strangers about the details of their personal finances."

"Will there be a section," he asked smoothly, "on how it's illegal to bilk senile little old ladies out of their social security checks?"

As accusations went, that one hadn't even been thinly veiled, but she wasn't about to launch into a spirited self-defense. That would imply a guilty conscience. And since she didn't have a damn thing to feel even the least bit guilty about, she wasn't going to give him the satisfaction of so easily putting her on the defensive. No, she was going to make him say it straight out.

"Who do you think is bilking whom, Mr. Preston?"

"I suspect that you are bilking—or at least attempting to—my grandmother."

Emily silently counted to five before she allowed herself to ask, "And what, exactly, leads you to think this?"

"My grandmother thinks supporting this…this…" He glanced around the old office, cocking one eyebrow and looking decidedly less than visionary.

"The building itself used to be a produce warehouse," Emily explained. "I'm in the process of turning it into a fine arts center for senior citizens. And you should know that I haven't taken so much as a single solitary cent from—"

"And if I have my say in it, you're not going to, either."

She had to count to six this time. "Look," Emily said tightly, her pulse pounding furiously, "let's get something straight, Mr. Preston. Your grandmother hasn't said a word to me about donating anything other than her time and considerable artistic talents once we're up and running. If she were to offer me money, I'd turn her down. This—"

He made a sound that was part sigh, part snort.

If the sander hadn't weighed a ton and a half, she'd have snatched it up and beaten him with it. "Do you make it a habit to go around insulting the ethics and integrity of everyone you meet?"

"Just those I think are attempting to take advantage of my grandmother's failing mind."

Clearly there was no reasoning with the man. He was going to believe what he wanted to believe and neither the facts nor any assertions from her were going to make the least bit of difference to his thinking. And given that unfortunate reality, there wasn't any point in pulling her punches. "You have to be the most insuf—"

The door bell jangled and Emily instantly snapped her mouth closed. She was just giving him a try-to-be-civil-for-two-seconds look when a familiar voice said brightly and cheerfully, "Oh, I was hoping you two would get to meet today."

"Yes, we've just met, Ida," Emily replied as Cole Preston smiled and planted a kiss on the cheek of his elegantly slim, silver-haired grandmother. Emily added, "Although, I really gotta say that I can't imagine why you'd want us to."

Ida chuckled softly and patted his arm. "Cole's all

bark and no bite, dear. If I don't want to go to one of those retirement villages, I'm not going. He can stamp his feet and gnash his teeth all he wants. It's not going to make any difference."

Retirement home? Again Emily's mind put the all the pieces together in a single second. Inching her way into what—by her quick count—was the third round of her and Cole Preston's "How Many Ways Can I Dislike You?" game, she asked, "Are we talking about an assisted living facility?"

"Yes," he answered with a crisp, brief nod. "She would be better off there."

"Really?" Emily answered, accepting his challenge. "Says who? You?"

Ida chuckled again. "Give him hell, Emily. Is Beth around somewhere?" She patted her Gucci handbag. "I brought her some of that jojoba oil I got out in Santa Fe last year."

How such a sweet and generous person could be related to such a pompous... "She's back in the rear section talking with the electrician," Emily supplied, squarely meeting Cole Preston's self-assured gaze.

Ida nodded and walked off toward the rear office door, saying as she went, "Cole, help Emily, please. That machine, whatever it's for, is much too big for her to handle all by herself."

He didn't move. And despite the fact that he didn't look as though he had any intention of doing so, Emily wanted to be sure. "Touch it and die."

"I wouldn't lift a finger to help you," he replied. "I

don't want to be considered even a minor accessory when you're hauled off on fraud charges."

"Yeah, defending yourself would really distract you from your efforts to get your grandmother locked up nice and tight in some veggie bin."

Both brows went up. "Veggie bin?" he repeated as the corner of his mouth twitched upward and the cool distance in his eyes turned into a sparkle of amusement.

Her pulse skittering and her heart fluttering, Emily glared down at the floor and collected what she could of her suddenly scattered outrage. God, she couldn't even remember what she'd said that had triggered the unnerving change in him. And her. Damn. Round One had been about his belief that the elderly shouldn't do anything more physically strenuous than sit in a rocker and drool the day away. Round Two had been his baseless assumption that she was a con artist preying on the elderly. Round Three had started with the mention of Ida being put in a home. Ah, now she remembered where she'd been going!

"Are you the only grandchild?" Emily asked bluntly.

His amusement was gone in a heartbeat. "I'm Ida's only living relative," he responded, his tone cool again, but this time with a slightly wary edge to it. "It's my responsibility to see that she's cared for and that she doesn't do anything physically dangerous or financially unwise."

"By financially unwise you mean write checks to questionable charitable causes like…" Emily paused to

FREE BOOKS OFFER

To get you started, we'll send you
2 **FREE books and a FREE gift**

There's no catch, everything is **FREE**

Accepting your 2 **FREE** books and **FREE** mystery gift
places you under no obligation to buy anything.

Be part of the Mills & Boon® Book Club™ and receive your favourite
Series books up to 2 months before they are in the shops and delivered
straight to your door. Plus, enjoy a wide range of **EXCLUSIVE** benefits!

- Best new women's fiction – delivered right to
  your door with FREE P&P

- Avoid disappointment – get your books up to
  2 months before they are in the shops

- No contract – no obligation to buy

2 **FREE** books
and a
FREE gift

We hope that after receiving your free books you'll
want to remain a member. But the choice is yours.
So why not give us a go? You'll be glad you did!

Visit **millsandboon.co.uk** to stay up to date
with offers and to sign-up for our newsletter

D9HI9

Mrs/Miss/Ms/Mr   Initials

BLOCK CAPITALS PLEASE

Surname

Address

Postcode

Email

The Mills & Boon® Book Club™ – Here's how it works:

Accepting your free books places you under no obligation to buy anything. You may keep the books and gift and return the despatch note marked "cancel". If we do not hear from you, about a month later we'll send you 2 brand new books including two 2in1 titles priced at £5.25*each. That is the complete price – there is no extra charge for post and packaging. You may cancel at any time, otherwise every month we will send you 4 stories a month which you may purchase or return to us – the choice is yours.

*Terms and prices subject to change without notice.

NO STAMP NEEDED!

@ MILLS & BOON®
Book Club

FREE BOOK OFFER
FREEPOST NAT 10298
RICHMOND
TW9 1BR

NO STAMP
NECESSARY
IF POSTED IN
THE U.K. OR N.I.

look around her for the dramatic effect of it. "Oh, just for the sake of an example, let's say a senior citizen fine arts center."

"You would be just one and the latest among many of the questionable hands stuck out, looking for a sizable donation from her."

Since the man just didn't have any bounds at all… "Well, I can certainly understand your perspective on the matter," Emily drawled. "What she gives to charity would probably come out of your inheritance."

"I don't need her money," he countered, sounding truly offended. "I happen to be very well-off financially."

"Or so you say," she allowed with a shrug, pleased with having so easily pushed his buttons. Fair was fair, after all; he'd certainly been pushing all of hers. "Then again, the Porsche could be a rental and you could have picked up the Brooks Brothers suit and the fancy Italian shoes at a Goodwill store in an upscale part of town. You never know. Appearances can be deceiving."

"In my case, I can assure you that appearances are reality."

Big Woo. As if she cared. "Would it come as a great shock to you to learn that maybe you aren't the only person in this room who's financially secure?"

He laughed, the sound striking her as way more condescending than amused. "Nice try, Miss Raines. You get points for attempting the bluff. Aside from the fact that it was a poorly executed effort, I've had you investigated and—"

"Investigated?" Oh, the low-life son of a—

"The first time my grandmother mentioned this…" He looked around the office again.

"Fine…arts…center," Emily supplied slowly, crisply. "Three words, Mr. Preston. A total of four whole syllables. Let's try to remember them."

"I had my assistant do some checking on you."

"Oh?" *Couldn't be bothered with doing it yourself?* "And what interesting tidbits did your personal ferret find?"

"You're relatively well-known in the historic preservation community for your stained glass repair work."

She decided not to mention that there was no "relatively" about her professional reputation; he'd probably never heard of the Smithsonian Institution. The impressive fact that she was in their go-to contact file would be completely lost on him.

"And, of course," Emily said with a tight smile of frayed patience, "me being well-regarded professionally led you to immediately suspect me of being a scam artist who specializes in fleecing the unsuspecting elderly. Yeah, I can see how you came to that conclusion. Pure logic at its best."

He shrugged. "You make a decent enough living for an artist type."

"An artist type. Boy, are you racking up the points. Do you refer to your grandmother as an artist type?"

For a second the corners of his mouth tightened. "But your credit rating suggests," he said, plowing ahead, undeterred, "that you don't make enough with your glass chips to qualify for a bank loan to buy a building like this. At least not a loan with a reputable bank."

There was so much fodder for offense in that statement that she could go off in ten different directions for a week, but if he wasn't going to be sidetracked, she wasn't either. "Isn't someone's personal credit information considered confidential?"

"Except to industry insiders," he replied offhandedly. "My sources say you paid cash for this building. Where did you get that kind of money, Miss Raines?"

Insiders? Sources? She considered him again. Finely chiseled nose and brow, a perfectly square, utterly masculine jaw. Dark eyes with lush lashes. And his mouth... His lips might be full and soft in the rare moments he wasn't scowling. All in all, he sort of reminded her of Hugh Jackman. Yeah, he was definitely handsome. Too bad he was way too abrasive to pull off a successful information schmooze. But none of that really mattered at the moment. No, what mattered was drawing a line of acceptable behavior and holding it.

"Forgive my bluntness, Mr. Preston, but Ida's grandson or God's grandson, insider or outsider of whatever industry—I really don't care. My personal finances are none of your business."

"I can find out," he countered.

"Well, you just put your pet ferret right on that," she challenged, wondering what law he was violating and what it would take to get him charged. "Do let me know what he turns up. I'm sure it'll be fascinating stuff."

"I'm absolutely certain of it. I'll bet it's a very long list of names like Edna and Ralph and Ida."

Hell, she'd take any name. Not that she was going to tell Cole Preston that. She'd been calling her anonymous benefactor "Secret Santa" for the last three weeks and while it worked in a casual way, she wanted to have a real name and an address to go with it so that she could write a proper thank-you note. Without Santa and the cashier's check for fifty grand, the center would still be nothing more than a dream.

"Like I said," she retorted as she pushed off the old desk and reached for the handles of the sander, "go for it. Now, if you'll excuse me, I have work to do."

She paused, smiled at him and added, "The first rule of running a successful con is to look like you don't need anyone's money, you know. I'm figuring that refinished oak floors ought to be enough to lull Mrs. Flores into giving me her weekly bingo money. And if I can get two or three other old ladies to do the same… Look out, Vegas, here I come."

"Sarcasm—"

Emily flipped the switch on the handle and the motor on the sander roared to life. His next few words were drowned out by the clatter of the accelerating blades. Whatever else he might have been intending to say was swallowed as the blades bit into the floor with more force than Emily had anticipated and the machine lurched forward out of her control.

While Emily tightened her grip and dug in her heels in a desperate effort to gain control of the wildly surging monster, Cole Preston displayed a keen sense of self-preservation and jumped out of the way.

The machine was making a slow left turn with Emily fighting it every inch of the way, when he stepped to her side and flipped off the power switch. The motor stopped instantly.

"You're a menace," he declared as the blades clattered to silence.

Her hands white on the handles and her cheeks hot with embarrassment and anger, Emily retorted, "Better than being a pathetic excuse for a grandson."

He glared at her in silence. Emily glared back and, not suffering from any sudden onset of muteness, added, "Kindly haul your sorry ass out of my *fine… arts…center.*"

His jaw clenched and his pulse clearly pounding in his temples, he turned on his heel and strode out of the building without another word. Emily watched him go, hating herself for having noticed that he wore a really yummy aftershave. A deep and dark spice with woodsy notes and just a hint of some sort of flower. She sighed and shook her head to dispel the ridiculous preoccupation.

At least, Emily consoled herself as she left the office in search of Ida, Beth and the electrician, she'd delivered a fabulous last line. The "sorry ass" part of it had been pure inspiration. Not the least bit physically accurate, of course, but…

She smiled, imagining him frantically checking out his butt in the first mirror he came across. Yeah, it was a shallow and probably fleeting triumph, but she'd take it. She had a niggling suspicion that in a contest of wills with Cole Preston, even the smallest of victories counted.

Two

Cole Preston walked down the sidewalk beside his grandmother, telling himself that he'd had worse days. Lots of them. Not that he could recall any of them at this particular moment. In looking back at the day so far… No, actually his world had gone off the rails yesterday afternoon when Grams had called him wanting—out of the absolute clear blue sky—to liquidate part of her investment portfolio so she could give it to a new friend of hers who was doing wonderful charity work.

The alarm bells had gone off in his head. Two hours later Wendy had been furious with him for canceling their date to the symphony—again—and he was heading for the middle of nowhere to do his family duty.

Six lanes of bumper-to-bumper Kansas City rush-hour traffic and then dodging pot holes on eighty miles of narrow two-lane road later, he'd arrived to find his grandmother with a heating pad in the small of her back, popping ibuprofen like candy and gushing over darling Emily Raines and the chance to dance again.

Darling? *Darling?* Yeah, okay, he'd allow that Emily Raines was drop-dead gorgeous. Legs from here to eternity, luscious curves in all the right places, and he couldn't remember the last time he'd seen a T-shirt stretched so invitingly over what looked like a perfect set of breasts. Add in a smile that lit up a room, curly blond hair, a perky little nose and a chin that she could square in the blink of her incredibly green eyes. No doubt about it, his Grams's new friend was a knockout.

But she was no darling by any stretch of even the most creative imagination. He'd been ten miles outside of town yesterday when Jason had called with the information from the first run of the background software. An artist who, until the last year, hadn't lived anywhere in her adult life longer than six months, a woman who suddenly showed up in a little bitty town with a wad of cash to buy a rundown building and saying she wanted to make life better for the elderly. It met the classic definition of suspicious.

Not that anyone but he and Jason thought so. Grams was absolutely convinced that her precious Emily was nothing short of an angel, an angel sent by the God of Days of Faded Glory Returned. Yeah, right. How anyone with such a quick temper and a sharp tongue could be considered angelic was beyond him. An angel from hell, maybe.

But since Grams didn't see Emily the same way he did, he was in one helluva bind. His original plan to blow into town, lay down the law, make arrangements for Grams to move to a more protected environment and blow out again obviously wasn't going to cut it.

And that first meeting with Emily Raines… He hadn't mangled a face-to-face with a woman that badly since junior high. He'd been pacing the living room of his grandmother's house desperately trying to come up with a workable plan B when she'd come home to chew him up one side and down the other for the way he'd behaved toward her Little Miss Perfect. She'd concluded the verbal lashing with the demand that he be nice to Emily, even if he had to fake it.

And in that moment, he'd found his solution. There was a saying about keeping your friends close and your enemies closer. If ever there was a situation when that advice applied, it was this one. So what if Grams thought he was a cross between a choirboy and a Boy Scout for saying that he would apologize to Emily Raines? It was the end result that mattered. And the odds of Emily Raines being able to commit mischief, mayhem and criminal fraud would be considerably lessened if he could keep her in his hip pocket. While being perfectly nice about it, of course.

"Oh, good, Alma's here," his grandmother said brightly.

Cole nodded absently as his gaze swept over the small crowd gathered in little groups on the lawn of the Augsburg public library. "And so is Emily," he replied as he took in the long length of her jean skirt and how she'd left the top buttons of her Hawaiian shirt undone so that everyone could have a delightful glimpse of her cleavage.

"Remember your promise, Cole," Grams admonished as she waved to another silver-haired lady.

"I will. In fact," he added, "apologizing is the very first thing I'm going to do. If you'll excuse me?"

She beamed up at him. "Of course, dear. And thank you."

He smiled, planted a quick kiss on her cheek and then stepped off the sidewalk and headed across the lawn toward his tall, curvy prey.

Just when she'd become aware of him, he couldn't say, but she watched him advance on her, pursed her lips and then took a long slow sip from her red plastic cup. Her gaze never left his. As he came to a stop in front of her, she arched a perfectly winged brow and sweetly asked, "Are you here to make sure I don't run off with the library's late fees?"

He had to give her credit for being quick-witted. But then again, successful con men—and women—were notorious for being able to think on their feet. He took a breath and cleared his throat. "I'm here to apologize for the way I behaved this morning and to see if perhaps we might be able to start all over again on a better foot."

Her brow inched higher and one corner of her mouth twitched. "Ida laid into you, huh?"

"I'd already come to the conclusion that I'd been an ass." Not exactly the truth, but it was the smart thing to say. "Grams came home soon after that and very quickly reinforced my thinking on the whole thing."

She took another sip of her drink, then studied him, her green eyes dark and serious. "Just for the record, I didn't say a word to Ida about our…exchange."

"She made sure I knew that," he assured her. "Apparently she was only a few steps out of the office when we picked up where we'd left off when she came in. She overheard and stopped in her tracks to eavesdrop."

"Just so that you know that I'm not a lowlife ratter-outer."

As though that was even in the top ten of her sins. "Ida is right," he went on. "I was rude and I really am sorry." He stuck out his hand. "Truce?"

Was it his imagination, or did she lift one brow ever so slightly? Did she suspect his real motives for making nice with her?

"Apology accepted," she said, putting her hand in his and wrapping her fingers around it.

He had a vague thought about how perfect her grip was, but his ability to analyze why melted away as a warm current surged up his arm to his shoulder and then flooded through every fiber of his body.

A buzz, his mind whispered in awe. *An honest to God electric buzz.* How long had it been since…?

"Shall we get something to eat?"

Called back to reality, he blinked and took his cue.

He released her hand and tried to look as though he'd been totally unaffected by the physical contact.

She smiled up at him and there was no uncertainty about the arch of her brow this time. And neither was there any mystery as to what she was thinking. She knew full good and well that she'd sizzled his socks. He could see the amusement sparkling in her eyes.

"I've heard," she said silkily, "that Alma Rogers makes the best fried chicken in the county."

He ran her statement through his mind. Twice. No, he hadn't imagined it; the tone in her voice was unmistakable and the message that eddied through her words was crystal clear. He smiled and wondered if for the rest of his life the words "fried chicken" would translate to "let's get naked."

"Well, let's go judge for ourselves," he said, stepping to the side and motioning for her to lead the way toward the buffet tables set up under the library's giant old elm trees. Falling in beside her, he placed his hand in the small of her back and savored the warmth that radiated through him as he added, "If food hasn't come out of a drive-through window or been delivered by a waiter in the last fifteen years, I haven't had any."

She looked up over her shoulder at him. "I gather you don't get back home much."

Back home? "I've never lived in Augsburg," he clarified. Even to his own ears he sounded critical, so to save himself, he quickly added, "And Grams moved here just a few years ago—five, I think—when the dance company finally forced her to retire."

She handed him a paper plate from the stack at the end of the table and a bundle of napkin-wrapped plastic silverware, forcing him to take his hand off her back. The tingling warmth in him quickly ebbed away. Maybe if he crowded her at the serving table, brushed up against her not-so-accidentally… He took a half step before the voice of reason growled from the back of his brain. He froze in place and took a slow, steadying breath. An inviting smile, a silky voice and one sultry innuendo…. Geez, if there was a con artist Hall of Fame… He was beyond pathetic for letting himself get sucked in so easily, so quickly.

"Really? Listening to Ida talk," she said brightly as she selected a crispy drumstick from the heaping roaster of chicken, "I had the distinct impression that Augsburg was a long cherished ancestral home."

As far as he was concerned, Augsburg was nothing more than a bump in the road he was forced by family duty to visit once—or if things went to hell in a hand-basket—twice a year. But actually saying so wouldn't be a good strategic move in his campaign to be a paragon of pleasantness. He followed her, putting a chicken breast on his plate and saying, "Grams's sister, my great-aunt Imogene, married a local man whose family was waiting here for God to invent dirt. Since he wasn't about to move on, Imogene lived here all of her married life. Which was a long time. They didn't have any kids and when she passed away, she left the house to Grams.

"Personally," he went on, "my recommendation was

for Grams to sell it or rent it out as an income-producing property, but she very conveniently went deaf on the whole deal, sold her New York condo instead, and then packed up everything she owned and moved here. She says she likes being able to see from one end of town to the other. As for why, I don't have a clue."

"Oh, I do," his companion claimed, plopping a big scoop of homemade potato salad on her plate. She attacked the platter of sliced tomatoes next as she added, "The older people get, the more they tend to find larger spaces confusing and disorienting. Smalling down their world makes everything more predictable and less stressful for them. I guess I've never really thought of Ida as being old enough for those to be real concerns for her."

"Are you some sort of an expert on old people?" he asked, opting for coleslaw and a pretense of innocent inquiry.

The afternoon sunlight glinted softly in her blond curls as she shook her head and picked up another serving spoon. "Not really," she admitted, chasing a deviled egg around the plate. "What I know about the elderly comes from practical experience. My grandmother moved in with us when I was a teenager. For her, the final straw was the stress of driving in a bigger city. It's just too intense for most older people."

"Well, yeah. It's too intense for *me*. Does that make me an oldster?"

She paused to look over at him—and look him over. "Not hardly."

Okay, so he knew that it was really stupid to be

turned on by her open approval, but the thinking part of his anatomy was a full two ticks behind the rest of him—the rest of him that believed that nothing logical should ever get in the way of having a well-hello-there good time. Yep, by the time his brain had kicked in, it was too late; *his* smile of approval had made the effort pointless.

Grinning, she put down the spoon, reached out to snag the egg with her fingers and then plopped it onto her plate. She flicked the tip of her pink tongue over her fingertips, then laughed softly and asked, "Where do you live?"

"Kansas City," he supplied, quickly deciding to run with the whole thing for now and deal with her possible ulterior motives later. His basic plan, after all, was to keep her close. Real close was even better. "The town of Blue Ridge, to be precise," he went on. "In a two-bedroom, two and a half bath condo with a view of nothing in particular."

"Sounds like a regular real estate dream come true."

Clearly not to her, though. He shrugged and helped himself to the tomatoes. "It's a decent investment property. I'm not there very much so resale value is all I really care about."

"Ida mentioned that you travel a lot. Are you in sales?"

"I'm a venture cap—" The sudden blast of cold air nearly knocked the plate of food out of his hand. He caught it just in time and blinked in amazement at the flurry of paper napkins and plates and plastic lids winging across the library yard. "What the hell?"

"The dry line's here about four hours early," his companion laughingly offered above the wind and flapping storm of debris. Pivoting, she used her hip to keep the plastic wrap from a plate of chocolate chip cookies from being blown away. She set her plate down and while securely covering the cookies, added, "At least it's moving fast. That's kinda good news in the whole big scheme of things."

Women were dashing toward the tables from all over the yard. The men were folding up chairs in their wake. "The *what* line?"

The wind whipping through her blond curls, she turned her head to give him a brief, but puzzled look. "You know, cool dry air slams down on a mass of warm moist air? The wind gust is the leading edge of the storm front. Wicked bad nasty stuff usually rides on the back edge of the dry line."

"But—" He gripped his plate with both hands as another wind gust tried to strip it from his grasp. He looked up through the whipping leaves of the trees overhead. "There isn't a cloud in the sky."

"Look in the direction the blast came from."

He did as she'd instructed. Wicked bad nasty... Yeah, that pretty well described the flashing mass of greenish-black sky barreling at them from the west. He'd add deadly and mean and brutal to the list, too. "I take it that the picnic's over."

"Good looks and keenly observant, too."

He grinned. Good-looking, huh? Now, why her appreciation for his handsome self mattered was beyond him. It wasn't as though he hadn't heard compliments all his life. But still… He watched her lean over the table to put a lid on the potato salad container.

"You might want to finish loading up your plate before they get all the lids on," she said, interrupting his appreciation of her sexy curves. She'd no sooner made the suggestion than a speedy little old lady whisked away the potato salad container. The coleslaw was carted off a half second later by another equally fast and ruthlessly determined elderly woman. The cookie plate was gone in the same fraction of time. A blue-haired lady slammed a lid on the big roaster pan full of chicken and then stepped back to let her husband haul the mass of metal and poultry off the table and toward the cars parked along the street. For an old guy, he covered the ground in really good time.

"Well, okay, that's no longer an option," Emily Raines said, chuckling as she straightened and tried to push her hair out of her eyes.

"Good God, it's like someone yelled, 'Raid'!"

She tipped her head back and laughed outright. The sound was full and throaty, genuine and full of life. He more felt it than he heard it. At least that's the way it seemed. The comfortable, almost settling warmth that had instantly bloomed deep in the center of his chest at her amusement didn't fade as the sound of her laughter trailed off. Marveling, he watched her lift her partially filled dinner plate just enough to pull the tablecloth from underneath.

"You probably need to get Ida home before the rain gets here," she said, giving the cloth a vigorous shake.

Grams! What a lousy grandson he was. He quickly looked around the library yard, half expecting to see that she'd been trampled into the grass by the geriatric stampede. "She's over by the front steps, stacking chairs," he said in relief. He stepped over to a metal barrel trash can and dropped his plate into it, asking, "Do you need help with anything?"

"I'm fine for now, thanks." She tossed down the folded tablecloth and yanked the one off the next table in the line. "But if you want, once you get Ida home, you can come back and help us carry the tables and chairs back into the library storage room."

"Okay. I'll be right back."

"I'll be right here." She laughed again, more softly this time, but the warm fullness in his chest wasn't any less for the difference. "Somewhere."

He nodded, forced himself to tear his gaze away from the windblown opening of her shirt front and turned away. He was a half dozen steps away and still impressed with how sheer a bra could be when she called out, "Hey, Cole!"

He turned around just in time to see her pull her hand from the pocket of her jean skirt.

"You guys walked down from the house. It'll be easier on Ida if you drive her home." Before he could say anything, she tossed him a set of keys. "Green Range Rover on the north side of the library. And don't mess with my radio station!"

Grinning, he saluted her command and then turned away to make his way across the lawn. "Hey, Grams," he called as he reached the library steps. He held up the keys for her to see and jangled them. "How about a chauffeured ride home before the storm breaks?"

She smiled and glanced uptown the six blocks to where his red Porsche was parked in the drive of her house. Her gaze came back to him, a mischievous sparkle in her eyes. "You haven't stolen a car, have you?"

"Emily has loaned us hers so neither one of us has to see if we can do the hundred-yard dash in under fifteen seconds."

"I take it that your apology was accepted?"

"She was very nice about it."

"That's because she's a very nice young lady," his grandmother assured him, waving goodbye to her friends.

Cole fell in beside her, cupping her elbow to steady her as they crossed the lawn and made their way toward the Range Rover. Nice? Yeah, he'd have to allow that Emily had good social skills. The jury was still out on how deep that niceness went, though. It could all be part of the con-artist show. After all, people weren't generally inclined to give their Social Security checks and life savings to strangers who were rude and unpleasant.

Of course, if he had to make a bet one way or the other at this point… Okay, he was usually a good judge of people so, yeah, he'd be willing to put a small amount down—a couple of grand, max—on Emily Raines being a sincerely nice person all the way to the center of her lovely bones.

Time would tell whether or not he should up his ante on her in that regard. Of one thing he was absolutely sure right this moment, though. He'd put about ten grand on her for being the most intriguing woman he'd met in a long, long time. And while he was at it, and as long as he was being honest, he'd put another twenty on keeping her close as eventually turning out to be one of best short-term romantic decisions he'd ever make in his life.

He jangled the keys in his hand and smiled. It was really nice of the weather to have helped him out. There was way more potential in a private dinner for two than a public picnic for fifty and he had every intention of making the most of the unexpected opportunity he'd been handed.

Emily stopped on the top of the library stairs, waiting for Cole to close the door behind them and join her. *Decision, decisions. To take a chance or to play it safe. It's do or die time. For today, anyway.*

He'd be back to shadow her tomorrow. Odds were that he wasn't going to give up his suspicions over-night without some sort of real effort on her part. She'd made a bit of progress in disarming him as they'd made their way down the picnic table. She could press on and hope she didn't come off as pressing too hard, too fast. Or she could just let it go for the night and take another run at him tomorrow.

"Is the door locked?" she asked, watching the wall of shimmering silver coming in from the northwest.

"Yep."

Oh, what the hell. "We have about two minutes before we're drenched," she told him. "Do you want me to run you up to Ida's in the Rover? Or would you like to come over to my place? I can put together a bistro-esque meal. Nothing fancy. Certainly not as good as the meal we had to throw in the trash, but it's something."

"A can of chicken noodle soup with my grandmother or any kind of fare with a gorgeous blonde. Strikes me as a no-brainer."

"Then c'mon," she called, dashing down the steps and toward her car, hoping that everyone in town was glued to their TVs, watching the weather radar, and not the least bit interested in looking out their windows to see her and Cole Preston heading off together to her place. Not that she really cared if they did, she admitted to herself with a smile as she climbed behind the wheel and put the key into the ignition.

Cole dropped into the passenger seat and pulled his door closed as she cranked over the engine. Rap music blasted out of the Rover's speakers.

She punched the power button—hard—and the torture instantly ended. "You messed with my radio station."

He grinned. "I wouldn't have thought of it if you hadn't mentioned it."

Chuckling, she backed the car out of the parking space and headed for her driveway at the other end of the downtown block. It took all of a whole minute to cover the distance. It took just shy of another minute to let them into the warehouse and make their way to the elevator.

The outer doors slid open as soon as she pushed the call button. She was pushing back the scissor gate when a heavy roll of thunder rattled the windowpanes and the man behind her asked incredulously, "How old is this thing?"

"I think Mr. Otis himself installed it," she answered over the hammering arrival of the rain and leading the way in. "But it was inspected and serviced last year. It'll get us to the second floor just fine."

He pulled the scissor gate closed. "It's an unexpected trip to the basement I'm worried about."

"Life is supposed to be an adventure." She pushed the button to take them up. "A bit of danger makes it extra interesting."

"True."

She thought he held his breath until the elevator doors opened again, but couldn't really be sure. There was no doubt about his reaction when she opened the door to her apartment, though.

Three

"As digs go, it's not much, I know," she offered, hanging her car keys on the cup hook someone had long ago screwed into the wall next to the doorjamb. "I've been traveling light for years."

"You have the basics," he observed, his gaze skimming over the sofa, the one end table and the thrift-store coffee table as he walked into the main room. She saw his appraisal move through the open bedroom door to take in the queen-size bed and single nightstand. "All the rest of the stuff people pack into their houses is mostly in the way."

"Thanks, but you don't have to be nice. I know that it looks like there ought to be a Gideon Bible in the nightstand and the Rescue Mission's free meal and mandatory prayer service schedule taped to the back of the front door."

She laughed outright as he automatically looked over his shoulder. "Made you look!" At his chagrined smile, she moved into the kitchen, saying brightly, "Have a seat and I'll put together a quick something to eat. Do you drink wine?"

"Every chance I get."

"Any preferences?" she asked, collecting items from her sparse cupboards. "I have a Zin and a Merlot. We're having fruit and cheese and marginally fancy crackers."

"I'm not a wine snob," he promised as he settled into a corner of the big brown leather sofa, one of her only two brand-new, never-been-used-by-anybody-else furniture purchases. "Whatever you want is fine by me."

Deciding that she'd take both and let him choose, she put the bottles and a corkscrew on a tray with a pair of cheap wineglasses.

"Great windows."

"They're the only redeeming feature to the place." She paused in her collecting to smile at the four huge windows spanning the front wall of the living room. Ten feet high, four feet wide with thick, carved moldings and perfectly sized window seats… Looking at them always gave her hope, always reminded her that the rest of it—the leak-stained ceiling, the long past faded wallpaper on the walls and the plumbing that groaned and moaned like a moose in distress—could be fixed, could be brought up to the standards set by the windows.

Emily shook her head and went back to the task at hand. "When the gust front came through, I'd just asked you what you did for a living," she said, pulling open the refrigerator. "You didn't get a chance to really tell me."

"I'm a venture capitalist."

"Which is what, exactly?" she asked as lightning flashed bright white outside the windows and thunder boomed in the near distance.

"My specialty is providing money for start-up or expanding businesses," he answered above the noise of the storm outside. "I do the research and crunch the numbers and if it's all good, we draft a contract and I write a check. Then I stand back and let them do what they do. After a set period of time, they pay me back with interest."

"And you have to travel a lot to do this?"

"Absolutely. I never invest without meeting the borrowers in person and laying my own eyes on the operation. I have more frequent flyer miles than your average airline pilot."

"Ah," she challenged, slicing a block of cheddar cheese, "but do you know all the flight crews by name?"

"My pilot is Bob. My copilot is Randy and my flight attendant is Collette."

"You have a private plane?"

"A Cessna Citation."

A rich man…. Obscenely rich. He'd probably never in his life been in an apartment this tacky. And she was serving him some slightly too old green grapes, and Monterey Jack and cheddar cheese with crackers out of box decorated with elves. With five-bucks-a-bottle wine to wash it all down. "Your ventures obviously return a good deal of capital," she offered as she carried the tray of poor peasant fare into the living room.

"I do well enough," he replied, watching her set their pathetic excuse for dinner on the coffee table. He slid forward on the sofa and took the merlot and the cork-screw off the tray while adding, "I don't think my father would be at all disappointed in what I've done with my inheritance."

"Has he been gone long?" she asked, taking her conversational cue as she sat down beside him and snagged a piece of the Jack.

"Seven years. He was a heart surgeon who, in a cruel and ironic twist, died of a massive coronary."

"What about your mom?" she asked as she wondered just how many bottles of wine a person had to open before they got as smooth at it as he was.

"My parents divorced when I was in high school. My mother died my sophomore year of college. Ten years ago this spring."

"I'm so sorry," she offered in all sincerity.

He shrugged and poured the wine. Handing her the glass, he said, "I never have been able to understand why a woman who couldn't swim would sign up for a white-water rafting expedition."

"Maybe she was trying to overcome a fear of water."

"Who knows. She didn't talk to me about much of anything except alimony payments and child-support checks." He poured himself a glass of wine, returned the bottle to the tray and leaned back into the sofa. "What about your parents? Still living?"

"Living very well, actually. Mom teaches textile arts at the University of New Mexico at Albuquerque and Dad teaches high school Social Studies."

"Are they cool?"

Emily grinned around the rim of her glass. "Your regular Kum Ba Yah–singing sort of hippie holdovers. It was *so* embarrassing when I was a teenager. Add in my grandmother who, in her last year or so, thought she was living in a clothing-optional world..." She shook her head, remembering, and then lifted her glass in salute to the sweet insanity of her comparatively happy family. "Looking back, it really wasn't as awful as it seemed at the time. I probably should have risked having at least a few slumber parties."

He nodded and leaned forward to make himself a cracker and cheddar sandwich. "Why didn't you follow your parents in the education business?"

"Hey, it wasn't for a lack of trying," she assured him. "My first degree is in secondary education with an emphasis in fine arts. But, just in case you haven't been paying attention to the whole cultural trend thing, funding for art education isn't exactly at the top of the priority list for most school boards these days." She shrugged and took a sip of wine.

"So, throwing good money after bad," she went on as he ate, "I went back for my masters in fine arts. Halfway through I did a summer internship on a resto-ration project funded jointly by the Smithsonian and the

Rockefeller Foundation. I let them talk me into going in the special projects direction."

"What sort of projects do they do?"

"All kinds, all sizes, all over the country," she supplied, taking a cracker from the plate. "Historic preservation, the performing arts, the visual arts, the sciences in support of the arts. The most famous Rockefeller project is Williamsburg, Virginia, of course. Restoring the historic city, not building the theme park."

"I was wondering."

"Sure you were," she said, chuckling. "I did my internship working on a stained glass window project in the National Cathedral in Washington, D.C., and then on a railroad depot restoration in Seattle. I can't tell you all of the places I've worked since then."

"Your basic nomadic lifestyle."

At least he hadn't said *gypsy*. Nomads ranked considerably higher on the Homeless Integrity Index. "Yeah," she allowed, "I've pretty much lived out of a suitcase for the last few years. Have toolbox, will travel and all that. Which is cool in that I've seen a lot more of America than most people have. If you want a restaurant recommendation along any road, or in any city, just ask me."

He grinned, amusement sparkling in his dark eyes as he met her gaze in good-natured challenge. "Okay. San Francisco."

"Forget the sit-down places. Eat your way along Fisherman's Wharf. Your dollar goes further and you get a whole bunch of great eats. The clam chowder there is awesome. The best I've ever had."

"How are their crab cakes?"

"If you want crab cakes you need to go to Annapolis, Maryland. I don't remember the name of the place, but you can't miss it. Two-story clapboard on the water. It's yellow with brown trim. The best crab cakes in the world. Way more crab than cake. And when you're done eating, you can go over to the Naval Academy and sign up for the tour. They have John Paul Jones in the basement of the chapel."

"Who?"

"John Paul Jones," she repeated. At his cocked brow, she ventured, "The Bonhomme Richard versus the H.M.S. Serapis? There's a famous painting of the battle." He shook his head and she sighed. "American Revolutionary War?"

"I was a finance major with a minor in economics."

"John Paul Jones is the one who said 'I have not yet begun to fight.'"

"Oh, okay," he declared happily, his smile wide. "Why didn't you just say so?"

She rolled her eyes and went on. "Anyway, they have his sarcophagus in a rotunda under the chapel at the Academy. It's a really cool marble deal. Very Davey Jones and Neptune-esque. You do know who Davey Jones is, don't you?"

"Of course." He chuckled and reached for another slice of cheap cheese. "He played with the Monkees. He was the short English guy."

"You're culturally hopeless."

His laugh said he didn't much care. "You know, if

the artist gig doesn't work out, you can be a travel agent.
Or a tour guide."

"I guess a person should always keep their options
open."

"Are you working on a stained glass project around
here?"

He really was good at the pumping for information
deal. Very smooth, very easy and conversational. "I
have one on the table at the moment. It came in special
freight two days ago. But that's it. Nothing local for
the time being. I'm a little bit otherwise engaged for
the next few weeks. The grand opening is scheduled
for the fifteenth of June and there's a ton of work to
do between now and then."

He cocked a brow in a silent but eloquent "no
kidding" response. "So tell me," he said aloud. "How'd
a girl from New Mexico and who's traveled all over the
country end up putting down roots in Kansas?"

"I came here last year to repair a church window down
in Wichita and took a few day trips on the weekends. One
of them was on the Fourth of July. Augsburg has the best,
the absolute best, fireworks display you've ever seen. If
you can stretch out your visit this time to be here for it,
I promise you won't be disappointed."

"I'll give it a shot," he causally offered in the way of
commitment. "At the moment, I don't have any crises
on the radar, but it's the stuff under the radar that always
nails you. So what made you decide to live here between annual fireworks extravaganzas?"

"Real estate here is an incredible bargain and—"

"That's because there's no demand for it," he interrupted with a chuckle. "If it weren't for the weekend tourists, this town would be dead."

"Kansas City will grow this way," she offered confidently. "In twenty years I'll be able to sell my place at an embarrassingly huge profit."

"Twenty years is a long time to wait for a return on an investment."

She shrugged. "Money isn't everything. There's also the logistical considerations. With Kansas being in the middle of the country, it's a shorter flight to anywhere from here. The less time I have to spend in airports and making flight connections, the better. Aside from that…"

She took a quick sip of wine. "Big cities are nice and all. There's lots to see and do. But in the end… Well, I suppose that for me the bottom line is that I can visit big cities anytime I want, but I like living in a place where they call me by name when I walk into the grocery store."

With a quiet snort, he countered, "There are no secrets in a small town."

"True. But that's really not a problem if you're not doing anything that you wouldn't want everyone to know about. Or if you don't give a damn if they do know."

"You have a point. I prefer to remain anonymous while shopping, though."

"Why?"

"It keeps things simple."

Emily chuckled. "I've got to say that I've never considered saying hello to people to be a real complicated social transaction."

"To each his own. I buy a quart of milk, I pay for it, I leave the store, I go home and drink it."

"All alone," she teased in a pitying tone.

"I didn't say that," he drawled. "You're presuming."

She leaned toward him and said in her best imitation of a prosecutorial voice, "If you weren't going home to an empty house, you probably wouldn't be the one buying the milk. And if you were sharing, you'd be buying a gallon, not a quart."

"I'm not a monk."

"I didn't say you were." No one would ever say such a thing. Not once they caught a whiff of that incredible cologne he wore. She'd bet money his was called something like "Yeah, I'm That Good."

He considered her a moment, his eyes sparkling and his smile quirking slowly. "Do you buy milk by the gallon or by the quart?"

She laughed and confessed, "I buy it by the *pint*."

"Are you a nun?"

"Not unless they've *really* changed the rules," she answered through her laughter. With a sip of wine to sober her, she added, "I've never been a big fan of milk. Positively un-American, I know, and I can't tell you how often I've regretted the fact that I'll never be asked to do one of those mustache ads, but a little bitty splash on cereal once or twice a week is pretty much it for me."

"So there's no significant male other?"

Interesting. Whether or not she had a boyfriend wasn't at all relevant to the Fleecing Granny Investigation he was conducting. Had they crossed a trust line? "Well, my dad's pretty significant to me, but there's no boyfriend," she said. "And there hasn't been in I don't know how long. Is there a significant female other for you?"

He pursed his lips for a long moment and then answered, "I'd describe her as decidedly casual and mostly convenient."

"Geez, you're such a romantic." And way more direct than she'd expected.

"It's never really been necessary."

Yeah, believing that wasn't the least bit of a stretch. "Did they call you Mr. Lucky in high school?"

"Naw. I was…" He shifted his shoulders back and bobbed his head while looking at her through his lashes. He dropped his voice extra low and said, "The Stallion."

She couldn't help herself. She fell back into the sofa, laughing so hard she almost spilled her wine.

"So," he said, his voice sounding tight. He paused, cleared his throat, and tried again. "So why did you decide to give up the road to buy this building and make it into a *fine…arts…center?*"

"Well, it's kind of a long, complicated story."

He reached for the merlot bottle. "As it happens, I don't have a curfew tonight. More?"

She held out her glass and let him pour a generous amount into it before she began, "There's a church up in Wiebeville that—"

"Wee-bee-ville?" he asked, his grin wide and the mouth of the bottle poised motionless above his glass as he looked at her.

"Founded by Mr. Franz Wiebe a hundred-plus

years ago. It's a cute little town about forty miles
north of here that's pretty much a retirement community these days. All the old farmers turn the home-
stead over to the next generation and move into town.
They have a church that's listed on the National
Historic Register. *Gorgeous* stained glass windows."
She shook her head. "Hail the size of golf balls... Not
a good thing."

He emptied the last of the wine into his glass and
settled his back into the corner of the sofa, angling his
long legs partially across the center cushion. "And they
called you in to fix them."

"Yep. In the dead of this past January."

"Were you *that* desperate for work?"

"No," she corrected. "That busy. But it wasn't as
miserable as you might think. Cold, yes, but definitely
not as boring as I thought it was going to be."

"Boring?" he said, brightening. "Why, Miss Raines,
I distinctly remember you saying—mere moments
ago—that you prefer living in small towns."

"There's a big difference between small and oh-dear-
God-just-shoot-me."

"Oh, yeah? What would it be?"

She ignored his sarcasm. "I'll have you know that
Wiebeville is one of the most happenin' places on the
prairie. They have a kick-butt, state-of-the-art senior
center. Every Monday night is polka night. Second
and fourth Tuesday is big band or swing. They vote to
decide which."

"No square dancing?"

"Friday night. *And* Sunday afternoon. All that dancing is good for the heart and for keeping the bones strong, the muscles toned, you know. I think most of them could outrun me on my best day."

His gaze… There was something different about it as he looked at her. A kind of deepening, settling. Not that it was a dark thing. Not at all. More like an acceptance, a certainty of… Something right? No… Something…

Emily took a quick, healthy drink of wine and deliberately put her mind back on track. "During the daytime hours the seniors have all kinds of art activities. Painting and ceramics. Woodcarving and woodworking and model making. Weaving and quilting and you name it. Everyone comes and goes as they please. Mostly they come in right after breakfast, stay through lunch— there's an ethnic cuisine cooking class three days a week and leftovers on the other two—and they take off for home about four to eat supper and to get into the dance outfit *du noir*."

He gave her a lopsided smile. "Any clothing-optional devotees in the bunch?"

"No, and that's exactly what I noticed," she supplied excitedly. "Everyone is mentally alert and interested in life. Oh, yeah, one of their favorite conversations is about the latest meds their doctor has them on and what tests they're scheduled for, but the important part is that they're having that conversation while they're turning a wooden bowl on the lathe, putting a quilt on a frame and buckling up their square-dance shoes. They're active. They're involved. The creative parts of their brains are kept engaged. They're alert and mentally sharp and young at heart."

"And so you decided that Augsburg needed a place like that, too."

It would be easy and safe to take the story leap he offered, to blow right on past the hard to believe part. Easy, yes, but only in the short run.

"Actually, I wrote a letter to the area newspaper, complimenting the taxpayers for funding such a great place for the retirees. And then I waxed a bit poetic about how wonderful the world would be if there were more senior centers in rural areas to keep our aging parents and grandparents involved in life and physically and mentally active for as long as possible.

"The next week a man walked into the church while I working and asked me if I was Emily Raines. I said I was and he handed me an envelope, and then walked out. Inside the envelope was a clipping of my letter to the editor and a cashier's check for fifty thousand dollars."

He lowered his chin and tipped his head slightly to the side. "Who was the guy?"

"I have absolutely no idea. None," she admitted. "No return address on the envelope. Nothing at all to give me even a little bitty hint as to who my Secret Santa might be."

"Someone just gave you fifty thousand dollars out of the blue."

"Yeah. I know. I didn't believe it, either. I looked at that cashier's check at least a dozen times a day for a week, just trying to wrap my brain around it."

She shrugged and sighed. "And I eventually decided that since it came with a clipping of my Wouldn't It Be Lovely letter, I was supposed to use the money to set up a senior citizen fine arts center somewhere."

"You could have given the money to a foundation and specified that the interest be used for the support of existing senior programs."

"If Secret Santa had wanted to do that with the money, he would have done it himself," she countered with a shake of her head. The room moved back and forth a little longer than her head did. "I honestly think he gave it to me because he wanted to invest in my vision of spreading Wiebeville across America."

"Why'd you pick Augsburg?"

"Lots of elderly. Well, and the man who owned this building was only asking thirty grand for it."

"You got took."

"I did not," she asserted with a chuckle. "Between the two floors, I have almost twenty thousand square feet and, except for this apartment, all of it is wide-open space for doing whatever I want with it. Don't forget the elevator, either. And I talked him down to twenty-two five and into paying half of the closing costs."

He lifted his gaze to the stained ceiling tiles. "What kind of shape is the roof in?"

"That's an old stain," she explained. "The roof in this section is about fifteen years old and it's holding up fairly well. The rest of it…. Okay, it leaks like a sieve." She turned on the sofa to look out the front windows.

The rain rolled past in gray sheets, so thick and fast that she couldn't see the park across the street.

She turned back to face him, realizing as she did that she'd had a tad too much wine, too fast. She looked at her glass, noting that only a sip or two remained. "If it rains like this for very much longer, I'll be able to have a swimming party in the front office. B.Y.O.F."

"B.Y.O.F.?"

"Bring your own floaties." She grinned, finished the contents of her glass and then leaned forward to put it on the coffee table. Picking up some crackers and a few slices of cheese, she added, "I have some roofing bids and I'll get it taken care of in the next week or so."

"Ten thousand square feet of roofing... You don't have enough of the Secret Santa money left to pay for a new roof."

"I have a piggy bank," she assured him.

"Unless your piggy bank is the size of a Hummer, you're severely undercapitalized."

"I'll be just fine." Well, financially, anyway, she allowed as she very carefully folded a slice of cheese in half. Functionally... Hopefully the wine was done creeping up on her. It would be really embarrassing to fall off the sofa. She needed to eat something. And focus. She needed to keep her mental focus until the fuzziness wore off. What were they talking about? Hummers the size of pigs. No, that was backwards. Piggy banks. Costs.

"I plan to start small and add stuff over time as I can afford it," she said, feeling incredibly pleased with picking up where she figured she'd left off. "It doesn't take much to have a polka night, you know. An MP3 player loaded with Big Joe Polka tunes and a decent pair of speakers, some munchies and a cooler full of well-iced brewskies... Hey, we're good to dance 'til dawn. Or until the cops come to break up the party. Whichever comes first."

"You could ask for donations."

"For what? The beer?" Was it the wine, or was his smile considerably more quirked than before?

"The roof, Emily. You could ask for donations for the roof."

"No. It's really bad form to ask people to chip in to buy their own gift."

He chuckled and smoothly eased out the corner of the sofa to set his glass of wine on the table beside hers. "How about applying for foundation grants? I hear that they love this sort of thing."

She ate a cracker and two pieces of cheese while she nodded like a bobblehead dog on the rear window deck of a '62 Chevy Impala. It was hard to swallow it all down, but she immediately felt better for having made the effort.

"Foundations run on strict timetables for applications," she explained, folding another piece of the cheese. "There's a...well, a *season* and you have to have your paperwork ready to go in the second it opens. Miss it and you have to wait until next year. I didn't get the Secret Santa money in time to be part of this year's charitable dash for the cash.

"My friend Beth—she's an accountant—is working on some applications for next year. I'm going for the wood-working machines. You know, table saws and planers and lathes. That sort of stuff. I'm also going for a professional kitchen. The rest of what's needed is small-ticket stuff that I can buy on sale at a hobby store up in Kansas City."

"What about insurance, taxes, utilities?" he asked as he pulled a clump of grapes off the main stem. "How are you going to pay those expenses?"

"This year it's coming out of the piggy bank. Next year…I'll figure it out. Maybe I can go for some oper-ating money through a grant."

"Is your piggy bank a real piggy bank?" he asked, handing her the grapes. "Or is that what you call your investment portfolio?"

"It's a savings account at a reputable bank." Given the look on his face at that announcement… It was nice to know that she might not be the only one falling off the sofa. She ate a grape and waited for him to collect himself.

"Earning what? Two percent a year?"

"I actually have no idea. I think I made about twenty dollars in interest last year. Enough, anyway, that the IRS wanted to know about it. *And*," she added confi-dently, "it's FDIC insured."

"Theoretically," he declared. "It's also not working for you as hard as it could be."

"Well, if you're suggesting that I add 'learn how to play the stock market without losing my shirt' to my list of things to do this week… Sorry. I'm already signed up for the 'how to sand and refinish wood floors' class."

"I've seen you with a floor sander. You need the class…bad."

"And basic bathroom plumbing and simple tiling come right after that," she told him, popping another grape in her mouth. "Restrooms are a very high priority for the elderly."

"You need to let a professional invest your money for you."

"I agree. But right now I need the cash on hand. I can't afford to have it tied up for the long haul."

"There's this thing called day trading…?"

She snorted. And managed to suck a piece of grape skin hard against the back of her throat. Even as her brain was saying what an incredibly uncool thing she'd just done, her cough reflex kicked in. "Unless you're volunteering to do it," she struggled to say through the fit, "you can forget it. I'm totally clueless."

Handing her his wineglass with one hand, he slid close and gently patted her upper back with the other. A sip didn't accomplish anything toward dislodging the peeling, but a second, heftier one, did. "Thanks," she whispered hoarsely, feeling like a complete and utter idiot.

He didn't move away, didn't take his hand from her back when he reached down to his hip and pulled his cell phone out of the holster. Holding it in his free hand, he flipped it open, hit a single button with his thumb and then held it to his ear.

"Hey, Jase," he said a second later. "What you got going on this evening?" There was a short pause during which Emily resisted the urge to lean into him and lay her head on his shoulder.

"Good," he said. "I need the mini station down here."

She breathed deep and decided that his cologne should be made illegal. Or at least available only by prescription.

"Sounds perfect to me. Eight it is. And thanks, Jase." He flipped the phone closed and holstered it, saying, "There, Miss Raines. You may consider yourself as having hired an investment guru."

"Can I afford you?" she asked, tilting her head to look up at his face.

"I don't think the charges will be all that outrageous."

Oh, God. That soft, low rumble of his that melted her bones. She drew a slow breath and kept herself from leaning deeper into the curve of his arm. "Give me a ballpark idea of what kind of fees we're talking about."

He tipped his head and lowered his lips toward hers. She closed her eyes and stopped breathing altogether as his lips slowly, softly and thoroughly took possession of hers. Swaying, she slipped an arm around his neck and held on, savoring the delicious warmth flooding through her.

He drew back just enough to meet her gaze. His smile knowing, his eyes sparkling with amused certainty, he asked, "Steeper than you expected?"

Actually, it wasn't nearly as steep as she was suddenly wanting. No, *needing*. "I can't remember ever enjoying paying a bill quite so much," she replied, threading her fingers through the hair at his nape and hoping it was enough of a blatant-but-just-shy-of-tawdry hint to keep things moving forward. Preferably quickly. Before she exploded—all by herself—right there on the sofa.

His smile quirked slowly. "Oh, yeah?" he whispered as he took his wineglass from her hand and blindly set it on the table. "Wanna make some advance payments on your account?"

"I'd love to," she admitted, twining her other arm around his neck. He chuckled, put his arms around her waist and drew her against the hard heat of his body. She went, her lips parting beneath his, her senses flooding with a deliciously desperate kind of hunger. She felt him pull her shirttail from her skirt and whimpered in delight as his hands skimmed upwards over her bare skin to undo the hooks on her bra. She was on fire, completely, gloriously, thoroughly—

The 1812 Overture?

At least she wasn't the only one surprised. Cole abruptly broke their kiss and freed a hand from her shirt, saying, "Sorry," as he yanked his cell phone from the holster and flipped it open. "Hi, Grams," he said without preamble. "What's up?"

His wince at whatever Ida was telling him didn't take a rocket scientist to interpret.

"Yes, he is. And, yes, it was very nice of him to let you know."

Augsburg, we have a problem.

"No, of course not. Nothing we can't pick up again some other time. I'm on my way right now."

He flipped the phone closed with a heavy sigh. She spared him from having to actually announce that the good times weren't going to roll for them that night. Taking her arms from around his neck, she put some distance between them, saying, "You've been called home to get ready for Jase's arrival."

He sighed hard again, put his hands on his knees and leveraged himself to his feet. "She can't let Jason see the house in such a mess. And she has to bake a cake and freshen the bathroom towels and get the second guest room ready and, and, and." He scraped his fingers through his dark, already tousled hair. "And since he's my employee, I need to go help her be an impressive domestic goddess."

Emily stood, too. Reaching up one arm of her shirt, she grasped the strap of her unhooked bra and pulled it down her arm while she admitted, "I'd pay money to see you in an apron, you know."

"I don't think so," he replied, watching intently as she dragged the other strap down and out. "What else besides an apron?"

"Absolutely nothing at all."

He blinked and grinned at her, arching a brow. "*That* I'd be willing to do."

She laughed, pulled the bra from under her shirt, and dropped the sheer scrap of fabric on the coffee table between them.

His smile disappeared in an instant even as his brow inched higher. Considering the bra, he asked, "How long does it take to bake a cake and freshen towels?"

"Longer than you're hoping," she laughingly replied as she moved around the coffee table and toward the apartment's front door. "But I'll give you a rain check for tonight. Redeemable anytime." She heard him mutter under his breath, but he followed.

"Here," she said, opening the door and handing him her car keys. "Take the Rover to Ida's. You'll drown if you walk. You can bring it back in the morning."

"Thanks." He frowned at the keys and looked up at her, his smile inching back for a moment as though he might be thinking about kissing her good-night.

"I'll see you tomorrow," she said, putting the kibosh on letting him get her wound up for nothing all over again.

He grinned and winked, then nodded and walked off toward the elevator, calling over his shoulder, "I'm really looking forward to it."

She closed the apartment door behind him and leaned her head against the cool wood of the carved doorjamb. Tomorrow. She could wait until tomorrow, she assured herself. She had to wait. She didn't have any other real choice because having Ida catching her climbing through her grandson's bedroom window in the middle of the night would be just too much for a genteel little old lady's heart to take.

Four

Emily considered the pale gray light coming weakly through the warehouse windows and rolled her already cramping shoulders. A night of restless sleep, a good hour of literally sweeping the water out the warehouse front door, of answering a thousand questions about a million details from five electricians all at once… The stuff the dreams of social do-gooders were *not* made of.

She looked at her watch and sighed. Seven minutes. All of seven minutes since the last time she'd checked the time and wondered when Cole was going to get there.

"Pa-thet-ic," she muttered, taking her watch off her wrist and setting it in the open lid of her toolbox. "He'll get here when he gets here," she admonished. "And not one second sooner. So buck it up and get something done while you wait. Nothing sadder than being caught sitting by the phone and waiting for it to ring."

She studied the old, battered stained glass window lying on the table in front of her, her gaze tracing over the lines of solder. Picking out the subtle signs that told her in what order the small glass pieces had originally been put together, she followed the course backward to where the next piece needed to be removed, and then picked up her tools again.

Carefully laying the hot tip of the iron on the solder, Emily slowly melted the joint where three pieces of glass met and then used the scraper she held in the left hand to pull the excess liquid metal off the ancient copper tape below. The silvery stuff pooled on the glass, the molten surface instantly skimming over as it cooled, darkened and eased back to a solid state. She moved the iron to the next juncture and repeated the process, melting, dragging and letting it cool, working steadily to release the individual antique glass shapes from the intricate floral and vine pattern some unknown artist had just as painstakingly assembled over a century ago.

It took several minutes—no more than usual—to completely melt the metal holding the two-inch curved piece of swirled green glass in place. Propping the iron in its insulated holder, she picked up a bare utility blade and inserted it in the sliver of space she'd created and gently leveraged the glass shape free of the pattern. Stepping to the other side of the table, she scraped the old copper foil off all the edges with the blade and then held the piece up to the light.

No cracks, no chips that she could see. "Four down," she said to herself as she wrote the number on the glass piece with a black grease pencil. "Seventy, eighty, ninety or more to go," she added as she laid it on the number four spot of the vellum template she'd made last night. She adjusted how pieces one, two and three laid in relation to four, making sure that all the spaces were equal.

"Sorry to have to bother you, Miss Raines."

She looked up from her work, smiled at the electrician—Mike?—and assured him, "It's not a bother at all. What can I help you with?"

"On that wiring for the woodwork shop you're going to put in… Do you want two outlet receptacles? Or four?"

"What would be your recommendation?" God, was she smooth? Total ignorance and not a sign of it.

"I'd go with four."

"Then four it is."

"Okay," he said, writing on his little notepad. "Let me check to make sure there isn't something else so I don't have to bother you again."

While he flipped through his notes, she moved back around the table to the larger piece.

"I thought you were supposed to be taking a floor sanding class today."

She looked up, grinning, to watch Cole Preston close the distance between them. "Good morning," she said, wondering if he'd ever thought about modeling for a living. Not every man could make a pair of khaki trousers and a light blue oxford shirt look like a million bucks.

"Morning," he replied, stopping a perfectly respectable distance away and dropping her car keys beside the toolbox.

"I don't see anything else, Miss Raines. Thanks."

"Don't hesitate to ask if something else comes up," she called after the departing electrician.

Turning back to Cole, she said, "After I drained the pool in the front office this morning, I gave the sander a shot, but it was an absolute no-go. Everything is way too damp. The dust is miserable, but gum paste is even worse. This weather system is supposed to clear out tomorrow afternoon. Until things dry out, though, there's no sanding, no painting, no staining and certainly no divinity making."

"Divinity?"

"A candy made with egg whites," she explained, propping her hip against the worktable. "Egg whites don't beat up right when there's high humidity. There's no hope for a seven-minute frosting, either. Although I gotta tell you, even under the best weather conditions, I have never been able to make a seven-minute frosting in under fifteen minutes."

He knitted his brows as he fought to keep a smile contained. "Do you suppose I've ever had seven-minute frosting?"

"It's usually on angel food cakes. Frothy and light with soft little peaks. Basically it's the cake version of the meringue on a pie."

"Well, you learn something new every day." His attention went to one of the electricians backing through the warehouse, uncoiling a big spool of yellow wire. "I see that the sparkies aren't worried about working in the damp."

"They're running the new electrical wiring today. They've *sworn* to me that nothing they're doing is hooked up to the juice."

His attention came to back to her. "So what are you working on?" he asked, stepping up to the table beside her and looking down at the battered window.

"It's from a couple in Minneapolis," she explained, breathing deep the delicious scent of him. "They're restoring an old Victorian mansion and the Smithsonian sent them my way. Since I couldn't get there to do the repairs on-site, they crated it up and shipped it to me. Money is no object for these people."

"Apparently. It looks complicated."

"It's not a Stained Glass 101 project, that's for sure."

"It also looks like it's taken a lot of abuse over the years."

"Apparently the mansion has been vacant for the last thirty years or so. Vandals had done a number on it and then some kind, well-intentioned soul thought it would be a good idea to take it out of the window and store it in a damp basement. Why people feel compelled to break glass…"

She shook her head and then resolutely brightened. "By the time I'm done with it, I'll probably have around fifty or so hours and a good grand of new materials in it. Antique glass and reproduction glass are high dollar.

But when it goes home, it'll look every bit as good as the day it was first made."

"Shipping will cost more than the repairs."

"I told you, money is no object here. And speaking of money," she hurriedly added, "I forgot to ask you last night how you want the check made out for the trading you're going to do for me."

"Don't worry about it right now. I set up a separate account under my name and spotted you ten to get started last night. I'll take the seed money out of the proceeds when I transfer the profits to you."

"Ten? I can chip in more than ten bucks. I'm not a total pauper." She grinned and added, "I just look like one."

"Ten *grand*."

There was beholden and then there was *beholden*. "That's a lot of money to loan someone," she protested. "And while I really appreciate it, I have twenty grand in the Secret Santa account that—"

He held up his hand, palm toward her. "You never gamble with what you can't afford to lose," he kindly but firmly advised her. "If your twenty goes up in smoke, you can't get a new roof put on this beast. I've covered you. I can easily afford it. It's a done deal."

In other words, there was nothing left for her to do but be gracious about it. "Thank you."

He smiled. "You're welcome."

Since it was a done deal… "So what stocks do I own?"

"I put you in short on financials before the market opened this morning," he answered crisply and with what sounded like great satisfaction. "I'm trading you long on oil and wheat futures for the time being, but I've set the auto trade program with triggers to sell and go short at the first sign that the bubble is going to pop."

Emily didn't even bother to run any of it over in her mind. She knew it wouldn't make the least bit of difference. She leaned toward him and whispered, "I've never heard Greek before. It's kinda sexy."

So was the incredible warmth radiating from his body. It crossed her mind to simply throw herself against him and be done with any pretense of decorum. She eased away, her sense of deprivation not all that assuaged by the thought that her mother would be pleased that she was behaving like a lady.

He laughed and then said through a wide grin, "We're betting that the banks lose big money and—"

"That's not very nice."

"Nice isn't an investment strategy," he replied, chuckling. "Anticipating whether stocks will go up or down is."

She frowned. "How do you make any money if the stocks you own go down?"

"Okay," he said on a sigh. "Technically, you don't own any shares in the banks. You've borrowed them from someone who does own them with—"

"How do I know this person?"

"They advertise."

"Okay. Go on."

He smiled, closed his eyes for a second and mouthed *thank you*. "All right," he said, returning to his explanation. "You borrow them with the promise that you're going to give them back in a few weeks with a little interest payment. While you have them, you sell them to someone else."

"You can't sell something you don't own." What had he gotten her into? "That's illegal."

"Only outside the stock market."

He sounded so sure of it. Still… "You're kidding me, right?"

"No, I'm not," he said with absolute confidence. "Now, say you've sold the shares for ten bucks each and the price drops to five. You buy them back at five and return the stocks to the guy you borrowed them from. Net profit on the trade itself is five bucks a share. If you traded a thousand shares, what's your profit?"

"A math story problem!" she gasped. Leaning back, she held up her hands between them, her index fingers crossed one over the other. "Get back, Spawn of Satan!"

"It's five grand," he declared, shaking his head and rolling his eyes. "It's also really simple math."

"It sounds too easy. The trading part," she quickly clarified. "Not the math. No math is easy."

"Yes, it is easy to make the money on the trade. Unless you bet wrong on the market direction and the price you buy back at is higher than when you sold. Then you lose not only your shirt, but your pants, socks and underwear, too."

"Ooooh. Strip stock trading," she said, her mind filled with delightful images of Cole Preston at the end of a bad trading day. "You could sell tickets, you know. The Chippendales of Wall Street. Do a little peep-and-tease dance with briefcases."

His eyes sparkling, and fighting back a smile, he cleared his throat and said, "Anyway, we're also betting that the price per barrel of oil keeps going up and that a bushel of wheat does, too. Not, mind you, that I think those are long-term positions. Current price trends in commodities are more a reflection of money looking for a safe haven from the market's volatility. That says speculative bubble to me."

Whatever. She hadn't heard much more than a half of what he'd said. "Ooooh, more Greek," she said on a whimpering sigh. She undid another button on her blouse and fanned her shirtfront. "I'm feeling a little breathless."

"So am I," he admitted, his gaze slowly coming up from her chest. Had he noticed that she wasn't wearing a bra at all this morning? "What time does this crew plan to clear out of here for lunch?"

"They're working through lunch and breaks today because they need to get this done so they can start another job tomorrow."

"Where's a strong union when you need one?" he muttered, scowling down at the stained glass window. He suddenly lifted his head and met her gaze, his eyes smoldering with undisguised desire. "Wanna come over to Grams's place and see my trading desk?"

"Is that anything like asking a girl if she'd like to see your etchings?" she teased, fanning her shirt again.

"In this case, it's a straight translation."

Oh, he was wound tight; she could hear it in his voice, could see the smoldering in his eyes and the tense lines at the corners of his mouth. "I take it that Ida's over at the Senior Center this morning?"

"And planning to play bridge all day."

"I'd *love* to see your trading desk," she admitted, relenting. "Let me get things unplugged and put away. It won't take me any more than a couple of minutes."

Even as she spoke, she bent over to unplug the iron from the outlet. The sensation of his hands boldly skimming up the backs of her jean-clad thighs took her breath away. The heat of his palms as he laid them flat over the curve of her rear and ever so slightly squeezed... Her insides instantly molten and pounding, she straightened and looked at him over her shoulder. "Do that again," she said, her voice husky, "and you're going to get your bones jumped right here in front of God and any sparky that wanders through."

"Life should be an adventure, remember?" he reminded her as she stepped out of his easy reach. "A little danger..."

"Danger is fine," she retorted, retrieving her watch and closing the lid of the toolbox. "Exhibitionism is another thing entirely."

"Then stop bending over like that and tempting me. I'm only human."

And so was she. A human female with apparently no fuse at all. "Let me get my purse out of the apartment and we can go."

He caught her hand and pulled her back, saying, "You're not going to need it."

Did that mean he intended to drive them to Ida's? she wondered as she let him lead her to the elevator. Or did it mean he had his own condoms and that she could keep the ones she'd been carrying around in her purse for the last eon or two? Now that she thought about it, there were probably expiration dates on condoms. Any he had were a sure bet to be at least current. Hers, just as certainly, weren't.

Emily waited until he pulled the scissor doors closed and then punched the down button. The outer doors were barely closed when he suddenly straightened beside her, happily declared, "Hey, I have an idea!" and reached out toward the control panel.

"No!" she cried, catching his arm, knowing exactly what he had in mind and why. "An alarm will go off. And it's *loud*."

He let his arm fall back to his side, muttering regretfully, "Damn. It was a fabulous fantasy."

"No kidding," she agreed on a long, hard sigh. "Short-lived, but reeeallly good."

He looked over at her. The brightness of his smile said it all; he was clearly surprised by her honest reaction and just as obviously intrigued with the possibilities in her being a good sport. "Is there any way we can shut off the alarm?"

"Well, yeah, but not right this moment and not from in here."

"I'll take care of it when we come back," he promised as they reached the first floor and the doors opened.

"Just as a point of information," she offered while he

pushed back the scissor door. "I was wearing a halter top, a short skirt and pair of stilettos in my version."

"Oh, yeah? How short?"

"If I had bent over," she said casually, walking past him out of the elevator, "you would have seen that I wasn't wearing any panties."

He stopped in his tracks. She paused and waited for him to recover his wits. He had to swallow twice before he could get his feet to move. As he reached her side and together they made their way toward the front door, he asked, "How late do you think this electrical crew is going to be here finishing up today?"

Well, there was no grass growing under the feet of the Cole Preston side of her fantasy. "They said probably seven or so," she supplied as they stepped out onto the sidewalk. "Hold on a second."

She called out to the electrician taking a box out of the back of their work van. "John?"

"Yes, ma'am?"

"I'm wondering if I could get you to disconnect the alarm on the elevator while you all are working? When I'm moving stuff between floors and having to prop the doors open for a while, the ringing drives me nuts."

"I'll take care of it for you right now, Miz Raines."

"Thanks, John! I'll be back in a little bit. If there's a problem, I have the cell on."

"That was smooth," Cole said softly as he held open the passenger door of his car for you.

"Hey, the fantasy doesn't include us down in the

basement with me holding a flashlight while you figure out which fuse to pull."

He laughed, closed the door and trotted around to his side of the car. He backed them out of the parking slot and had them pointing toward his grandmother's house when he asked, "What was I wearing in your version of the fantasy?"

"A huge smile."

"That's a given. Other than that."

"Let me see." She wiggled into the curved back of the luxurious leather car seat and closed her eyes. "A gray suit. White shirt. Red tie." She smiled. "Interesting." Opening her eyes, she turned to look at him. "You weren't wearing any underwear, either."

"Well, I do believe in being prepared to seize any opportunity that presents itself."

"I seized first. Boldly, confidently. Just so you know."

Grinning, he said, "That's okay with me," and eased the car into his grandmother's driveway. "It's your elevator. I'm only along for the ride."

"Yeah, well, I have a news flash for you."

He laughed and got out of the car. Knowing that she was perfectly capable of doing the same without gallant male assistance, Emily didn't wait for him to come around and open the door for her. She met him at the headlights and followed him up the steps and into Ida's house.

She wasn't even all the way across the threshold when she saw that her elderly friend's living room had been utterly transformed. The serving buffet that usually sat against the far wall of the living room was gone. So, apparently, were the silver candelabra and the collection of porcelain figurines that normally sat atop it. In the buffet's place was a huge but sleek, minimalist high-tech-looking desk and chair. And on top of the desk's glass top…. Emily counted. Seven flashing monitors, four hard drives and two laser printers. She looked again. No, no partridge in a pear tree.

"Jeez Louise, Cole. Was NORAD having a garage sale? Or is that stuff just on loan?"

"This is my traveling setup," he explained. "Nothing more than the bare minimum."

"So I guess I'm not going to get to watch you call in an air strike, huh? Bummer. Talk about sexy. Even better than Greek."

He chuckled, caught her hand in his and headed across the living room toward Computer Central. "Would you like to see where your account balance is at this point in the day?"

As if she could say no while she was being towed across a beige berber sea? But there was seductive potential in gadgets and blinking lights; she could work with it. "I should probably have a fair idea of just how much I owe you in management fees already."

When he came to a stop in front of the desk, Emily slipped up against his side and wrapped an arm around his waist. He draped an arm over her shoulder and looked down at her, his brow cocked. "You believe in seizing opportunities," she said silkily. "I believe in paying my obligations in full when they're due."

He bent his head. Her heart racing, Emily closed her eyes and parted her lips. The computer dinged. She staggered, he let go of her so fast.

"Have a seat," he commanded, working a mouse across the desktop, his gaze riveted on one of the monitors.

"Since you're the one at the controls," she offered, pulling her blouse back to rights, "shouldn't you be the one sitting in the chair?"

He looked up over his shoulder at her to give her a sheepish grin. "Sitting right now would be more than a little uncomfortable for me."

"Really." She dropped into the chair, wondering if she was the cause, or if he actually got that big of a charge out of trading.

"Yes, really."

Well, she decided, there was only way to find out. She reached out and slowly drew her hand up the hard ridge lying beneath the fly of his khakis. "Do you have a day-trader fantasy?" she asked.

"Apparently you do," he answered, his hand over the now-still mouse, his gaze smoldering and locked with hers. "I'm liking it so far."

"Yes, I can see that." She ran her hand over him again, harder this time. "May I see more?"

He abandoned the mouse, straightened and turned to face her. "Your wish is my command," he said, unzipping.

"Such an accommodating gentleman."

"The jury's out on the gentleman part." He freed himself, then added, "Accommodating... Yes, definitely," as he set about undoing his belt.

She didn't wait for him to get as comfortable as he had in mind. She took him in her hand, stroking down the hardened length and then slowly stroking back up.

"I'll add appreciative, too," he said hoarsely, his hands still as he broadened his stance. She quickened the pace of her strokes and he drew a breath through his teeth. Tipping his head back, he groaned at the ceiling. "That feels so good."

Yes, it did. God, she was climbing the arc herself, her own tension coiling tighter, hotter, and building with the power of his arousal, with every sound he made in the throes of the pleasure she was giving him.

The sound was muffled, but distinct. Emily froze, listening. It was followed by another and then two more in quick succession.

"What?" Cole demanded. "Don't stop!"

The moment of possibility and promise shattered, she drew back quickly and looked up at him. "I hear car doors." The look of disbelief and frustration on his face…

Emily fought the urge to laugh as he growled and made a rather penguin-esque—no, pissed off penguin-esque—trip over to look out the front window.

"Hell!" he cried, whirling back and frantically trying to get himself tucked back behind his trouser fly. "It's Grams and the bridge club!"

Emily leaned back in the chair and stretched out her legs as she watched him arrange himself, tug at his clothes, then put a hand on the back of one of Ida's wingback chairs and stare off in the general vicinity of the crown moldings. Emily sighed softly around a smile. If only he'd had a keg and a parrot....

Outside the window, Ida and three blue-haired ladies were making their way along the front walk. Emily looked back at Cole. "That's your *best* casual I-wasn't-doing-anything pose? Gotta tell ya, it's *not* working for you."

"God," he groaned, his shoulders sagging. He glanced around the room and then moved toward her saying, "Out of the chair."

She did as he commanded, saying, "I thought sitting was uncomfortable for you."

"Not a problem now," he declared crisply as he dropped into the seat and grabbed the mouse. "Grams and her friends coming up the walk took care of it."

Standing behind him, she put her hands on the back of the chair . She leaned close and said softly, "I always wondered what they meant by 'deflationary pressure.' Now I know. You learn something new every day."

"Your economic education was appalling."

Listening to Ida insert her key into the door lock, Emily kissed the curve of his ear and whispered, "Wanna tutor me?"

"You're not helping me here."

"I know," she laughingly admitted as she straightened and focused over his head at the monitor screen right in front of them.

"Cole!" Ida exclaimed happily as she entered the living room. "Emily! What a pleasant surprise, my dears. Are you playing one of those computer games?"

Emily turned to smile at her friend. "Hi, Ida. No

games. Cole's trying to teach me the basics about investing in the stock market. So far I'm proving to be a less than stellar student."

"She's very easily distracted," Cole supplied without looking away from the chart on the computer screen.

"Would we be a distraction to you if we play bridge in the dining room?" Ida asked as her friends trooped past her into the adjacent room. "They fumigated the kitchen at the Senior Center last night and the smell is still just horrendous today. We were hoping we could ignore it, but it's given Gladys a headache."

"No distraction for me at all, Ida," Emily assured her. "I really think that your poor grandson has had his frustration quota met for today and I need to head back to the warehouse to check on the electricians."

"I'll drive you there," he offered, putting his hands on the chair arms and starting to gain his feet.

Putting her hands on his shoulders to stop him, Emily brightly replied, "Thank you for offering, Cole, but the walk will do me good." Before he could protest, she turned and walked away, adding, "Got to keep the muscles toned and the stamina up. You never know when you're going to have to do a marathon."

She stopped at the front door and with a hand on the doorjamb, turned back to find him watching her departure, looking like a man watching the rescue boat sink twenty feet from shore. "Oh, what time did you say for dinner tonight, Cole?"

He instantly brightened and grinned. "I seem to recall that we decided on sevenish."

"Perfect. I'll meet you at Vito's. I'll be the one in the green dress."

"I'm thinking a gray suit, red tie. Would that be too upscale?"

"Sounds perfectly yummy to me." She smiled at his grandmother. "Win big, Ida. Kick their butts."

Ida laughed and Emily left the house, bounding down the stairs and feeling utterly, thoroughly delighted with life. She could only hope that Cole would spend the afternoon trading stocks and making her a huge, huge pile of money for which she would owe him huge, mind-blowing fees.

Making her way down the sidewalk toward her warehouse, she made a mental list of what had to be done in the next few hours. At the very top of it was to make sure that she could still get into her green dress. If she couldn't, she was going to have to make a dash up to Kansas City and find a new one.

Everything else on the list behind the dress was optional. Yeah, clean sheets on the bed, some votive candles and a couple of bottles of chilled white wine would be nice. But they would be damn small consolation at the end of even a slightly disappointing elevator ride.

No, anything less than total fantasy fulfillment was not acceptable. When she walked into Vito's that evening, Cole Preston's jaw was going to hit the linen-covered tabletop. And by the time they finished licking the cannoli cream off each other's fingers, the only challenge would be to hold back until they actually got into the elevator. But once those doors closed...

Yes, life was good and it was only going to get better as the day turned into night. And as the night turned into a dawn they could wake up to wildly, breathlessly celebrate together. Maybe, if the sun were shining like the weatherman had promised it would, they could celebrate its return twice, once wherever they happened to have collapsed in exhaustion in the night, and then...

"Gotta clean the shower," she said as she walked into the warehouse. She stopped, her mind clicking through a household and bedroom inventory list that sent her heart racing in a barely contained panic. She checked her watch and did the calculations. Two hours to Kansas City and two hours back, an hour to get the apartment ready and an hour to get herself irresistibly gorgeous. Yeah, she'd have to make every minute count, but she could do it.

Cole Preston was most definitely worth the effort. Okay, she admitted to herself as the took the elevator up to get her purse and car keys, maybe it wasn't so much Cole Preston himself as it was the promise of a night of hot, torrid, panting, sheet-twisting, world-shattering sex. Cole Preston, Greek god, hunky and every bit as hungry as she was, might well be no more than the icing on the cake.

Not that she was going to spend a lot of time trying to figure it out for sure, she decided as she let herself into her apartment. He was here, he was willing, and there didn't appear to be anything wrong with his ready and able.

She woke up her computer and executed a search.

While the map and directions were printing, she took her sexy green dress out of the closet and gave it a quick try on.

Emily checked her watch. What a difference ten minutes could make. She dropped down on the sofa and tossed the computer printout onto the coffee table, sensing that the impromptu trip was slipping out of her grasp by the second.

"What brings you here this morning?" she asked as her friend Beth poured herself a cup of coffee.

"The roofing crew is setting up out back."

Well, talk about unexpected news. "I didn't know that I'd hired a roofing crew."

"This company had two days of downtime they needed to fill and were willing to put a roof on for you for seven grand less than any of the other companies who bid it. I jumped at the deal before someone else could grab them. You, by the way, have a very easy signature to forge."

And her friend made it sound like such a good thing.

She'd been right; the trip to Kansas City was now out of the question. Timing-wise it was perfectly doable, but with a crew climbing around on her roof with buckets of hot tar... The roofers might have questions. There could be problems that she needed to be there to solve. Conscience-wise... No, as much as she wanted to, she just couldn't give herself permission to spend the entire day getting ready for a night with Cole Preston.

Five

Emily gritted her teeth, poured more of the chemical onto the rag, set the open can back on the kitchen counter and rubbed on the palm of her left hand some more. Of all the stupid things she'd ever done in her life… She paused to consider the coating of tar. Maybe, if she squinted, it looked like a little of it had come off. A glance at the rag said otherwise.

God, what was she going to do if she couldn't get the stuff off? She couldn't go anywhere in public all covered with tar. And she sure as hell couldn't go to dinner with Cole. No dress on earth was sexy enough to make a man blind to the fact that the woman wearing it had spent the day swimming in a tar pit. Fighting back a wave of desperation, she poured more of the solvent on the rag and and rubbed harder.

"Whoa, there."

Her stomach clenched and fell to the bottom of her feet. "Cole," she said flatly, lifting her gaze to where he stood in the open doorway of her apartment. "What are you doing here?"

Cole cocked a brow, but otherwise ignored her less than enthusiastic welcome. "I got bored watching computer screens," he answered, ambling toward her. "And I thought I'd come down and see if you needed help with anything."

She went back to scrubbing her hand. "I'm fine, thank you."

Yeah, he could see that. He could also smell the fumes. He glanced at the can on the counter. Ah, good ol' automotive chrome cleaner. The roofer's friend.

He leaned a hip against the edge of the kitchen counter and took in the extent of the damage she'd suffered. There was tar on her knees, her hands, even in her hair and on the curve of her left ear. He very causally tilted his head to change the angle of his view. Good Lord, the entire back side of her jeans was covered with the stuff.

He waited, but since she didn't volunteer an explanation for why she was standing in her kitchen, covered with tar and bathing in solvent… "Okay, I'll come right out and ask. Have you been rolling around on your new roof?"

She stopped scrubbing and her shoulders sagged as she sighed. "Well, if you must know," she replied, meeting his gaze. "In a moment of pure, unadulterated kindness, I took a plate of freshly baked chocolate chip cookies up to the guys working on the roof. While up there, in a moment of pure, unadulterated *grace,* I backed up, tripped over an empty tar bucket and landed flat on my fanny in front of God and the whole cookie-munching, horrified crew."

As he fought the urge to grin, she went on, "And while they speed-ate their cookies with one hand and held steaming tar mops with the other, I spent about ten of the longest, most humiliating moments of my recent life trying to get to my feet without making matters any worse than they already were."

He cleared his throat softly before he dared to observe, "I'm guessing, by the looks of you, that the effort wasn't terribly successful."

"Duh," she countered testily. "I'd only managed to get to my knees before one of them finally got a hand free and pulled me to my feet."

"Look on the bright side. You gave them a great story to tell in the bar tonight."

"Wonderful." She picked the can up from the counter and showed it to him, saying, "They told me this stuff would take the tar off. They didn't mention that I'd have to rub hard enough that it would take the first two layers of my skin with it."

"Would you like some help?" The look in her eyes was a fascinating mixture of mortification and resent-ment. "I spent the summer of my freshman year in college working construction," he hastily explained. "I actually have some experience at getting the stuff off fairly easily and without sacrificing too much of your hide."

"How?" she asked instantly. Okay, it was a bit warily, but at least her eyes weren't shooting daggers at him anymore.

"You start with a good, long, hot shower. The heat softens the tar, washing away some of it and making it easier for the solvent to do its thing on what's left. You go hop in, get it pliable and I'll take it from there."

She lowered her chin as she raised a brow.

"What?" he asked, recognizing a challenge when he saw one. "It really works. I wouldn't lie to you."

She picked up the can of solvent and walked off toward her bedroom saying crisply as she went, "I am not sharing a shower with you, Cole Preston. You are not going to see me naked."

Frowning, he watched her disappear. He wasn't going to see her naked? How in the hell had they come to this point? He thought back, step by step. He'd come over that morning. They'd headed over to Grams's for some privacy. The elevator fantasy had come up on the way out of the warehouse. Once at Grams's... They'd have been naked within minutes if Grams and the bridge ladies hadn't shown up. And then Emily had set up a dinner date slash elevator rendezvous on her way out.

And now she wasn't going to let him see her naked? Shaking his head, he went after her.

The bathroom was off on the right side of the

bedroom, directly opposite the foot of her bed. There wasn't a door. But there was a shower-tub combination with a definitely non see-through curtain. Her jeans and shirt lay in a stained heap on the floor beside the tub.

"Okay, I'm officially confused," he announced, stepping into the doorway just as a pair of panties appeared from behind one edge of the curtain and were dropped onto the pile.

She turned the faucet on full blast while saying, "Pretend there's a door there."

Cole snorted. As if she was going to come out of there after him if he crossed the line. He walked in, closed the lid on the toilet and made himself comfortable. Over the groaning of the pipes and the roar of the showerhead coming to life, he asked, "Correct me if I'm wrong, but I'm under the impression that we have a date for a fantasy elevator ride tonight."

"We do. After dinner at Vito's."

Well, she hadn't hesitated in answering and she certainly sounded like she might be looking forward to it. "Did I miss a memo or something? Is the evening over after the elevator ride?"

"I sincerely hope not."

Again, no hesitation and what sounded like anticipation. Which really didn't do a damned thing to clear up his confusion. "Well then, won't I see you naked at some point tonight?"

"That's tonight," she replied. "This is the afternoon."

If she thought that made any sense at all to him... "What difference does it make?"

"It makes a difference. A huge one."

So she said. Not that he could see it for the life of him. He fell back on the only explanation men had for such mysteries. "Is this one of those deals where it's some official Girl Rule that us guys have no clue about?"

"Yes."

The strangled sound of her reply… The odds were she wasn't drowning. "Are you crying in there?"

"No."

For God's sake. Tears over a little tar? "What are you crying about, Emily?"

It took a few moments, but she finally answered, her voice thick with tears and frustration, "This is *not* how it's supposed to go."

Cole closed his eyes and scrubbed his hands over his face. Part of him wanted to offer a few curt suggestions about putting things in perspective. The greater part of him, though, the insensitive part that was probably a genetic holdover from the Neanderthal age, wanted to laugh.

"Okay," he said, trying to take the middle ground, "take a deep breath, let the water run over your head for a minute and then kindly tell me what's not supposed to be whatever way that's upsetting you to the point of not crying."

Emily stood under the hot water, letting it sluice down over her body, and turned his words over in her mind. His request was convoluted, but she knew what he was asking. She was tempted to tell him that it was all beyond description, but that wouldn't have been honest.

Swiping away her tears, she sniffled and began, "I was going to go up to Kansas City this afternoon and do a whole day spa thing. Get a manicure and a pedicure and waxed and buffed and tanned so that..." Okay, there was such a thing as *too* honest. She sighed hard and long. "But, oh no, I decided that I needed to be responsible and stay here in case there was a problem with the roof."

"Being responsible is good, Emily."

"Yeah, right," she countered. "And now I'm standing in a hot shower trying to melt the tar off my body while you sit on my commode offering me words of encouragement and reassurance, and to scrub what I can't reach. This is *not* part of the elevator fantasy."

"Well, no," he quickly and brightly agreed. "The elevator fantasy begins when the elevator doors close and ends when they open."

He didn't get it. "You were supposed to think of me all day, envisioning me in a hot dress," she explained. "You weren't supposed to see me until I walked into Vito's tonight and blew your socks off. And now it's all ruined. The illusion has been shattered."

He didn't say anything, at least not that she could hear over the sound of the chugging plumbing and the running water. Stepping out from under the showerhead, she listened. And heard a low, rumbling, almost choking noise that sounded a lot like... "Are you laughing?" she asked.

"No. Absolutely not," he said, obviously lying through his teeth. "In fact, I'm thinking about crying, too."

"It's not funny, Cole."

He cleared his throat and had managed to control his outright laughter when he asked, "Would you like for me to go away? I will if you want me to."

"As if that would make any difference at this point," she countered, stepping back under the heated stream of water. "As if you could pretend you never saw me like this. You couldn't even pretend there was a bathroom door!"

"Emily, darlin'," he replied, his voice rippling with both amusement and patience. "I'm a guy. Reality doesn't ever get in the way of our fantasies. My socks are still going to get blown off tonight when you walk into Vito's."

Surprisingly, she believed him. Emily smiled and, because she didn't want him to think she'd surrendered too easily, observed, "It just won't be the same as it could have been."

Despite knowing that she couldn't see him, Cole grinned and held up his hand. "I swear to you that the wonder will be the same for me tonight. Nothing has been ruined at all."

The edge of the shower curtain drew back just enough for her to look out out at him. Her skin pinkened from the heat of the water, her hair a mass of wet curls around her face, she smiled sheepishly and said, "If you'd be so kind as to hand me the can of tar and bug remover from the top of the tank behind you."

He stood, picked up the can and then took the single step to stand right next to the tub. "Do you have any idea of just how adorable you are right this minute?"

The tips of her beautiful, deliciously soft lips curved up into the smallest, shyest smile. "Cole…"

His gaze fixed on hers, he blindly passed the can of solvent to her, murmuring, "Sugar and spice. Everything naughty and nice."

He slowly trailed a fingertip through the droplets along the length of her nose, then down to those luscious, tempting lips. She ever so slightly kissed his fingertip, sending a jolt of pure, demanding desire shooting to the center of his bones. If he stayed one second longer…

"See you tonight," he said softly, dropping his hand and backing away. "I'll be the guy with his jaw on the table."

Emily nodded. Or at least she thought she did. All she really knew for certain as she watched him leave was that somehow he had made her forget all about the disasters and disappointments of her day and made her feel special. And that made him something very special.

Cole rubbed the towel over his head, tossed it on the end of his bed and then tightened the sash of his bathrobe as he headed for the closet. Out of the corner of his eye, he saw his grandmother heading down the hall toward her own room. "Hi, Grams," he called. "What are your plans for the evening?"

She came back to stand in his doorway and answer, "I'm going to a nine-pin tap tournament at the bowling alley."

He froze, his suit halfway out of the closet. "Excuse me?" he asked, turning his head to look at her.

"Oh, for heaven's sake, I'm not bowling," she assured him, laughing. "I'm going for the front-row seat to watch Edgar Moore bowl."

"Is he that good?" he asked as he resumed his routine.

"I have no idea. But I do know that he's the only man over sixty in town who's still packing a fanny in his pants. The rest of them are as flat as boards back there."

"Grams!"

"Oh, he's married to Edith," she said with a dismissive flutter of her elegant hand. "And besides, that whole ear hair thing of his…" She shuddered and then smiled to add, "I may be old, Cole, but I am a long way from desperate. And there are certainly limits to my selective blindness. Do you need me to press your shirt?"

"It should be fine, Grams," he assured her as he laid his clothing on the bed. "But thanks for offering."

"I'm so glad that you and Emily have resolved your differences. You two look very cute together, you know. I hope you have a wonderful evening out. I'll leave the light on for you, but I hope you don't feel an obligation to be in by any certain time. I'm not going to wait up for you."

Well, as blessings went, that was as good as roundabout ones came. "Thanks, Grams," he called after her.

It was nice to know that his grandmother approved of—

Part of his brain running ninety to nothing and the other part of it sitting at a dead, totally numbed stop,

Cole dropped down on the side of the bed. How could he have... Damn, she was... Of all the... Not that he had... Maybe it really...

He pressed his hands into the sides of his head and squeezed, desperately trying to get his thoughts to slow down just enough to actually finish one. With a deep breath, he got to his feet.

He began to pace his bedroom, sorting the random stream of his thoughts into neat little mental categories. And when the last of them had been grasped and organized, he sat back down on the bed and logically went through them, analyzing each in turn.

Why was he in a bedroom at his grandmother's house in a town that wasn't anything more than a bump in the road? Because he'd been so alarmed at Grams's request to liquidate part of her portfolio to fund a new friend's community project that he'd slammed the brakes on his own life, jumped in the car and driven here to put things right.

And what had he discovered when he arrived here? A gorgeous, perky blonde with long legs, perfectly shaped breasts and an apparent willingness to turn his every fantasy into reality.

Emily was all that and intelligent, funny and delightful, too. He couldn't deny that and wouldn't even try.

And therein laid the problem. That was all he'd been aware of for the last... He tried to think back and coordinate the moments of the calendar. "Well, for however long," he muttered. "Doesn't really matter, anyway."

What mattered was that he'd completely lost track

of why he'd come to Augsburg, what his suspicions were, and the plan he'd had as he'd walked across the library lawn, stuck out his hand and made a truce with the green-eyed devilette.

Cole frowned at the floor between his bare feet. Actually, now that he thought about it, his plan to keep Emily Raines close so that she couldn't pull a con on Grams—or any other gullible old person for that matter—was working perfectly. So well, in fact, that he'd forgotten that it was a deliberate plan. But since it seemed to be working even better than he'd hoped... Okay, no harm, no foul. He didn't have a thing to be worried about on that front. As long as he remembered from time to time that it was a carefully calculated strategy, of course.

Now, as for the other issues that he needed to be concerned about... What to do about Grams was the most important. He couldn't spend the rest of his life in Augsburg. Well, he could, what with computers and high-speed Internet and all, but it made for a long drive to the airport where his plane was parked. And he wasn't likely to get any work done as long as Emily was anywhere around.

He cocked a brow. He was assuming that the fling with Emily wouldn't fizzle out by the end of the week. Since he knew himself and the way affairs typically went, the assumption was based on shaky ground.

Once a physical relationship was taken out of the equation, the situation changed considerably. He was right back to where he'd been when he'd turned off the highway and rolled into town. Grams was a soft touch for every cause that came down the pike with a sob story or a slick brochure. He didn't have the kind of life that would let him watch her every move every single second of the day.

And Emily Raines... While Jason's comprehensive investigation had turned up nothing and his own instincts said that she wasn't a con artist, that her motives were sincere and aboveboard, the logical part of him was tallying up some interesting observations. The fifty grand from a Secret Santa was a great story, but so good it was slightly suspect. And while, technically, he hadn't handed her so much as one real red cent, he was running an aggressive brokerage account for her with his money. In fairness, though, he had freely offered his expertise.

"And not exactly for free," he admitted, smiling and checking his watch.

A half hour would be plenty of time to do a quick, basic Internet search on elder care and get a general idea of what the range of options were. Narrowing them down to two or three should be fairly easy; most choices, even the hard ones, usually came down to a very limited number.

And if he did all that before he headed off to Vito's Italian Gardens, it would give him something to think about while he waited for Emily to arrive. And Lord knew he was going to need a handy mental distraction if she showed up looking even half as delicious as he was imagining.

Cole studied the two sheets of paper on the linen-covered table before him and took another sip of wine. Having narrowed the options down to two hadn't made the choice a slam dunk. Not by any means. One place, in Florida, looked a lot like a cruise ship on land. Twelve dining rooms, an activity staff of twenty, an on-site state-of-the-art medical facility and a campus that was nothing short of palatial. The price per month was palatial, too, but that wasn't his concern. The cost wasn't even a minor factor. Grams being happy there was, though, and he was having a hard time trying to mesh what Emily had said about the elderly needing to have their worlds small with the obvious massive, sprawling size of the Florida retirement complex.

The second option met the small requirement very easily. It was in Sedona and offered a spalike existence to no more than eight residents at any one time. Private chefs, physical therapists, a medical team on-site twenty-four-seven… He read the description again. No mention of planned activities for the clients. Well, that was a strike against it. The cost was right in line with the Florida facility, so the question boiled down to whether his grandmother would be comfortable there.

Huge, active and palatial versus small, personal and luxurious. The choice was Grams's, of course, but he really wanted to have a choice made in his own mind before he presented the whole idea to her.

His waiter appeared at the edge of the table. "Pardon the intrusion, sir. You asked to be told when your dinner companion arrived."

"Thank you," Cole replied, folding the papers and hastily tucking them into the inside pocket of his suit jacket. He slid out of the booth and stepped out from

behind the foliage to watch Emily make her way toward
him down the center aisle of the restaurant. She smiled
as she saw him, her happiness and confidence every bit
as sparkling as the crystals that surrounded the edges
of what had to be the deepest plunging neckline he'd
ever seen off the beach. One hooked finger and a little
bit of a tug and he could kiss her navel.

As she'd promised, the dress was green and it was a
halter type. He couldn't tell at the distance how easy the
halter would be to undo, but undoing it wasn't going to
a major factor. There wasn't all that much fabric there.
All he had to do was slip his hands in under the crystal
edge, push it aside and he'd be in heaven. His gaze
traveled lower.

Her skirt wasn't as short or as tight as he'd expected,
hitting her a few inches above the knee and skimming
softly over her skin with every step she took, but he
wasn't at all disappointed. No, his only regret as she
reached his side and smiled up at him was the realization that if she hadn't been willing to make love with him
with sparkies wandering around her place, it was a safe
bet she wasn't going to be all that receptive to the idea
of going for it on top of a table in a public restaurant.

"Good evening, Miss Raines," he said, bending down
to brush a light kiss over her dark pink lips. "May I say
how absolutely radiant you look this evening?"

"Thank you, Mr. Preston. You look quite handsome
yourself."

"I'm afraid that all the tables were reserved when I
called this afternoon. I hope a booth is all right?"

"It's perfect," she declared as she slid into the seat and slipped over to her place setting. "It's rather like being in a private little jungle all of our own," she added, looking around them. "Very nice. Very private."

"That crossed my mind, too," he supplied as he slid in beside her. "I took the liberty of ordering our wine."

"Have you thought of everything?"

"I sure hope so." He lifted his glass to her. "To adventure."

She tapped her rim ever so lightly against his. "With a bit of danger."

Yes, and speaking of danger... "How are the sparkies doing over at your place? All done?"

"They were cleaning and packing up as I left. Which is why I opted to wear the overskirt. I didn't want to give any of them whiplash."

"Overskirt?" The just above the knee thing wasn't the real skirt?

"It's kind of like a bathing suit cover," she explained. "It wraps around and hooks at the waist to give the appearance of a bit of modesty when one's out in a very public place."

"What's underneath?"

Her grin was delightfully wicked. "A very short, very well-fitted skirt that very eloquently says that going out in public was never so much as a minor, fleeting consideration." She paused for a second and then asked, "Would you like a peek?"

"No." She blinked at him, clearly stunned. He leaned close and whispered, "I want the whole reveal deal."

Her gaze darted to the world outside their sheltered enclave even as she reached for the front of the skirt's narrow waistband. Pooling the overskirt on either side of her on the seat, she leaned back, shifted slightly and crossed her long, lean legs.

Sweet Jesus. She hadn't been kidding about how short the skirt was or how well it fit her body. His blood heated. His jaw must have dropped, too, because she laughed softly and reached for her wineglass.

"So how is my stock portfolio doing this evening?" she asked after taking a sip.

"None of the trading triggers have activated yet," he explained, grateful to her for providing a much-needed momentary distraction. "A couple of them came close this afternoon, but didn't hit the magic number. You're still at your initial investment."

"Bummer."

Her little sigh of disappointment... He couldn't tell if she was seriously disappointed, or if she was simply continuing the bantering and teasing game they'd been playing over the matter of his management fees. "A lot can happen in overnight trading," he assured her. "You could wake up tomorrow morning the richest woman in Augsburg."

Her smile was absolutely, adorably wicked. The delightful sparkle in her eyes as she met his gaze sent his heartbeat into overdrive.

"Rich certainly isn't necessary," she said. "But it would be a nice bonus."

He laughed outright, delighted with her and with

himself for having had the good fortune of meeting her. Actually, now that he thought about it, he was delighted with the way life was going in every single respect.

With a little wink, she picked up the oversize menu, saying, "I'm not really very hungry, but we should probably look at the menu and order at least a little something."

"Agreed." He picked up his menu and opened it.

"What looks good to you?"

"You," he answered honestly from behind the restaurant's bill of fare. "That is some dress."

"Thank you. I was hoping you'd find it...inspirational."

"Inspirational is an understatement." Still holding his menu, he leaned over to whisper in her ear, "If I thought I could time the arrival of the waiter, I'd be licking my way up your thighs right this minute."

She didn't say a word, but her breath caught and her gaze, locked on the menu she held in front of her, went vacant. With a smile, he reached out and slowly, deliberately scraped the pad of his thumb over the hard bud pressing against the fabric of her bodice.

She blinked, drew a deep breath and shifted on the seat. "So tell me about some of the companies you've invested capital in," she said softly, angling her menu to block the access of his hand.

"Chicken," he laughingly countered as he settled back into his seat and quickly adjusted himself.

Ever so innocently, she said, "I had the chicken marsala the last time I ate here. It was good, but I think I want to try something different this time."

"Lasagna is usually a pretty safe bet."

"True, but it also tends to be heavy. I don't want to finish supper ready to take a nap."

"That would be a bummer."

"I think I'll have the shrimp scampi with the angel-hair pasta. What about you?"

He chuckled. "You can have me anytime you want. Just say the word, sweet Emily, and we're out of here."

She shot him a considerably less than dire warning look and laid aside her menu. "So tell me about some of the companies you invest in."

"Persistent little thing, aren't you?"

"I can be."

"I've noticed that. You have an exciting penchant for risk taking, too. I can't tell you how stimulating I find the combination."

Her gaze dropped to his lap, but even as she parted her perfectly pink lips to speak the waiter stepped through the opening in the foliage.

"Good evening, sir, ma'am," he said. "My name is Gino and I'll be your waiter this evening. Are you ready to order?"

Cole poured the last of the wine into their glasses and wondered exactly when and why his focus had become so damned one-tracked, how it was that she could sit there, her elbows on the table and her chin resting on her laced fingers while she asked him questions about his venture-capital projects, and he thought it was the sexiest dinner conversation he'd ever had.

"So," she said brightly, as the waiter silently cleared away their plates, "are you going to invest in the Louisiana Cane Conversion company?"

"I haven't decided yet," Cole admitted.

"What's the concern that's keeping you from making a commitment? Is it the technology?"

He shook his head. "No, that's been proven. LCC isn't reinventing the wheel. Their engineers have built a good dozen biorefineries in Brazil in just the last five years. They're considered to be the best."

"So why the holdback?"

"I'm not convinced that our government is willing to support anything other than corn as a source for biofuel production," he explained. "The corn belt has a well-organized, well-funded and laser-focused lobby working for their interests. The Louisiana sugar cane growers don't have any of that."

"But," she posed thoughtfully, "if you gamble on them and they actually make it as big as Brazil's growers have…"

"Move over Bill Gates, there's a new mega billion-aire in town."

"Impressive," she allowed. "What's the price tag for the gamble?"

"Ten million in the initial funding outlay. More if it actually takes off."

"Can you afford to lose ten million?"

He chuckled ruefully and admitted, "I'm not a good sport when I lose a buck in a bad vending machine, so losing ten million of them would not make me happy. But, yes, I can afford the risk."

"Do I get to vote on it?"

"No," he said, already knowing what her vote would be. "Sorry."

"Well, I thought I'd give it a shot. I find all of this wheeling and dealing and future shaping…"

"A little like Greek?"

"It's way better than Greek." She sighed deeply and shifted on the seat. "Trust me."

"Oh, yeah?" he dared her. "How much better?"

He'd expected her to offer him another of her deliciously provocative innuendoes, not to silently take his lapels in her hands and deliberately draw his lips down to hers. Any thought of a waiter evaporated from his awareness as she traced the seam of his lips with the tip of her tongue. His awareness of place remained, but just barely. He opened his mouth for her and slipped his arms around her waist, drawing her closer so that she could more thoroughly wage her assault. In reward for his consideration, she eased her leg over his and sent his mind reeling.

The voice of restraint reminded him that they were in a restaurant. The voice of need pointed out that it was a long tablecloth. He slipped his hands down over the perfectly well-rounded curve of her rear, loving the way she moaned her approval into his mouth. With one hand he held her still while he slid the other down to the hem of her skirt and then around to the front and up beneath it.

As his fingers brushed over wet curls, she drew back

to meet his gaze and whisper, "I'm ready for dessert. How about you?"

He smiled, said, "Let me take care of the check and we'll be on our way," and eased her back onto the seat beside him. Taking a hundred-dollar bill from his wallet, he tossed it onto the table and then slid out to offer her his hand. She took it and allowed him to assist her to her feet. She reached back for her overskirt and held it up as though she intended to put it back on.

"Oh, I don't think so," Cole said, taking it from her hands.

She considered it for maybe half a second, then gave him a sultry smile and tiny shrug just before she slipped her arm around his and said, "Arguing would be such a waste of time."

With her overskirt draped over his forearm, Cole pulled the scissor door closed and stepped back against the elevator wall next to the control panel. Her smoldering emerald gaze boldly locked with his, Emily reached out blindly and punched the button for the second floor. The outer doors slid silently closed. As the car started upward, the corners of her mouth lifted in a wicked smile of expectation.

Far be it for him to disappoint her in any way. He punched the stop button, and as they gently lurched to a halt, dropped her skirt at their feet and reached for her, sliding his hands beneath the inside edges of her bodice and dragging his palms down over the firm mounds and hard peaks that had taunted him all through dinner.

She shuddered in delight as he cupped her fullness and scraped his thumbs slowly and firmly back and forth over her nipples.

Emily drew a deep breath as she savored the incredibly sweet aching his touch triggered in her breasts, the demanding heat he ignited deep in her core. There was no resisting the urge. No point in it, either. Not with the speed at which he was fanning her need. She ran her hands down his chest, caressing through his shirt the chiseled planes of heated flesh and hard muscle, and then moved lower, trailing her fingertips over the ripples of his abs. Reaching the waistband of his trousers, she said, "I hope you don't mind."

She already had his belt undone when he murmured, "Not at all," and abandoned her breasts to reach into his pants pocket. A second later he produced a small foil packet. As he tore it open, she undid his zipper.

"Shall I?" he asked. "Or do you want to?"

"You," she answered, pushing his pants and shirt out of their way. No underwear, bless him. "I'll help, though," she added, taking his hardened shaft in her hands. She heard him suck a hard breath through his teeth, heard it catch deep in the center of his chest as she drew her palms up the heated length of him.

As much as he hated having to interfere with her attentions, Cole couldn't risk letting her set the pace. What self-control he normally had had been largely shredded in the course of dinner. No way did he want to leave her frustrated and wanting. He gently but firmly pushed her hands away and rolled the condom on.

A wicked, appreciative smile tipped up the corners of her mouth as she looked up to meet his gaze. God, she was beautiful. Sexy beyond anything any man had ever seen in a magazine. She was real, flesh and blood, fiery desire and unstinted passion. And she was all his. He slipped his arms around her, cupped her bottom and drew her hard against the full length of his body.

Her arms twined around his neck, she tipped her head back and offered him her parted lips. She could feel the hammering beat of his heart everywhere their bodies touched, could feel her need curling low and building deep inside her. Her legs weakening, she melted into him as the heat in her core fanned out to fill every fiber of her body. God, she couldn't ever remember wanting so much this fast. If she didn't get control, didn't tamp her hunger down...

But even as the last remnant of rational thought was offering advice, she instinctively knew there was absolutely nothing she could do to alter the course or the pace. What was, was. All of her senses were intensely aware, so wondrously alive, there was no putting them in a bottle, no calling a time-out for a steadying breath.

Her breasts throbbed with sweet pleasure as she and Cole moved against each other. The heat and hardness of his erection pressed into her abdomen, taunting her, teasing her, feeding her hunger. She rose on her toes, pressing herself closer, tightening her arms around his neck, and deepened their kiss, wordlessly begging him to match the frantic pace of her spiraling need.

He moaned, low and deep in his chest, and scraped

his hands down the back of her thighs to the hem of her skirt. She whimpered in desperate approval, dragging her leg up the side of his as he pulled her skirt to her waist. She wanted to climb, needed to climb. *Now.*

His mind saturated with the feel of her hot, silken skin, Cole barely heard the word buried deep in the sound of her pleasure. But he did. And if she wanted *now*... God knew he'd wanted *now* since the doors had closed. He cupped her buttocks and lifted her up. She instantly wrapped her legs around his hips and he whirled about, pressing her hard against the elevator wall and bending his knees. She kissed him deeper, her quick, hard moans vibrating through him and urging him on, begging him for more, for faster. For *now.*

And he obliged her, obliged himself, driving upward and burying himself deep within the throbbing heat of her need. She drew her head back and gasped for air, her gaze locked with his, silently commanding. He smiled and drew back slightly, then drove into her again, filling her, hard and fast.

"More. God, more," she moaned, her eyelids drifting down. He drew back and thrust again, and again. "Yes," she whimpered as he set the rhythm of his strokes. "Don't stop, Cole."

Her senses reeling and awash with pure, pulsing pleasure, she clung to him and rode the rocketing crest upward. Power and strength. Heat and hunger. All that was her world in this moment, all that she had ever wanted, all that she would ever need.

She cried out in relief and happiness as the bloom

of completion began to unfurl deep in her core. She arched back against the wall and pressed her hips against the power of Cole's magnificent body, demanding, begging that he understand how desperately she needed to reach the end.

And he heard her plea, shifting his hands to hold her hips tight and driving deep. The heavy coil of her need shattered in an explosion of utterly pure, exquisitely raw pleasure. She gasped in happiness and called out his name as wave after gloriously intense wave of body-wracking wonder and delight consumed her.

When the last one ebbed away, her soul was left quiet, and her mind calm enough to note more subtle sensations. She smiled. Cole. Slowly pressing soft little kisses to the side of her neck, his breathing every bit as ragged as hers was. She pried open her eyes and let the real, everyday details around her bring her mind back to center.

His body was relaxed against hers, the fierce driving tension that had been in all his muscles washed away. She sighed in contentment and thought about offering an apology for having been so wrapped up in her own moment of incredible pleasure that she'd missed his entirely. Moistening her parched lips with the tip of her tongue, she drew a steadying breath. Even as she did, his chest and shoulders began to gently shake.

Twining her fingers through the hair at the nape of his neck, she quietly asked, "Are you laughing or crying?"

He lifted his head from her shoulder to grin lazily at her. "Laughing. Sort of."

"Why?"

He leaned forward and bushed a light, butterfly kiss over her lips. "Because," he said as he drew back, "I'm so thoroughly drained and satisfied, I'm thinking I may not be able to move anytime real soon."

"I'm sorry I missed yours," she offered. "I was too busy selfishly enjoying my own to pay even the slightest bit of attention to anything else."

He chuckled and gave her an easy hug. "Well, if it makes you feel any better, I only caught the first few seconds of yours. And then I was off in my own world, too. Next time maybe we can take it a bit slower so we can properly savor each other's moment."

Well, that was good in theory. "I think it's only fair to mention that it may be a while before I can work up another want that intense. I've never been anywhere near this satisfied before."

"Oh, yeah?" He gave her another quick kiss. "I'm going to take that as a personal challenge, you know."

God love him. And more power to him. "Am I getting heavy?"

"Not really. I've got you fairly well pinned against the wall."

"Beautifully, I'd say. I have no complaints. I could stay like this for another lifetime or so." Even as she spoke, a warning twinge shot down her leg. "Well, okay, now that I think about it, my hips are getting a little stiff."

"All right," he offered, laughing. "Let me see if we can't get ourselves slightly less tangled without ending up in a heap on the floor."

He managed the task just fine, shifting his hold on her ever so slightly so that she could ease her legs down and put her feet under herself. The world swayed a bit as she took responsibility for her own balance, but he steadied her until everything came right.

And then with another quick, light kiss, he let her go and stepped away to deal with his own need to put himself back together. Her skirt pulled back down, she waited until he'd fastened the button on his waistband, and then hit the stop button to release the car.

As they eased upward, he smiled and opened his arms. She stepped into his embrace, tipped her head back for his kiss and let him fan her fires to life again.

Six

Life is good. Emily cradled her hands behind her head on the pillow, smiled up at the ceiling and listened to the shower run in the bathroom. If she had an ounce of energy left in her, she'd roll off the bed and have another turn at that fantasy, too. The first shower together had been when they'd first come into the apartment. The plan for going slow enough to savor each other's climax had... Emily chuckled softly. Gone down the drain.

Oh, well, it was impossible to be disappointed. Satisfied was satisfied. And fast and furious, part two, had been every bit as mind-blowingly wonderful as the elevator interlude. Maybe even better for her having had a sturdy towel bar to hang on to as Cole had held her hips in front of him and sent them both way over the moon.

They'd slept a bit after that, so spent that they'd awakened sprawled across the bed in each other's arms and still wrapped in damp towels.

Yep, life is good. And she'd never again look at a case of bed hair as an inherently bad thing. The quick wetting to put it back to a semblance of nonweird shape… Finally, slow and easy and savoring had been possible. And so well worth the attempt.

But like all good things… Emily sighed and rolled off the bed and onto her feet. Dawn had been hours ago and the world was calling them. The least she could do was gather up Cole's scattered clothes and have them ready for him when he got out of the shower. She pulled on her silk robe and while tying the sash, padded out into the living room.

She laughed at the trail that laid in a fairly direct line from the front door to the bedroom. If that didn't tell a story…. She bent down and picked up his socks, then retrieved his pants. His shirt was next in the line, only a few feet away from his tie. His shoes were next and last, just inside the front door was his jacket, laying right beside the green pool of her dress.

She picked up his jacket first and gave it a good shake, hoping that it would help to ease away come of wrinkles. A square of paper flipped out and landed on the floor with a hefty *whack*. Emily scooped it up, her gaze automatically skimming the words as she went to put it in one of his pockets. She stopped and read it more carefully.

Damn. Damn, damn, damn. It crossed her mind to

put it away and pretend that she'd never seen it, to act as though she didn't know—or care—what he was thinking and planning. But she did care. And while, no, it wasn't the way she had had in mind to end their night together, what would be the point of wandering over to Ida's later in the day and confessing to what she'd found hours earlier? She'd found it, she knew what it meant, and she needed to deal with it square up and straight on.

She took his clothes into the bedroom, gave them another shake and laid them out on the foot of the bed for him. The shower tap went off as she sat down on the corner of the mattress, unfolded the papers and gave them her first detailed inspection.

The Florida place looked like a cross between a casino and cruise ship. Glitz, glitter and a slick Web site presentation designed to impress. For four grand a month for the most basic package, she wasn't as impressed with the actual deal as she knew they wanted people to be.

The Sedona place… Why on earth did she have the feeling that the owners had tried and failed at running a posh dog kennel and were taking another run at making the ol' ranchero pay by pampering old folks instead of pooches? If they'd charged just under four grand a month for doggy retreats, it was no wonder they'd gone bust. She wouldn't hold out much hope for them being all that much more successful at housing people.

She stacked the two printouts, neatened the edges and refolded them into the neat little square that Cole had made of them. It was only after she'd finished the task that she realized that he'd come out of the bathroom. He stood in the doorway, a towel wrapped around his waist, another draped around his neck. He scraped his fingers through his tousled hair as he looked at the papers she still held in her hand.

She'd been caught. He'd been caught. There was no denying that they both knew what was hanging in the air between them.

Emily tossed the papers down on the bed. "This fell out of your jacket pocket when I was gathering up your clothes. Is it another venture-capital thing?" she asked lightly, hoping for an answer that would probably fall in the minor miracle category.

"You know that it's not," he said, crossing the room to stand by the end of the bed.

Part of her was glad he was being honest. Another part of her was sick at heart for what they stood to lose in locking horns over his grandmother's care. "What does Ida think about these places?"

He picked up his shirt, checked to make sure that she'd left him a few buttons and replied, "I haven't shared them with her yet."

"Smart choice," she observed dryly, arching a brow. "If I were you, I'd think real hard—a couple of times— before I brought up the idea of sending her off to pasture."

"These places can't be considered pastures in any way," he countered, tossing down the shirt and snatching up the papers. He opened the folds and held them out, one in each hand, as if she hadn't seen them before. "Not by a long stretch. They're incredibly nice. Didn't you read the details of what kind of services they offer to the residents?"

The insistent way he shook them at her... She took them with a silent sigh and prayer for patience. As she read over them a second time, he pulled on his shirt and fastened the only three remaining buttons on the front.

"Okay, there," she said, laying them on the bed in front of her as he noticed that a cuff button was missing, too. "I've read them. Now let me ask you, Cole... Why would you spend four thousand dollars a month for Ida to live in either one of these places when she can have very much the same thing for a whole lot less while living right where she is now?"

"You don't understand," he growled, rolling up his shirtsleeves.

"Obviously. Enlighten me."

"She's my grandmother. Not yours."

If he thought claiming proximity was going to be good enough to avoid making a case, he had another think coming. "Well, she's my friend and I'll bet you one sugar cane biofuel refinery that she would rather *die* than be shipped off to live in an old-folks home."

"These are hardly your typical old-folks homes."

She stopped herself from bluntly asking when he'd ever been in a retirement home and took a more indirect approach to make the point. "Oh, yeah? Do they have a preschool on-site? An after school latchkey program? Do the Girl Scouts make the rounds selling cookies? The

Cub Scouts their popcorn? Do the high school couples drop by to do a promenade of their rented tuxes and fancy gowns before the big night out? Do you see anyone in those pictures that's a day less than sixty-five?"

"They're *retirement* communities," he shot back, dropping down on the bed, his back to her, and yanking his pants on. "They're places where people go to live so they don't have to be guilt-tripped into buying cookies and popcorn they really don't want. Or put up with badly behaved toddlers and teenagers."

Yeah, that was the standard myth, the candle that drew the moths to the fatal flame. "That may be true in part. But mostly they're places, Cole," she said patiently, "where people go to quietly fade away and die without their families having to watch, feel guilty or be the least bit inconvenienced."

He stood, stripped away the towel and quickly pulled his trousers up around his waist. "They're places where the elderly are protected and safe."

"Protected from what?" He gave her a look that said she really shouldn't have had to ask. Well, she did, because she had no idea what he was talking about. "God, don't tell me you're one of those people who think that there's a serial killer lurking behind every bush waiting to jump out and hack granny to death when she goes to the mailbox for her Social Security check."

"Now you're being ridiculous."

"So answer the question," she challenged. "And answer it specifically. What is it that Ida needs to be protected from?"

He sat back down on the bed and picked up his socks. "Unrestricted access."

"What?" Emily asked, astounded. "You think she should be the human version of Area Fifty-One?"

His shoulders sagged and he heaved a sigh of surrender. "Grams is a notoriously soft touch," he said, slowly turning to face her. "You know all those solicitations that come in the mail every other day? The crippled children, the burned children, the third-world children, the orphans, the soldiers, the sailors, the missionaries, the dolphins, the whales, the caribou, the bison, the blind dogs, the tailless cats, the trees in Brazil, the ice in Antarctica, the—"

"I got it, Cole," she gently interrupted.

He shook his head. "You're on the go-to list for the Smithsonian when it comes to stained glass. Which is great. It's how you make a living. But my grandmother is on the go-to list for every lunatic and fringe cause known to mankind. They need money, they fire a set of address labels and a form letter out to Ida Bentley. Ida can be counted on to zip them a check the day she gets it."

He sighed and scraped his fingers through his hair again. "For God's sake, Emily, she's got a dozen shoe boxes in her bedroom closet right this minute, all of them stuffed full of fricking address labels."

"Not every charity is lunatic or on the fringe," she pointed out, trying to help him deal with a situation that had clearly frazzled his coping strategies.

"The point," he said crisply, sadly, "is that my grandmother doesn't make the distinction. Last year she bought six Holstein heifers for a village in Guatemala, eight pairs of rabbits for a village somewhere in India and paid for reconstructive surgery for three orphans with harelips somewhere in Lower Transylvania. Or maybe it was Upper, I don't know. I don't care. The important fact is that, altogether, it totaled close to fifteen grand."

"Was it money she didn't have?"

"She has the money," he assured her morosely.

"Then what exactly is the problem, Cole?" Emily pressed gently. "If it's her money, then she's entitled to spend it any way she wants. Clearly she thinks she's making a difference in the world when she writes a check. What's wrong with that? We all want to make the world better."

He gave her a tight smile. "Last year was also a group who wants to outlaw the internal combustion engine, the group who is publishing a dictionary of whale-speak, the group who blew up three family planning clinics, the—"

"I heard about that one," Emily admitted, suddenly understanding that his frustrations were based on a reality that had actually moved beyond eccentric and into dangerous.

"Yeah, well," he said, gaining his feet and beginning to pace, "Ida Bentley's generous contribution bought the dynamite." He threw his arms up and turned to her. "And let me tell you, you have not had a real nightmare until the FBI shows up on your doorstep asking questions about your grandmother's subversive activities."

"Okay, I understand your concerns," she allowed. "But why do you think moving Ida to some retirement village is going to change things? Do they restrict what mail the residents get?"

"I don't know." He came back to the bed and picked up his socks again. "It's one of the many questions I have to ask before I make any sort of decision."

"Well, if they can do that at those places, then it can be done right here, too. There's no need to ship Ida off into exile."

"It's not exile. These are extremely nice places."

"They're not real communities, either, Cole. My grandmother has gone before yours. I've been down this road. These places are really nothing more than very expensive, very profitable warehouses for old people on the end-of-life conveyor belt. You start in the independent living apartments, then you move over to the assisted living ones, then they roll you over to the nursing home, and then they load you in the wagon and haul you off to the morgue."

At least he seemed to be thinking about what she'd said. Either that or he was really having to concentrate on getting his socks and shoes on. "And the alternative?" he finally asked.

"You stay in your home, live your life as you always have, arrange for in-home living and nursing care when you need it, and when you have to have more intensive or specialized care than a visiting professional can provide... That's when you look at the nursing home. You don't climb on the conveyor belt before you absolutely have to. You sure don't do it so that your mail can be screened before you get it."

He stood, picked up the papers from the bed, folded them and then picked up his jacket to tuck them into the inside pocket. All without saying a word, without so much as a quick glance in her direction.

"Why don't you go talk to Jay, the postmaster here in Augsburg," she suggested kindly, "and see what you can do about controlling the solicitations?"

He nodded and then slowly looked up from his jacket to meet her gaze. "Who do I see, Emily, about controlling the appeals and pitches made twenty times an hour on every single TV station out there, twenty-four-seven? And who do I see about keeping the fraudulent contractors from knocking on her door and asking to fix her roof or trim her trees or clean her gutters or paint her house?"

"Maybe it's time for Ida to let someone else handle all the hassles of keeping a checkbook."

"You think?"

She ignored his sarcasm and countered with deliberate optimism, "Which is quite doable without upending her whole world by sending her off to live in a swamp or a desert."

"But that's based on the assumption that she'd agree to go along with it. I don't think she would."

Good God, if he thought she'd fight him over giving up control of a checkbook, had he really given any thought at all as to what her reaction would be to the notion that she move into a home? He wasn't just frazzled over the whole thing, his brain was fried.

"Then you just have to figure out some way to

restrict her access to checks," she offered diplomatically, climbing off the bed. "And debit and credit cards,
too, I suppose."

Again he gave her a tight smile. "She used a credit
card to donate the dynamite money. It took the FBI all
of five seconds to come up with her name and maybe
ten minutes for the credit card company to give them
mine. There's now a flag on all of her cards that goes
up when someone off the standard retail and golden
charity list sends through a request for payment. And
the credit agencies have flagged her reports to let me
know if she applies for new cards."

"Well, you obviously have that under good control.
I assume that you've enrolled her in one of those
identity protection services, too?"

"Yes."

She walked to the end of the bed and slipped her
arms around his waist. "You're a good man, Cole
Preston," she assured him as she smiled up at him.

He put his arms around her and managed a close imitation of a genuine smile. "I'm a hard-hearted bastard
who wants to ship his grandmother off to a plush prison,
remember?"

"Yes, but I'm sure that, in the end, you'll consider
all the options and choose the one that's best for her. You
would never do anything that you know would make her
unhappy. If there's anything I can do to help, all you
have to do is ask."

"Which job do you want? Tripping the mailman, or
grabbing the mail sack?"

She grinned. "Both are federal offenses. I'm pretty sure we can think of a solution that isn't going to land us in Leavenworth."

"At least the FBI would know where to find me when the Japanese Prime Minister gets *harpooned* by Greenpeace."

She laughed and hugged him. "Life has a way of working out like it should, Cole. There's no point in borrowing trouble in advance. When it's time to really deal with caring for Ida, you'll know exactly what the right decision is. Today isn't the day."

"You're sure of that?"

"Absolutely."

"Thanks, Emily," he whispered, lowering his mouth to hers.

"Yoo-hoo! Emily! Are you in here?"

He jerked back and cocked a brow. They both looked toward the front door at the same time to find her friend Beth standing just inside the apartment, holding the green dress at arm's length and blinking furiously.

"The party's over," Emily said, taking her arms from around him with a regretful smile. "I'll introduce you on your way out."

"Oh, damn, Em," Beth gushed as they came out of the bedroom together. "I'm so sorry. I didn't know. Didn't even suspect!"

"It's okay," Emily assured her.

"Yeah," Cole added. "Although it would be a different story if we'd still been hanging from the chandelier."

Beth's gaze instantly went to the ceiling, to the simple glass cover over the single light bulb.

"He's kidding," Emily assured her friend. "Beth, meet Cole Preston, Ida Bentley's grandson. Cole, my friend Beth Hardesty, the CPA and very literal thinker."

Cole stepped forward and with a grin, stuck out his hand and said, "Nice to meet you, Beth."

"Me, too," she stammered. "I really hope I'm not interrupting anything."

"Not at all," he said, giving Emily a quick kiss on the cheek. "Life is just working out the way it should. See you tonight?"

Her heart swelling, she nodded. "I'll be here."

"Have a good one," he called over his shoulder as he walked out of the apartment, his jacket slung over his shoulder. "Don't mug any mailmen without me!"

Emily laughed, watched him get on the elevator, and waved goodbye as the doors closed.

"Mailmen?"

"It would take too long to explain it," Emily replied, closing the apartment door and taking her dress from her friend's hand. "I should probably get dressed."

Beth nodded and headed into the kitchen, saying, "Yeah, I don't think Augsburg is quite ready to consider a peekaboo peignoir acceptable day wear."

"It's not peekaboo," Emily retorted, moving off toward the bedroom, checking the fabric of her sleeve just to make sure.

"Reach for something and it is," Beth called, getting a chunk of cheese out of the refrigerator. "Amazing how much so little fabric can cost, huh? Was he worth it?"

"Oh...my...God," Emily replied, pausing in the bedroom doorway.

"Don't tell me any more," Beth groused as she got a knife from the drawer. "I'd have to slit my wrists."

Emily went into the bedroom, grinning and feeling more alive than she could ever remember. Gathering up Cole's damp towels, she found his tie lying forgotten in the twisted sheets. She picked it up, too, and breathed deep the heady scent of his cologne. Oh, yes, he was most definitely worth a whole new lingerie wardrobe.

Maybe she should just accidentally leave a catalog on the coffee table before he came over this evening. Discussing possible purchases would be an easy, nonthreatening way to get an idea of just how long he intended to be around. If he was a one-week wonder, she could save her money. But if he wasn't making any plans to head for the hills anytime soon, well, then it was Katy bar—

Emily stopped, took a slow, deep breath and lifted her chin. They'd had one night together. A fabulous night, yes, but it wasn't the stuff on which a smart woman built a whole new wardrobe. Not even for a week of fun and breathless games. And she sure as hell didn't have any business even vaguely hoping that blow-the-top-of-your-head-off-curl-your-toes sex would bloom into a long-term relationship they could take outside the bedroom.

"Scratch the catalog idea," she muttered to herself as she opened a dresser drawer and collected her clothes. "Just play it as it goes and don't get greedy."

* * *

He'd managed to remember, of all things, most of the words to the song "Zip-A-Dee-Doo-Dah" by the time he bounded up the front walk of his grandmother's house. A blast from the past, of days of his childhood spent sprawled on the floor of the living room of Grams's Manhattan forty-second-floor condo, watching videotapes of old Disney movies. Damn, if he couldn't still see and hear Uncle Remus and the pudgy-faced bluebirds.

"It *is* a wonderful day," he said as he let himself into the house.

"Hello, dear!" his grandmother called from the dining room.

"Hi," he said in greeting, hanging his jacket on the back of a chair as he noted that she was sorting papers on the table. There were three stacks of brand-new address labels. "I see the mail's come already today."

"With lots of goodies in it," she answered happily. She handed him a small rectangular cedar box, stamped on the top with the name of a Native American tribe he'd never heard of. He opened the lid and found it neatly packed with pencils, also made of cedar and stamped with the name of the tribe.

"This was a gift, I presume?"

"Last month I sent them thirty dollars for vocational development programs."

Cole expelled a long, slow breath and considered the box of pencils in his hand. "You could have bought these at an office supply store for less than a buck."

"The ones at the store aren't made of cedar," she

countered, still sorting her mail. "Nor are they stamped with the tribal logo."

"That's really beside the point, don't you think?"

She stopped sorting and looked up to meet his gaze. "No, Cole, I think it's the whole point. Pencils bought at the store don't help anyone except the importer and the retailer. These go toward helping minority, disadvantaged young men and women learn a lifelong trade."

Yeah, there was a lot of demand for traditional number-two lead pencil makers these days. "Okay," he said, choosing to avoid the fight. "Point taken and accepted. More address labels?" He mentally kicked himself the second the words left his tongue.

"Are you planning to give me another of your lectures about charitable responsibility?" Grams asked crisply. "I have apologized I don't know how many times for that whole clinic bombing thing. I had no idea that was the sort of people they were, and I truly believed that I was funding the purchase of bassinets and receiving blankets."

He held up his hands in surrender. "No lecture, Grams. I promise."

"Thank you." She smiled and her blue eyes twinkled. "How was your dinner last night?"

Uh-oh. The Grilling. "Fine," he answered vaguely, knowing that she wasn't going to let him get away it.

"What did you have to eat?"

Damn, what a time for his brain to replay the image of Emily coming toward him in that killer dress of hers.

"You did go to dinner, didn't you?"

"Well, yes. I just don't…" *Make something up,* suggested a disgusted voice in the back of his brain. "Veal Parmesan. It was very good."

"And did Emily enjoy her meal, too?"

"She said she did."

"And how is she this morning?"

Oh, that was a new level for The Grilling. "I don't know," he replied with a cavalier shrug. Grams's brows slowly rose. "Well, you see, Grams," he said, "there was this really hot chick tending the bar named Bambi and—"

"Cole Edward Preston!"

"Emily is fine," he laughingly supplied. "And that's all I'm going to tell you."

"Are you seeing her again tonight?"

"She has a roofing crew going to work this morning. I don't know if she'll be able to get away this evening, or if the whole construction deal will leave her too exhausted to do anything but fall down and go to sleep. I'm going to play it by ear."

She nodded slowly, the way she used to when he maintained that he hadn't eaten the last six truffles in the box when they both knew he'd been the only one in the house. "Speaking of sleep, you look like you could use a good nap."

"Nice try, Grams," he said, grinning. "I'm going to go fix myself some toast. Would you like some?"

"Thank you, but no thank you. I had breakfast hours ago."

"Hours ago" implying, he knew, that he had obviously been too otherwise engaged to think about break-fast until now. He didn't say anything, though, just smiled pleasantly and left her to her sorting.

He was smearing peanut butter on his third slice of wheat toast when the swinging door from the dining room smacked against the kitchen counter. His grand-mother strode in a half second later.

"Cole?"

"Yes, ma'am?" he replied, his mind whirling through the list of his recent sins and how many she might know about.

She threw a familiar folded square of paper down on the counter beside the butter dish. "I am *not* going to a retirement home. Any*where*. At *any* time. I am staying in this house until Mr. Baker comes to haul me over to the funeral home."

He looked at the paper. "You went through my pockets?" was the only thing he could think to say.

"I was going to press the wrinkles out of your jacket."

Women and their damn war against wrinkles. This was twice inside of a single hour! "I think," he began, trying to think diplomatically, "it's something we should talk about, Grams. Not necessarily now, but sometime down the road. You're not always going to be able to—"

"You are *quite* welcome to have the conversation anytime you like, Cole. Do *not,* however, expect me to participate. I have made the last move of my life. I'm not leaving here unless it's on a gurney, feetfirst and cutting a *lovely* feminine figure under a blue velvet Baker Funeral Home cover."

And with that declaration, she turned around and stomped out of the kitchen. He took a bite of his toast and slowly chewed, pondering what appeared to be a universal female aversion to the whole concept of retirement living. Was it some sort of hormonal aversion to golfing and shuffleboard, to day trips on little buses with chirpy, cheerful activity directors? Okay, he could see that the day trip thing might wear real thin real fast, but… Hell, they could call a taxi and flip the activity director off as they rolled down the driveway and past the little bus.

Was there something about community dining rooms that they simply couldn't bear to think about? Or was it that there were, on average, ten females for every male in typical retirement communities and they didn't want to have to spend their last years in constant catfights? Not that he could picture Grams doing anything other than regally holding court at which all the men kneeled at her feet and begged for her favor.

Whatever the reason for their visceral aversion… Cole picked up the printouts his grandmother had tossed on the counter, then walked over to the back door and dropped them into the trash can.

"There," he said around another bite of toast. "Never to be mentioned again." He should have listened to Emily and thrown it away while he was at her place. Emily really did have a good handle on life and people.

Considering the whole matter resolved, he finished his toast, cleaned up the kitchen and then headed upstairs for a well-deserved nap. Odds were, after all, that Emily wasn't going to be hauling buckets of hot tar around her roof all day and wouldn't be dead tired by dinnertime. He'd pick up some deli sandwiches on his way over and maybe a six-pack of some good imported beer. They could have a quiet evening in together, curled up together on the sofa talking about… Cole grinned. Futures markets and commodity exchanges, international currency trading and the valuation of the Chinese yuan. She'd be putty in his hands.

Cole frowned. Private beach in Hawaii, palm trees and waves, Emily wearing nothing but a lei. Why was there suddenly a gushing, sloppy slurry operation in his dream paradise?

"Shole?"

There it was again.

"Shole? Wase up, pease."

Someone was shaking his shoulder. He pried his eyes open and struggled to focus his vision on reality. His grandmother sat on the edge of his bed, her one hand on his shoulder, the other dangling from an arm hanging limply at her side. His heart shot instantly into his throat. He sat up and took her hand in his. "What is it, Grams?"

"Somesings…" She sucked a wet, slurpy breath. A thin line of saliva trickled from the corner of her mouth.

"Smile for me," he commanded even as he was yanking his cell phone out of its holster on his hip. She tried, but as he had known would happen, only one side of her face lifted for the effort.

"Nine-one-one," said the dispatcher on the other end of the phone connection.

He didn't wait for her to ask what his emergency might be, he barked out the address, his grandmother's name and age, and choked back a sob as he uttered the dreaded, horrible word *stroke*.

Seven

Emily slammed the car door behind her and sprinted across the hospital parking lot, her car keys gripped tight in one hand, her purse strap in the other. The extra-wide emergency entrance doors opened to let an ambulance crew roll their empty gurney back to their wagon and Emily shot past them, slowing down once inside only long enough to get a bead on the reception desk.

She slid to a halt in front of it and gasped, "Ida Bentley."

The woman on the other side of the counter considered her for a long second and then slowly swiveled all of ten degrees in her chair to look down a list of names on her computer screen. Turning back the ten degrees, she folded her hands on her desk and said, "She's back in the examining room. If—"

"Which one?" Emily demanded, her gaze darting around in search of doors with numbers on them.

"Only immediate family may go back with the patient."

"I'm family," she said, the lie tumbling off her tongue without so much as a moment's hesitation. "She's my grandmother-in-law."

Ten degrees to the computer screen… "Your name?"

"Emily Preston," she supplied. "Her grandson Cole is my husband. We're her only living relatives. I was told that he came here in the ambulance with her."

Ten degrees back… She inclined her head ever so slightly toward a set of wooden doors on Emily's right and then absently pushed a red button on the desk top, saying, "Room three, second on the left."

"Thanks!"

The big doors whooshed open and she shot through the opening, turned to the left and came to another skidding stop before the open door of Exam Room 3. There wasn't any hospital bed in it, just the empty space where it was obviously supposed to be. Cole sat in a blue plastic chair against the far wall, his elbows on his knees, his face buried in his hands.

She paused, expelled a breath in a long, slow stream and then took two deep ones to calm herself before she called softly, "Cole?"

He whipped his head up as though he'd been shot. His eyes were red-rimmed and his dark lashes clumped from his tears. He swallowed, quickly scraped the heels of his hands across his eyes and then met her gaze again.

"Where's Ida?"

"They're doing a CAT scan," he said, pushing himself slowly to his feet.

"What happened?" Emily asked, tossing her purse down on another chair and crossing the room. "Did she fall?"

He opened his arms for her and she stepped into his embrace, wrapping her arms around his waist as he answered, "She's had a stroke."

Her cheek pressed against the warmth of his chest, she heard and felt the hard, rapid beat of his heart. "Do they know what kind yet?" she asked, beginning to gather the information she needed in order to help him get through the ordeal. "Did they give you any idea of how severe they think it is?"

"I don't know anything, Emily," he answered, his voice tight, his arms around her even tighter. "Not one damned thing."

All right, it was time to get him focused and thinking. Enough of the being passive and wallowing in his understandable, but pointless, misery. Staying within his embrace, she eased back far enough that she could meet his gaze again. "What did Tim and Larry tell you?"

His brows knit as he thought back. "Who?"

"Tim and Larry are Augsburg's EMTs, the first responders that came to the house and brought Ida over here. Did they say anything?"

He eased his arms from around her and began to slowly pace. "Okay, let's see," he began. "They got there, checked Grams out, asked me when the symptoms began and then put her on a gurney. I couldn't really tell them anything for sure, Emily. Grams was fine when I came in this morning and then she woke me up, slurring her speech and drooling, one side of her body just limp."

"Were you able to give them a best guess for a time between fine and slurring?"

"I said two hours maybe. But I honestly don't know. I didn't look at a clock before I fell down on the bed."

She was running her morning against the clock, ticking off the minutes in her mind to see if she could get a better idea of how long it had taken to get Ida help when Cole said, his voice tighter than before, "God, Emily, I don't know how she got to my room in that condition. She had to have dragged herself down... God, I'm the world's worst excuse for a grandson."

"Cole," she said firmly, stepping into his path in an effort to force him to pay attention, "it's not your fault that Ida's had a stroke."

"Oh, yeah? Wanna bet?"

Seeing that neither simple assertion nor logic were going to work, she opted for the ridiculous. "You didn't throw away her boxes of address labels, did you?"

He gave her a smile. A real one. It lasted for only a second. "She found the retirement home stuff in my jacket pocket and she was not happy about it. Her blood pressure probably went through the roof." He dragged his fingers through his hair. "Jesus. You warned me and I didn't listen."

"Unless you charged up the stairs," she countered, continuing her course, "pulled out her suitcases and started packing for her, I don't think you're going to be considered an accessory to stroke."

"No," he said, shaking his head. "All I said was that a retirement community option was something that maybe we should talk about sometime. Which, in twenty-twenty hindsight, I shouldn't have."

She sat down in the blue plastic chair. "Have you always had such an incredibly well-honed sense of guilt?" she asked, watching him pace some more.

"The doctor here didn't say much of anything at all," he replied. "He just did some quick reflex tests, checked her eyes and her heart and then they rolled her out of here at a trot."

"Well, at least it wasn't at a gallop," Emily offered. "That would have been bad. Was Ida conscious for all this?"

He nodded. "She waved goodbye as they rolled her off for the CAT scan. She said something, but her speech is really slurred and I didn't understand a word of it."

"Has anyone given you an idea of how long the CAT scan is going to take?"

"No. No one's told me anything, Emily."

Ah, he was on the verge of slipping back into poor, pathetic and helpless again. "Well, I've got a bit of news for you."

He stopped in his tracks and stared at her. "You can't be pregnant. How could you know so soon?"

Good God, talk about absolutely illogical leaps. For a captain of industry, he sure didn't deal with the unexpected very well. Throw him one curve and his mind hooked on everything that came after it. "No, I'm not pregnant," she assured him. "But if anyone around here asks, I am your wife."

He didn't react. Not a blink, not a breath, not a swallow. Nothing.

"I had to tell them that so they'd let me in here," she explained. "Only immediate family is allowed. I suppose I could have told them I was just another grandchild, but that option didn't occur to me until just now."

He nodded. Very, very slightly, very, very slowly. "Thanks for being here."

"I came as soon as I heard that the ambulance run was for Ida. And I'll stay for as long as you need me."

"What about your roofing crew?"

"Amazingly enough, they said they'd done this sort of thing a few hundred times and that they didn't need any help from me. Go figure. I was crushed."

He smiled. Softly and genuinely. And it didn't flicker out in an instant, either. "You are incredible, Emily Raines."

"Yeah, I know," she replied. "You told me that last night. Twice as I recall."

"This is a different kind of incredible."

She was trying to decide if she wanted him to explain what he meant, when a tall, lean man wearing a pair of blue scrubs and carrying a metal clipboard, stepped into the doorway and knocked. Emily stood as she looked at the corners of his mouth for the telltale signs of bad news waiting to be told. And didn't see them. The guy was calm, relaxed, not at all worried. She locked her knees to keep from falling over as relief flooded through her.

"Mr. and Mrs. Preston?" he asked as he advanced into the exam room.

"Yes?" Cole replied for them.

"I'm Dr. Wilson, the neuro specialist on staff," he began, too busy looking at the chart on the clipboard to offer a handshake. "I've examined your grandmother and am going to admit her for twenty-four to forty-eight hours of observation."

"Observation?" Cole asked warily.

Dr. Wilson put the chart against his chest and crossed his arms over it. Rocking between his heels and toes, he replied, "The CAT scan shows that Mrs. Bentley has had what we call an ischemic stroke. Of the two kinds of stroke, it would be the one you'd pick to have if you got to choose. While the symptoms are shocking for everyone, usually because they're so sudden and unexpected, timely treatment of ischemic strokes can often prevent significant and permanent brain damage.

"We've administered the usual drugs to break up the arterial blockage and we should see a dramatic improvement in your grandmother's condition within the next twenty-four hours. We'll decide at that point about ongoing therapies and releasing her. Do you have any questions?"

Not any that he could answer at this point, Emily knew. In twenty-four hours, though… She hoped he wasn't one of those doctors who scheduled his rounds down to the millisecond.

"What room is she in?" Cole asked.

"Admitting will be able to tell you that in an hour or so. We like to give the nurses time to get the patients settled in before the family takes up camp."

He looked back and forth between them. "Why don't you two go get some lunch. By the time you get back, Mrs. Bentley will be in her room and ready to receive visitors. For a while anyway. It probably wouldn't be a good idea to tax her too much. She's had quite a day and she could use some rest."

He tapped the clipboard against the side of his leg, once, twice, said, "Well, I'll see you folks tomorrow," and walked out of the room.

"Thanks, Doc," Cole called after him.

Emily chimed in with a, "Yes, thank you," of her own and then stepped up to slip her arm around Cole's waist. "I don't know about you," she said, smiling up at him, "but good news always makes me hungry. Does anything sound good to you?"

"Are you sure it's good news?"

"I'm sure it could have been a whole, *whole* lot worse, Cole. Drugs and observation are about as light-weight as stroke interventions get."

"Okay," he said as she literally felt the tension drain out of him. He cocked a brow and smiled. "We were at a luau on a private beach when Grams woke me up."

Another one in the fantasy bag. But since it was his, she was going to let him surprise her. Right now, though… "I'm thinking a whole pig and pot of poi aren't going to be all that easy to find. But there is a kick-butt barbecue place a half block up the street. They have hot links and pulled-pork sandwiches. Will it do?"

"Anything will do," he admitted, taking her hand in his. "I just need to get out of here and pull myself together before we see Grams."

She grabbed her purse from the chair as he led her out the door. Cole Preston, man of steel nerves and laser focus, was on his way back. Letting him get his wits back on an even keel, she strode along at his side in silence as they left the hospital and made their way up the block to the Smoke Shack. They had their trays of food on the table in front of them before he spoke again.

"Do you think she's going to be all right, Emily?" he asked, sounding considerably stronger, more in charge, than he had even five minutes ago. "I mean, do you think that the drugs they've given her will undo all of the damage?"

She shrugged and continued cutting her sandwich in half. "No one knows until they know. Sometimes there's a miracle and there's no telling there was ever a stroke at all. Sometimes there's damage, but other parts of the brain compensate and there's pretty near normal functioning. And sometimes…"

"Sometimes what?" he asked, delaying her first bite.

"The consequences depend on what part of the brain was damaged and how severely. My grandmother had a stroke and physically you couldn't tell, but she lost her ability to make judgments about appropriate social behaviors."

"That's why she ran around naked?"

She took a bite of the brisket sandwich, nodded and then put it down on her plate. "Just so you know, Cole," she said, wiping the corners of her mouth with a paper napkin. "My nana lived a long and actually happy life after her stroke."

"Much happier than the people around her?"

She knew where he was going, what he was really asking. "There were days when, yes, she was the only one having a good time. But there were a lot more days that were really good for everyone."

They ate while he mulled all of that over. Her sandwich was history and she was down to her last few bites of coleslaw when he finally broke the silence.

"If you don't mind me asking, how did your grand-mother die?"

He really did tend to dwell on the worst possibilities. "Nana walked into the front of a bus." The horrified look on his face was just what she'd been going for. "More accurately," she added, "she clipped the left front quarter panel of a city bus with the leg of her walker."

He chuckled silently and shook his head. "And the rest of the story?"

"She fell against the curb, broke her hip and went to a nursing home to heal and recover. For a while she did. And then she just slid away in a mental fog and her body eventually stopped. The term they use is clinical psycho-sis."

"That explains a lot, you know."

Yes, she did know. And maybe now that he knew,

too, it would make a difference in how he viewed the options for his grandmother. "There's usually a reason for the way people think about things," she allowed. "Reasons for what they do. People are far more rational and logical and deliberate than they often appear to be on the surface."

He leaned back in his seat and appeared to give that some thought, too. She watched as his gaze drifted off into his memories, saw the shimmer of tears form along the base of his lower lashes, heard him quietly clear his throat.

"Everything that I know about caring about people, about being a decent person, about being there when it counts, I owe to my grandmother," he said, reaching for his drink and blinking.

He took a quick sip and then went on. "When I was a kid, I spent all my summers and holidays with Grams. I never once heard her say a bad word about my mother or father. Not one, ever. But looking back as an adult, I can see that they were too busy with their own lives and ambitions and whatever to be parents. Grams picked up the slack.

"Every Thanksgiving, Christmas and Easter we served dinner at the homeless shelter. All those smelly, dirty, ratty… Most of them crazy… I can't tell you how many times I saw Grams sitting beside someone, her arm around their shoulder and looking at a tattered old picture they'd hauled out of their trash bag of belongings. Pictures of their moms, their kids, their war buddies, their beloved dog from childhood."

He laughed softly. "Pictures of people from magazines and newspapers they didn't really know but swore they did. She always took the time to listen and to care."

He sat forward to rest his forearms on the table. "She always carries a bunch of one-dollars bills, you know. The guy playing the sax in the subway, the bell ringer on the corner, the jars on the counters for a kid needing a kidney transplant. I think they've probably built at least a half dozen Ronald McDonald Houses with what she's put into the little collection boxes over the years. I guess, looking at it that way, pencils from an Indian Reservation aren't all that much different."

"Pencils?" she repeated.

"Three sets of address labels and a box of cedar number-two pencils came in today's mail. She sent the tribe money for vo-tech training. They sent her pencils as a thank-you."

"It's important to say thank you."

"And *please* and *may I?* and *excuse me* and *I'm sorry.* Grams has always been a stickler for the practice of good manners." He laughed again. "What I thought at the time had to be the worst spring break of any kid who had ever lived, I spent as a student at Miss Tanner's School of Social Graces. Day after day of which fork is for what, how to drink and eat, how to properly cut up anything that might show up on a plate. Sawing is done only by lumberjacks, you know."

"Well, I do now," she laughingly said.

"Good manners, Miss Tanner reminded us every morning, could ease the most awkward moment, open doors of opportunity that would otherwise be closed, and, if practiced with regularity, lead to a more civilized and peaceful world community."

He grinned and sighed. "Grams framed my certificate of completion. Next time you're over at her house, I'll show it to you. It's hanging on my bedroom wall. Right beside the door so that I see it and remember the lessons every time I walk out."

"And not just the ones Miss Tanner taught you. The lessons Ida has taught you, too."

His smile faded a bit, but didn't disappear completely. "You know what's really interesting? To me, anyway. I don't really have any strong childhood memories of times other than those I spent with Grams. The rest of it… It's all there, of course. I can remember people and places and things. It's just that in looking back at them, they don't mean very much."

Yeah, she could see how that would be. Ida was the one who raised him, the one who had given him all of her heart. It was perfectly understandable that she was in the center of his heart, his world, his life. It was just as understandable that her stroke had pulled the rug from under his feet.

Until today, the whole idea of Ida getting old and needing care was something that he hadn't really dealt with in any real, meaningful way. Instead of squaring up to the fact that Ida might someday be physically and mentally unable to care for herself, he'd put the whole solution thing into her needing to be protected from con artists and unscrupulous solicitors, from fraudulent contractors.

The day Cole Preston faced a world without his grandmother in it... He knew, deep down inside, the void he faced. And he was scared. It was that fear that lay under everything he did. The focus on business distracted him. The money he made, every cent of it, was earmarked for Ida's care, for buying the best medicine and any miracle he could find.

Ida was a very fortunate woman to be loved so deeply and completely. An ache bloomed in the center of Emily's chest and she felt her throat tightening with tears. Determined not to let emotion get the better of her, she picked up her drink, took a long pull through the straw and asked the first random question that popped into her mind.

"Was there ever a Gramps?"

Cole rolled his eyes and leaned slightly forward. "They eloped. He was killed in a tragic accident involving a third-story apartment, a grand piano and a frayed rope. In Chicago. Six months before my mother was born."

"Oh, that's too classic."

"Yeah, I've never believed it, either."

"Well," Emily offered in Ida's defense, "in those days there had to be a husband somewhere at some point, or you had to wear a big red *A* when you left the house. From what you've told me, I think that was probably the only concession to society's expectations that your grandmother has ever made in her life."

With a nod, he checked his watch. "They should have her settled in right about now. Are you ready to go back?"

Not that he really gave her much choice. "Anytime you are," she said, as he picked up her tray and carried it away.

As the nurse at the floor desk had told them, Grams was sound asleep. Cole watched Emily carefully smooth the blankets under his grandmother's arm and adjust the IV pole so that the line snaking into the back of her hand wasn't pulling at an odd angle. The little things Emily noticed, the kindnesses she so quietly and gently did…

"You look tired," he whispered as she came to stand beside him at the foot of the hospital bed.

"I am. A little," she whispered back.

"More like a *lot* tired. Why don't you kick back in the chair and catch a nap?"

She looked over at the huge green recliner that took up the corner of the room. "It's close to being a love seat." Looking up at him, she added, "Frankly, you look a little rough around the edges, too. We could share it and both catch a nap so that we're decent, cheerful company when Ida wakes up."

Hell, he was game for sharing anything with her. "This could be interesting," he observed, taking her hand and leading the way over to the corner.

"Yeah," she drawled as he dropped down into the chair, tipped the back and popped up the footrest. "Let's give your grandmother a heart attack on top of her stroke. I don't think so."

He held out his arms. Despite her protest, she didn't hesitate a second in climbing into the seat beside him. Turning on his side, he drew her into the curve of his body. She snuggled close, settled her head on the pillow of his arm and sighed in what sounded to him like utter contentment. He knew the feeling.

"Sweet Emily," he murmured, pressing a kiss into her golden curls. "You're—"

"If you say incredible, I'm going to buy myself a cape. With sequins."

He chuckled, his world suddenly so much brighter than he had imagined possible a few hours ago. "You're a very special person, Emily Raines. And I..." He swallowed hard and finished, "I'm thankful that you've come into my grandmother's life. Into my life."

She said something in reply, but sleep blurred the words into a soft purr.

Cole laid his cheek on her head and stared blankly out the window. It had been one helluva day, one helluva week, actually. Everything was turned upside down and inside out. His normal daily routine had been blown to smithereens. He was off his stride and not dealing very well with anything.

As soon as Grams was out of here and set up with all the caretakers and stuff she needed, he needed to get back to his regular life. And once he got his feet back under him and his world under control again... Then he could take a good look at his feelings, could decide if it was a matter of being caught up in the moment, or if he really did love Emily Raines.

And if he did... He closed his eyes, refusing to think about an entire lifetime of living upside down, inside out and out of control.

Eight

Cole held the front door open for Ida and her, sucking an audible breath through his teeth as his grandmother deliberately lifted her foot over the threshold. Emily understood exactly how nervous he felt; she had her hands up, prepared to catch Ida if the effort undid her balance and toppled her backward.

Ida managed to step back into her house without mishap, though, and Emily heard Cole sigh in relief in the same instant that she did.

"All right, you two," Ida firmly said, turning in the entryway to face them both. "We are going to come to an understanding right this minute."

"Wouldn't you like to sit down first?" her grandson suggested.

"Cole, dear," she replied crisply, "if I wanted to sit, I would. And I don't."

Cole was brave enough to mutter, "Okay," but Emily kept her mouth shut and tried to fade into the the grass cloth wallpaper. Man, she had never seen Ida the Queen before. Benevolent imperial command was the only way to describe the woman's approach. Well, okay. "Impressive" also worked.

"I have had a stroke, yes," she began, looking between them. "But as you clearly heard the doctor say as he was signing my discharge papers not more than an hour ago, I am a tough old buzzard. I am not in any way an invalid and I will not tolerate being treated as one. Is that clear?"

"Yes, ma'am," Cole said, sounding at least respectful if not exactly contrite.

"Emily?" Ida said, turning to her and making her heart jump. "Is that clear to you as well?"

Her stupid voice actually squeaked when she answered, "Yes, ma'am."

"Good." Ida turned and walked carefully into the living room, saying, "Now, I will sit down while we finish our conversation."

Cole followed her, pointing out, "Conversations usually involve more than one person talking, you know."

Ida, easing down in a wingback chair, countered, "You may talk all you like after I've gone into my office to write my thank-you notes." She tipped her head in the direction of the sofa and said quietly, but simply, "Sit."

They did as they were told, leaving the center cushion circumspectly between them.

"You both read the doctor's instruction sheet, did you not?"

They both nodded.

"And you are aware of the medications I'm to take? And how they are considered to be nothing short of miraculous in achieving positive results?"

They both nodded again.

"Good. Emily, has the barre been installed at the center yet?"

"The mirror wall went up yesterday morning," she explained. "The barre is supposed to go in this afternoon around three. At least that's what the installer promised me."

"Then I shall be there at four to begin my physical rehabilitation."

Cole shook his head. "I don't know, Grams. It—"

"Cole."

"Oh, God," he muttered, hanging his head.

"I understand that you and Emily have only the sincerest and best of intentions, but I do not need to be mothered and I will not tolerate being smothered. Independence is a fragile thing and it cannot survive coddling. I refuse to give mine up until my very last breath."

She looked back and forth between them and they dutifully replied in unison, "Yes, ma'am."

"Emily, my recollection is that you have slightly more than a week left until the grand opening celebration of the Augsburg Fine Arts Center. Am I correct?"

"Eight days."

"Don't you have a great deal to do in that time?"

Oh, damn. The queen was dismissing her. "Yes, I do."

"Then I suggest that your energies would be far better spent in seeing to the completion of your project than in hovering around me, waiting to catch me should I fall backward."

How had Ida known she'd done that?

"Cole," she said, turning attention to her grandson. "My understanding is that you have a business to run. Who has been minding it while you have been here visiting?"

He hesitated a moment and then finally answered, "There hasn't been much going on that's needed my input."

"Oh?" Ida said in what struck Emily as the epitome of a the-spider-said-to-the-fly tone. "Who called you this morning just before the doctor arrived for his final consultation?"

Oh, Cole was toast. Ida already knew the answer. They'd both known who was calling the second he'd answered his phone. The queen was setting up to dismiss her grandson, too.

"Jason."

"And what did your assistant have to say that required you to leave the room so your responses could not be overheard?"

He sighed and just looked at her.

"It is obviously time for you to go back to your life."

"Well, what if I don't want to?" he countered.

Ida slowly arched a silver brow. "If you think that re-sorting to the retort of a seven-year-old is appropriate, then it is most *definitely* time for you to be taking up your business activities again."

She looked between them again. "Thank you both for your loving attention the last twenty-four hours. I deeply appreciate and will forever treasure the depth of your concern for me. That having been said, please understand that I am returning the love and concern by my absolute insistence that you both go back to your respective lives. I will entertain no further discussion on the matter."

And with that pronouncement, she pushed herself to her feet with remarkable smoothness. "Now, if you will excuse me," she declared, walking out of the living room, "I have several dozen thank-you notes to write."

"Wow," Emily said in awe as Ida disappeared around the corner. "I've never seen this side of her before. Do you think that maybe the stroke has affected her personality?"

"Nope." He leaned back into the cushions and cradled the back of his head in his hands. "She actually took it easy on us. You should have been there the night the cops brought me home after catching me skinny-dipping in Central Park. I seriously thought about asking to be put into protective custody."

Emily smiled, but only until she saw his gaze. It was directed toward the ceiling, but focused on a distance far greater. She knew the look, knew what it meant. There was no point in pretending she didn't. No point in delaying the inevitable, either.

"So what did Jason have to say when he called

earlier?" she asked, trying very hard to sound way more casual than she felt.

"A congressional subcommittee is holding hearings on biofuels this week. The sugar cane lobby is scheduled to give their testimony on Thursday."

She supplied the next piece. "And they want to be able to tell Congress that they have the financial backing to be considered a serious player in the market."

"Yep. If they're taken seriously, then there will be government subsidies to fund further development."

"So you're basically the linchpin for their hopes."

He nodded, his gaze still far away. "If they're going to be ready to present the case they want to on Thursday, the deal needs to be done by tomorrow at the latest."

"It sounds to me," she quietly, "like you need to be headed for Louisiana tonight."

"They'd probably want me to appear with them before the subcommittee, too. Make the economic feasibility argument for them. And then make the pitch one-on-one during the weekend cocktail circuit."

It certainly sounded more glamorous than having a beer while sitting on the tailgate of a pickup truck in downtown Augsburg on a Saturday night. She couldn't blame him for being drawn to it. "Do you think C-SPAN will cover the hearings? I'd love to see you in action."

For the first time since Ida had left the room, his gaze came to hers. "You're assuming that I'm going to do all this."

"There's no assumption to it," she countered calmly. "I knew the second you walked back into the room after talking to Jason that a deal was on."

That seemed to take him aback. It only took him a second to recover, though. "Oh, yeah? How did you know that?"

"You were settled, centered, and I just knew. Ida knew it, too. She calls it your Hunter Look."

He considered her a moment as a myriad of emotions played across his features. She saw yearning and hunger, then doubt and regret. Resolve had slipped over his gaze when he reached for his phone. Her stomach tightened and rolled over, cold and heavy, as he flipped it open and hit the send button.

"Hey, Jase. What's the word from the flight crew?" he asked as she wondered how to extract herself from the situation with as much dignity as she could. "No way to fly around it or wait until it moves on through?"

She stood and looked at the door, wondering if maybe she should just make it easy on them both and walk out while he was still on the phone.

"Okay, I'm on my way," he promised his assistant. "Make the calls and get things ready to go. I'll meet you at the airport."

He flipped the phone closed and stood, saying, "There's a storm system moving in from the Gulf that's going to go stationary over the southeast for the next three days. I have a very small flying window to get in there before it does."

She nodded and put every bit of self-control she had

into a smile. "Then I'll wish you safe travels and smooth negotiations and get out of your way."

"Look, Emily," he said softly, kindly. "We've had a really good time, but—" His phone rang again and he snapped it open. "What, Jase?" He gritted his teeth. "Yes, forward it."

"Hang on a second," he instructed her, holding down the end button of his phone with his thumb. "I have to take—"

The phone rang and he instantly put it to his ear. "Hello, Mr. Brisbane. Yes, I am." There a very slight pause and then he walked over to his desk saying, "Yes, I had my assistant fax it here this morning. I've just come in the door and haven't had time to look at it. Okay, I have it right in front of me. I want Fontaine, Richards and Belleau there for sure. Tinley if he can make it on such short notice."

He was still talking, still organizing the players when she blew him a kiss he didn't see, and then left the house. She glanced back through the windshield of the Rover, hoping that the sound of the engine would at least bring him to the door to wave goodbye. It didn't.

"He's a money man," she told herself as she backed out of the drive and headed toward the warehouse. "And money men live to do the big-money deal. It's an addiction."

She managed to keep believing that was all it was until she closed her apartment door behind herself. The click of the latch echoed through her heart and filled her soul with an emptiness she had never known existed.

All the logic, all the rational pep talks about their relationship being a temporary fling, the caution she'd thought she'd exercised to keep her head squarely on her shoulders… Somehow, without her noticing, a hope for more, for love, had silently bloomed deep within her. Why the pain was ever so much deeper for not having realized that it had filled every corner of her heart until it died….

Tears welled in her eyes and spilled down her cheeks as she made her way blindly to her bed. Curling into a ball, her pillow clutched tightly to her heart, she sobbed for the loss of all that might have been.

"Another bourbon and Seven, Mr. Preston?"

He looked away from the window and up at Collete. "How many have I had already?"

"Two."

"I better call it quits," he admitted. "It's bad form to have the flight crew pour you down the steps when you land."

"Yes, it is. Would you care for something to eat now?"

The very thought of food made his stomach heave. He shook his head and looked back out the window.

He picked his cell phone up off the table, flipped it open and then stared at it as he sickeningly realized that he didn't have Emily's number in it. He'd never called her. Not once. She'd just been there whenever he'd wanted to find her. She'd come to him, without his having to ask, when she'd known that he needed her. She had become a daily, hourly part of his very existence and he'd never asked her for her phone number because it had never once crossed his mind that there would ever be a time that she wouldn't be an arm's length away.

He closed his eyes and mentally walked through Emily's apartment. No, no phone jack, no landline. With no four-one-one option, he scrolled through his contact list and found his grandmother's number. She picked up on the third ring.

"Hi, Grams. How are you doing?"

"I'm fine, Cole."

He took a steadying breath. "Did you get down to Emily's to work on the barre this afternoon?"

"I did. It's absolutely lovely. Emily does things with such panache, such… Well, in the popular vernacular, class."

Yeah, God knew she had way more class than he did. "How did your exercise session go?" he asked. "You didn't push yourself too far, did you?"

"Not at all. I know that I am not in dancing condition. I know how to pace myself."

He drew another deep breath. "Was Emily there to help you?"

"I allowed her to hover nearby to relieve her anxiety. But I didn't need any help, Cole."

"Of course," he said, wincing. Out of options, he bit the bullet. "You wouldn't happen to have her phone number, would you?"

"No. I've never needed it. If I want to talk to Emily, I simply go find her."

"Well, Grams, I can't quite do that at forty thousand feet over Louisiana." He hadn't meant to let his frustration show, but it was there, resonating in the air and demanding that his next words be an apology.

His grandmother cut off his attempt to spit one out by saying sweetly, "Well, Cole, dear… Again in the popular vernacular, it certainly sucks to be you."

"Grams!" he said, not sure whether he was more stunned or appalled.

"I would suggest that if talking to Emily by telephone were truly important to you, you would have seen that you asked her for her number before you left."

Okay, so much for being cool; desperate was desperate. "Could you ask her what it is and call me with it?"

"No. I did my part in bringing you and Emily together. You are responsible for what you ultimately do with the possibilities. Now, I hate to cut this conversation short, Cole, but *Dancing with the Stars* is coming on and I never miss it."

She was done and he knew that there was no hope of getting her to change her mind. "Good night, Grams."

"Good luck."

He flipped the phone closed and stared across the cabin, his mind numb, but not nearly numb enough. Grams had set him up. Deliberately. The whole thing about liquidating part of her investment portfolio to give the money to Emily had been a ruse. A ruse designed to get him to Augsburg and keep him there long enough for him to be…seduced. Seduced by Emily Raines!

No. He wasn't being fair. Emily had been just as much a victim of his grandmother's matchmaking as he was. He was absolutely sure of it. He'd bet the damned plane on it.

And, as long as he was engaged in an honest analysis, the truth was that neither one of them could claim that the other had seduced them. It had been mutual from the first moment. Every second had been exhilarating. Every second the stuff, literally, of his fantasies. He'd never been so happily oblivious to the rest of the world, or felt so utterly…loved.

He closed his eyes as the fullness of reality settled into his brain. His grandmother had set him up. Set him up to be seduced by the loving heart of Emily Raines.

And what had he done with such a wondrous, precious, undeserved gift? He'd put his world back on an even keel. He'd put his business ahead of Emily. He'd tucked his tail and run away.

There were no words to describe what a fool he was, what a coward he was and how badly he'd blown it.

Nine

Emily stepped back to get a better perspective of her handiwork. Work, yes, handy, no, she admitted as she considered how the *G* in *Grand* was a good three inches smaller that the *O* in *Opening,* and how all the letters in her sign went slightly uphill to the right. Well, add another thing to the long list of things she had bungled, screwed up, forgotten or just outright mangled in the last two days. Too used to failing to be disgusted anymore, she tossed her paintbrush in the water can and sat down on one of the empty wire spools the electricians had been kind enough to leave behind.

Maybe the fourth attempt at a front window banner would be the charm. Or not. She'd decide how she felt about trying tomorrow. Tomorrow might be the day when she woke up feeling rested and her brain would function right instead of four beats behind. That would help considerably.

"Where would you like these machines unloaded, ma'am?"

She looked over her shoulder. A man in a gray work uniform stood in the opening of the warehouse delivery bay. One label on his shirt front said George. The other one said National Freight. He held a clipboard stuffed with paper in his hand.

"What machines?" she asked, pushing herself to her feet.

"Well, let's take a quick look-see," he replied, leafing through the papers. "I got on board some lathes, planers, joiners, table saws, drill presses and what looks like more hand and power tools than Carter's got pills."

He squeezed the clamp and pulled the papers free. "Here's the bill of lading," he explained as he handed them to her. "I need your signature down there at the bottom where the red *x* is."

She had taken a pen from him, too, before what he was saying really registered. "I'm sorry, but there's been some sort of mistake. I didn't order these things. I don't have the money to pay for them. I wish I did, but I don't."

"The receipt's on the bottom of the stack there," George said. "I probably should have put it on the top for you. Sorry about that."

She pulled it out. Her name and address were in the delivery box. Other than that… She ran her gaze down the column of numbers to the total at the bottom. The amount was so staggeringly huge that even her befuddled brain wrapped instantly around it.

"Who bought all of this?" she asked, quickly turning the receipt over to see if there was anything on the back. There wasn't.

"I don't know, ma'am. They hand me the papers, give me an address and a map, and send me out. I don't need to know any more than that to do my job."

God, it was nice to have her brain back. She'd really missed it. "I don't know about this. I really think a mistake has been made," Emily persisted. "Can you hold off unloading for a few minutes and let me call the store?"

"Sure."

Heading for the office at the front of the building, thankful that Beth had reminded her to hook her cell phone up to the charger that morning, Emily looked down at the total for the machinery and tools again. Lord Almighty.

Ida was sitting on the office chair, changing into her dance shoes when Emily reached the office.

"Is there a problem, dear?" she asked as Emily found and unplugged her phone.

"There's a huge truck out back loaded high and tight with brand-new shop machinery and tools that the driver tells me someone bought for me," she explained as she carefully punched in the store's phone number and hit the send button.

"Perhaps your Secret Santa decided that you deserve more than he gave you."

"My Santa deals in cash."

The phone at the Home Center rang once and the automated system picked up. She was waiting to be told what number to push for customer service when Beth threw open the front door, grabbed the doorjamb and breathlessly exclaimed, "Emily! There's a kitchen design truck on the north side of the building and they want to know which door would be best to bring the stuff in through. Where did you get the money for a mega industrial be-still-my-heart all stainless steel kitchen?"

Aw, Jesus. "I didn't buy a kitchen," Emily assured her friend, snapping the phone closed and heading out the door. "I didn't buy shop machines and tools, either."

"Tools?" Beth asked as she blew past her.

The truck was right where Beth had said it was. This delivery man was wearing a blue uniform. His name was Edmond and he worked for Exclusive Kitchens and More. She'd heard of them. Upscale, high dollar, Kansas City.

She came to a halt in front of him and didn't even bother to ask questions. "Sir, I'm afraid that someone has gone way out of control in the practical joke department. I didn't order a kitchen. Right now, I'd have to take out a loan to buy a George Foreman Grill at Wally World. I'm sorry you drove all the way down here, but you're just going to have to haul it all back."

He stood there looking at her, probably waiting to see if she was really done with her rant. Either that or he was trying to decide if he could make it to the cab of his truck before she went totally berserk and attacked him.

"It's paid for, too, Emily."

From behind her. Cool, controlled, calm. Cole. Her heart swelled and her knees went weak. Drawing what she could of a breath, Emily lifted her chin and slowly turned, hoping that he wouldn't notice how her pulse was racing.

He stood just outside the front door, his hands in the pockets of his khakis, his dark hair, as always, just brushing the collar of his shirt. The wary hope in his eyes as he met her gaze... Her traitorous heart skittered and danced.

"You bought all of this stuff," she said. A statement of the obvious. An acknowledgment of an action taken. Nothing more. She couldn't give him any more of herself than she already had.

"Show them where you want the kitchen installed," he said easily. "And tell the guy out back where you want the equipment placed. Then let's talk."

God, she didn't want to talk. She didn't want to think. She wanted him to wrap her in his arms, hold her close and hear him say that he loved her with all of his heart. Not that that was the way their exchange was likely to go. The idea of having an audience watching her struggle to keep her composure...

"My apartment," she said quietly as she walked past him. "In twenty minutes."

Cole watched her march off with her shoulders squared, her hands fisted, and fought the urge to go after her, to throw his arms around her and beg her to forgive him, to beg her to let him back into her heart. It ached clear to the center of his soul to know that he'd so badly hurt her, that he'd been so incredibly stupid and selfish. He wanted things right between them, right now. He wanted to be whole again.

But that decision was Emily's to make and he had no choice but to allow her to make it on her terms, in her time. He expelled a long, hard breath, then tipped his face up to the warmth of the spring sunshine and deliberately tried to push the fear away long enough to figure out what he was going to say and how he was going to say it when the twenty minutes were up and the rest of his life was on the line.

It took her thirty minutes. Five to show George where the wood shop was, ten to turn Edmond over to Beth and fifteen to get her heart swallowed down and her hands to quit trembling.

Rising from the arm of the sofa as she came through the door, he turned to face her. He started to speak, but she cut him off, saying breezily, "I thought you were supposed to be in Washington today," as she headed into the kitchen on the pretense of getting a soft drink from the fridge. Anything to avoid having to face him square on and look him in the eye. Anything to keep him from seeing how broken her heart was without him.

"They can handle it without me. I have more important things to do."

She desperately wanted to hear him say that she was the most important thing to him, but since he hadn't…

"And playing Santa is more important to you than tes-
tifying before Congress?"

"Grams is today's Secret Santa, Emily," he informed
her quietly. "Not me. All I did was sell some of her stock
to cover the cost."

Oh. God. What he'd wrongly suspected at the very
beginning. And she'd thought that the mess of their relationship couldn't get any worse. "I never asked her to
do that," Emily protested, her pulse racing. "I didn't ask
her to do—"

"I know," he said, gently but firmly cutting her off. "I
know a lot of things today that I didn't know two days ago
when I left here. Grams set us both up. She admitted that
the whole I-want-to-give-Emily-money thing was a ruse.
She knew that I'd drop everything and make a beeline for
Augsburg to shut down her big donation effort *du jour.*"

"Which is exactly what you did."

"I'm nothing if not predictable, huh?" he offered
with a wry smile and quick shrug of one shoulder.
"Grams wanted us to meet and she figured that was the
quickest and most efficient way to get it done. And it
worked just as she'd planned."

"Ida the matchmaker," Emily said, turning over in her
mind all of Ida's comments, all the looks, all the questions. Now that it had been put out in the open… Damn
it all, she should have seen what her friend was up to right
from the beginning. She could have saved herself so
much pain if she'd only known and nipped it in the bud.

He nodded. "I had no idea she was so good at it."

"Well," Emily allowed, thinking she could at least try

to be gracious, "she gets points for recognizing the potential for good sexual chemistry, anyway. That part was really good. Beyond that…"

Emily dragged a deep breath into her lungs and willed her stupid knees to quit shaking. "So, if the suggestion of giving me a big donation was a ruse to get you here, to get us to meet, why did you sell her stocks? Why did you allow it to go from a ruse to reality?"

"Because she wanted to do it and it would have been wrong for me to stand in the way."

Well, there was an unexpected answer. Were there more of them? Could she really hope that this wasn't going to end with a cordial, mature adult handshake and an empty promise to keep in touch?

Her heart thundering and her mouth suddenly dry, she popped the top on her soda can and took a big sip. It didn't really help all that much, but it did at least give her a chance to put a coherent thought together that didn't sound totally desperate.

"You seem," she ventured, "to have had a considerable change in your thinking on the matter in the last forty-eight hours or so."

Finally. Thank God, they were finally to the beginning of what needed to be said. Cole tamped down the urge to walk around the kitchen counter and dispense with all the damn talking. Instead, he nodded slowly and confessed, "I've done a lot of thinking in the last few days, Emily. And one of the subjects I've given a bit of thought to is Grams and her charitable tendencies. You're right. Absolutely, one hundred and ten percent right. It's her money and if she wants to use it to make the world a better place, I don't have any right to stand in her way."

"Just how extensive is this newfound acceptance of yours? Does it go all the way to the funding of the whale-speak dictionary? Or does it go just far enough to cover a commercial kitchen and woodworking machinery for me?"

"I've done some real stupid things lately," he freely admitted, "but I do know better than to try to buy my way back into your good graces."

She gave him a small smile in reward for his honesty and then asked, "So now that you've seen that all of Ida's gifts have been delivered... What's next? Are you heading for Washington now?"

"No."

"I thought they really wanted you there to help present their project to congress."

"Plain and simple, Emily," he answered on the courage of his heart's desire. "I don't want to be there. I want to be here. With you."

With you. Her heart swelled and her soul danced. Her mind sadly warned that she was grasping for a hope that might not really be there. She put the soda can on the counter so he couldn't see how badly her hands were suddenly shaking.

It took everything she had to keep her voice from cracking as she asked, "How long are you planning to be here this time?"

"That's up to you."

Yes, it was. And she needed to draw the line so he knew precisely where it was. And as painful as it might turn out to be, she needed to draw it now so that she didn't hope for more than he would ever be willing and able to give her.

"Cole," she said, coming around the counter to stand in front of him. "I've discovered that I don't like being a disposable person. It hurts. Deeply."

He nodded as though he actually understood, then reached up to slowly trail a fingertip over her lips and whisper, "What would I have to do to get you to give me a second chance?"

A second chance at what? her mind wondered even as her heart said that it didn't matter. He was here and they were together. There were no guarantees in love.

"A second chance to get it right, Emily," Cole murmured, gently taking her face between his hands. She looked up at him and he saw the depth of his own hope in her searching gaze.

"I've never felt emptier or more alone than I have the last two days," he offered, pouring the desperation of his heart into each and every word. "I've turned to talk to you a thousand times and you weren't there. I've reached out to touch you and you weren't there. All the business, all the wheeling and dealing… I have no idea what I signed, Emily. I just put my name on the paper so that it was done and I could come home to you.

"I don't want to spend the rest of my life missing you. The ache is horrible and forever deep. Please, Emily. Please give me another chance. Let me prove, every single day for the rest of our lives, how much I love you."

Her heart brimming, Emily smiled up at him. "I love you with all that I am, Cole," she promised.

The relief flooding his soul nearly buckled his knees. Cole wrapped his arms around her and drew her close, holding her tight, letting her fill him with the strength of her endless love and the sweet, absolute certainty that his heart and soul had indeed come home.

* * * * *

Turn the page for a sneak preview of

The Magnate's Takeover
by Mary McBride

This exciting new story in the
GIFTS FROM A BILLIONAIRE *series*
is available from Mills & Boon®
Desire™ in September 2009.

The Magnate's Takeover
by
Mary McBride

"Here's to you, you magnificent building."

Libby Jost stared out the window and raised her wine glass once again to toast the nearly completed 20-story convention hotel on the other side of the highway just west of St. Louis. Now that it was autumn and the trees were nearly bare, and even across six lanes of traffic, the bright lights of the Halstrom Marquis flickered like rubies in what was left of her red Chianti.

"And here's to you, Mr. Halstrom, whoever you are and if you really do exist. Welcome to the neighborhood." She swallowed the last of the wine, and then a silly, not-too-sober smile played at the edges of her mouth. "What took you so long?"

She put down her empty glass, stood up and then immediately realized she had celebrated a bit too much. Way too much, in fact, for a person who rarely drank at all. Her last drink, incidentally, had been an obligatory glass of champagne on New Year's Eve. She was definitely out of practice, she decided, and figured it was time for a very sobering slap of cold October air, so she flipped the main switch for the outside lights and wobbled out the door.

Once outside, Libby glanced up at the ancient neon No Vacancy sign flickering above the office door. How sad was that? she thought. After all these years, all these decades, it was probably some sort of miracle that the *V,* two *c*'s and half of the *y* still managed to faintly sputter. The mere sight of the sign might have completely depressed her a few months ago, but it didn't tonight. It didn't bother her at all because she knew there would be a brand-new, far better sign very soon, and instead of perpetual vacancies, the old Haven View Motor Court would once more be full of guests and good times.

Again, as she'd done a thousand times these past few weeks, she gave silent thanks to the anonymous Santa Claus who'd sent her a check for fifty thousand dollars in appreciation of her recent book of photographs of old, downtrodden motels in the Midwest. Libby Jost was, first and foremost, a serious photographer who had worked for the St. Louis newspaper for nearly a decade. She'd garnered numerous awards in the past, but most of them came in the form of plaques or framed certificates usually accompanied by long, boring speeches and polite applause. She'd gotten a check for two hundred bucks once for a photo of the Gateway Arch in morning mist, but never anything close to fifty thousand dollars.

The huge, unexpected check not only sustained her pride in her work, but it also provided her the wherewithal to help her aunt Elizabeth, the woman who had raised her here at this run-down motel after the death of her parents in a car accident when Libby was just a toddler.

Aunt Elizabeth hadn't asked for her help, but then she didn't have to. As soon as Libby realized that the fifty-thousand-dollar gift wasn't a joke or a stunt of some kind, but was indeed good as gold according to her bank, she arranged for a leave of absence from the newspaper and began making plans to revive the derelict motel. It was her aunt's dream, after all, and Libby felt she owed it to her to keep that dream alive as long as she possibly could.

And while she was giving thanks, she directed a few of them to the Halstrom Marquis, which soon would be sending its overflow customers across the highway to the newly remodeled, all spiffed-up, ready-to-go Haven View.

Libby was determined to make it happen. The anonymous Santa had given her the money to set it all in motion. She had taken her time to nail down her plans and to budget the money properly. Now she was ready to begin.

Stepping out onto the pebbled drive that wound through the dilapidated little tourist court, she noticed that one of the lampposts was dark. Damn. If it wasn't one irritation, it was another. Exterior bulbs had gotten so expensive, even at the discount stores, and they seemed to burn out way too frequently these days.

Maybe she could let one light go dark for awhile. Maybe no one would even notice. There weren't any guests here, for heaven's sake. But, after another glance at the magnificently illuminated hotel across the highway, Libby sighed. Got to keep up with the Joneses now, she thought, or with the Halstroms as is in this case. She went back into the office in search of a ladder and a light bulb.

Well, this wasn't one of the best ideas she'd ever had, Libby thought ten minutes later as she wobbled and swayed high up on the ladder while trying to juggle a large glass globe, a dead light bulb, a fresh light bulb and the four screws from the lamp. If anything, it was a terrible idea. She could see the paper's headline already: *Woman, inebriated, expires under lamp.*

And if it wasn't a disaster already, it surely became one when a car engine growled behind her, headlights flooding the parking lot and tires biting into the loose gravel of the driveway just behind her. A customer at this time of night? That wasn't at all likely. The motel hadn't had a single customer in three or four weeks.

She tried to look over her shoulder to see who or what it was, but the fierce headlights blinded her. When she heard the car door whip open and then slam shut, her heart leaped into her throat and made it impossible to shout or scream.

This was not good. Not good at all. It was terrible. A strangled little moan broke from her lips.

Then Libby lost her grip and the globe and the light bulbs crashed onto the ground below her, and she was about to crash down, too, on top of all that broken glass when a deep voice said, "Hold still."

Two hands clamped around her waist.

"I've got you," he said. "You're okay. Just relax and let go of the ladder."

Libby, in her total panic, tried to jerk away from his grasp and she held on to the lamppost even tighter than before.

"Dammit," he growled, tightening his grip on her waist. "I said let go. It's okay. I've got you."

He did, indeed, have her.

What else could she do? Libby dragged in a breath, held it and then let go of the lamppost, wondering vaguely if her life was going to flash before her eyes now that it was about to end.

It felt like falling into a giant bear hug. The arms that caught her were warm and encompassing. Then glass crunched under the bear's feet as he turned, took several strides and finally and oh-so-gently set her down.

She was safe, but only for a second. The bear turned on her, his eyes flashing. "What the hell were you doing up there?" he growled. "You could have broken your damn neck."

Libby's heart was pounding like a jackhammer. Her legs felt like jelly, and she was still not exactly sober. Far from it, in fact. But now, instead of feeling tipsy and scared to death, she felt tipsy and mad as hell so she yelled back at the bear, "Well, it's *my* damn neck."

He merely stared at her then, stared hard, as if he were memorizing every feature and angle, every crook and cranny of her body, or else perhaps he was merely calculating the calories there just in case he decided to take a bite out of her.

Belligerently, Libby stared right back, into a face that struck her as more rugged than handsome. Even in the semidarkness of the driveway, she could tell that his eyes were a deep hazel and the line of his chin like granite. He was fairly good-looking, for a bear. She wobbled again, struggling to keep her balance and wound up standing even closer to him. He smelled divine, even though she was too tipsy to identify the scent. Then he smiled. It was a sudden, wonderful surprise of a smile that carved out sexy lines on both sides of his mouth.

"It's a lovely neck," he said, reaching out to touch the hammering pulse in her throat.

Libby blinked. "Thank you," she said. "I think."

Whatever hostility that had flared up so suddenly between them seemed to vanish into the cool night air. She glanced at his car—a dark, sleek Jaguar—and was fairly well convinced that this guy wasn't a thug or a rapist or, for that matter, a paying customer. People who stayed at the Haven View these days tended to drive dirty pickups and dented sedans.

But before she could ask the Jaguar guy just who or what he truly was, he asked her, "Is the boss around?"

Libby almost laughed. Her whole life she'd looked far younger than she actually was. Now, even at age thirty, she could still easily pass for nineteen or twenty. And obviously she didn't look like a "boss," either, in her current panicky and slightly inebriated state.

Well, in reality she wasn't the actual boss here. The Haven View Motor Court belonged to her aunt Elizabeth, after all, as it had for the past fifty years, but while her elderly aunt was in a nursing home recovering from a broken hip, Libby was most definitely in charge.

"The boss," she said, "is currently under the weather, which means I'm temporarily in charge around here." She attempted to stand a bit taller, a bit more steadily, even as her vision seemed to be blurring. Hoping to appear professional in spite of her condition, Libby stuck out her hand. "I'm Libby Jost. What, may I ask, can I do for you?"

His lips curled into another stunning and sexy grin. "I don't think you can do much of anything for anybody at the moment, little Libby." His hand reached out to steady her. "What do you think?"

What did she think? She thought she heard a bit of a Texas twang in his voice, and then she thought she was going to be very, very sick right here in the parking lot if she didn't make it to the office in time.

"Excuse me," she mumbled, then ran as fast as her wobbly legs would allow.

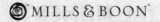

SPECIAL MOMENTS™ 2-in-1

Coming next month

BABY, I'M YOURS by Carrie Weaver

Rick's not ready to give up on the prospect of being a father – or of becoming more than just a friend to Becca. And he has nine months to ensure Becca feels the same way...

THE BAD SON by Linda Warren

Beau will do anything for Macy, even help fight for custody of an abandoned baby. But he suspects Macy's hiding something – and her secret could change everything between them.

ROMANCING THE COWBOY by Judy Duarte

Jared Clayton was sure the new accountant was stealing, however tempting her beauty. Until Sabrina showed him something he didn't know he possessed: his tender side.

THE DIAPER DIARIES by Abby Gaines

When someone leaves a baby on billionaire Tyler Warrington's doorstep, he panics. Then the sizzle between him and Bethany, the babysitter he hires, complicates everything...

HOMETOWN SWEETHEART by Victoria Pade

Was Wyatt ready to leave his past behind and take a chance on love? There was only one way to find out...

A SOLDIER COMES HOME by Cindi Myers

Single daddy Captain Ray Hughes and his little boy have to create a family. Starting with a new mother... But can the captain promise Chrissie what she needs to hear?

On sale 21st August 2009

SPECIAL MOMENTS™

Single titles coming next month

HAVING TANNER BRAVO'S BABY
by Christine Rimmer

Tanner Bravo was the type to settle down, free-spirited Crystal wouldn't hear of it. Now that Crystal is pregnant, will Tanner have his way after all?

HER FAVOURITE HOLIDAY GIFT
by Lynda Sandoval

Colleen Delaney would never forget her one night with Eric Nelson. Now the irresistible lawyer was going head-to-head with her in a high-stakes case. A meeting under the mistletoe seems inevitable…

HITCHED TO THE HORSEMAN
by Stella Bagwell

Mercedes had come home to the ranch she loved, not to get involved with a heartbreaker. Yet Gabe called to something deep within her, making her yearn to build a future with him.

THE DADDY PLAN
by Karen Rose Smith

It was a big gamble for Corrie to ask her boss if he'd father her child. But she absolutely didn't expect sceptical Sam's next move – throwing his heart in into the bargain…

On sale 21st August 2009

Available at WHSmith, Tesco, ASDA, Eason and all good bookshops.
For full Mills & Boon range including eBooks visit
www.millsandboon.co.uk

She came to take his company… but would she lose her heart instead?

New York Times bestselling author

DIANA PALMER

True Colours

As a pregnant teenager, Cy Harden's family had driven her out of town. Now Meredith Ashe runs a multi-national corporation – and she's back to take over Harden Properties.

Meredith plans to let Cy think she's the same naive girl he abandoned years ago. But when Meredith falls for Cy again, even her carefully made plans can't protect her.

Available 7th August 2009

www.millsandboon.co.uk

M&B

From No. 1 *New York Times* bestselling author Nora Roberts

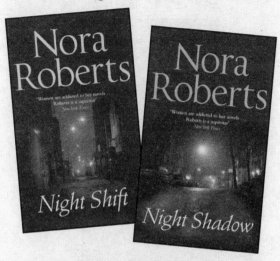

Night Shift available 7th August 2009

When her stalker's threats start to escalate, late-night DJ Cilla O'Roarke and Detective Boyd Fletcher are led into a terrifying situation that they might not both walk away from…

Night Shadow available 4th September 2009

Faced with a choice between her own life and the law, can prosecutor Deborah O'Roarke make the right decision – before someone else dies?

**Passion. Power. Suspense.
It's time to fall under the spell
of Nora Roberts.**

Rich, successful and gorgeous...

These Australian men clearly need wives!

Featuring:

THE WEALTHY AUSTRALIAN'S PROPOSAL
by Margaret Way

THE BILLIONAIRE CLAIMS HIS WIFE
by Amy Andrews

INHERITED BY THE BILLIONAIRE
by Jennie Adams

Available 21st August 2009

www.millsandboon.co.uk

M&B